HAITI NOIR

HAITI NOIR

EDITED BY EDWIDGE DANTICAT

Published by Akashic Books
©2011 Akashic Books

Series concept by Tim McLoughlin and Johnny Temple
Haiti map by Aaron Petrovich

Cet ouvrage publié dans le cadre du programme d'aide à la publication bénéficie du soutien du Ministère des Affaires Etrangères et du Service Culturel de l'Ambassade de France représenté aux Etats-Unis.

This work received support from the French Ministry of Foreign Affairs and the Cultural Services of the French Embassy in the United States through their publishing assistance program.

"Twenty Dollars" by Madison Smartt Bell ©2011 by Madison Smartt Bell; "The Finger" by Gary Victor was originally published in French as "Le doigt," in *Treize nouvelles vaudou* (Mémoire d'encrier, Montreal).

Hardcover ISBN-13: 978-1-61775-013-7
Hardcover Library of Congress Control Number: 2010935891

Trade Paperback ISBN-13: 978-1-936070-65-7
Library of Congress Control Number: 2010922715

Akashic Books
PO Box 1456
New York, NY 10009
info@akashicbooks.com
www.akashicbooks.com

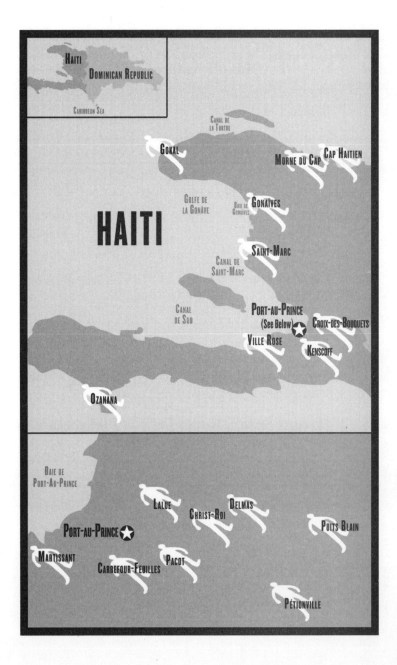

TABLE OF CONTENTS

PART III: WHO IS THAT NOIR?

INTRODUCTION
Noir Indeed

I began working on this anthology about a year before January 12, 2010, when Haiti was struck by its worst natural disaster in over two hundred years. The world knows now that more than two hundred thousand people died and over a million lost their homes in Haiti's capital and the surrounding cities of Léogâne, Petit-Goâve, and Jacmel. As I am writing these words, survivors remain huddled by the thousands in displacement camps, most shielding themselves from intermittent rain with nothing but wooden posts and bedsheets.

Even before the earthquake, life was not easy in Haiti. There was always the risk of dying from hunger, an infectious disease, a natural disaster, or a crime. But there was also hope, laughter, and boundless creativity. Haitian creativity has always been one of the country's most identifiable survival traits. Whether expressed in vibrant and colorful paintings, double entendre–filled spiritual or party music, or the poignant, humorous, erotic, lyrical (and yes, also dark) short stories and novels of its writers, Haiti's more nuanced and complex face often comes across in its arts.

When I began seeking submissions for this book, many of the writers I contacted, both inside and outside of Haiti, would comment on the suitability of the title *Haiti Noir*.

"I know you inherited it from the series," one of them said, "but it certainly is fitting."

Noir of course means—among other things—black, and

Haiti became the first black republic in the Western Hemisphere when it was established by former slaves in 1804. Noir (nwa in Creole), as the scholar Jana Evans Braziel points out in her book *Artists, Performers, and Black Masculinity in the Haitian Diaspora*, also refers to any Haitian citizen, regardless of race. The founders of the republic designated it that way so that even the Polish soldiers who deserted the French to fight alongside Haitians during their battle for independence were considered "noirs," while all other foreigners, of whatever race, were considered "blancs" (blan in Creole).

The irony of these designations struck me recently as I was rereading what I consider the most historically "noir" stories that link Haiti and the United States. The stories I am thinking of are those self-designated "dark tales" written by United States Marines who were stationed in the country during the American occupation that began in 1915 and ended in 1934. Over those nineteen years, Haiti was fertile ground for cannibal- and zombie-filled soldier memoirs and fear-provoking Hollywood B movies. Claiming to recount firsthand tales of "woolly-headed cannibals," books such as Captain John Houston Craige's *Black Bagdad* and *Cannibal Cousins*, along with William Seabrook's *The Magic Island* and Richard Loederer's *Voodoo Fire in Haiti*, shrouded Haiti in a kind of mystery that aimed to stereotype and dehumanize its people. I am certainly not one to censor any writer, but sentences like this one from *Voodoo Fire in Haiti*, send chills down my back:

> *Laugh at the negroes! You understand them as little as they understand you. The black race is far closer to the earth than the white, and for that reason they are happier than all the white men put together. A negro believes without asking why; he submits to nature.*

This is as understanding as it gets, folks.

What these narratives prove, however, is something that the Haitian scholar and intellectual Jean Price-Mars—a peer of those men—had been trying to convince his fellow Haitian writers for some time, that Haiti's own stories were worth telling. "Through a disconcerting paradox," he wrote in his seminal work, *Ainsi parla l'oncle (So Spoke the Uncle)*,

> *these people who have had, if not the finest, at least the most binding, the most moving history of the world—that of the transplantation of a human race to a foreign soil under the worst biological conditions—these people feel an embarrassment barely concealed, indeed shame, in hearing of their distant past. It is those who during four centuries were the architects of black slavery because they had force and science at their service that magnified the enterprise by spreading the idea that Negroes were the scum of society, without history, without morality, without religion, who had to be infused by any manner whatsoever with new moral values, to be humanized anew.*

Forget trying to rewrite the great works of French literature on which you had been raised, he exhorted the Haitian writers of his time. Turn to Haitian life and history and folklore and find your inspiration there.

Some of his contemporaries, and many among the generation that followed, took Price-Mars's advice to heart. Ida Salomon Faubert, one of Haiti's first published female writers, wrote of the country's tropical nights from both Haiti and France, where she eventually made her home. The ethnologist/poet/novelist Jacques Roumain placed his Langston Hughestranslated masterpiece *Gouverneurs de la Rosée (Masters of the Dew)* in a peasant setting. Jacques Stephen Alexis, Haiti's doctor/revolutionary/novelist, wrote about a massacre of cane workers in the Dominican Republic. Philippe Thoby-Marcelin's *The Beast of the Haitian Hills* took a satirical look at peasant life and Vodou through the eyes of a grieving urban shopkeeper who moves to the countryside. One of the grande dames of Haitian letters, Marie Vieux-Chauvet, wrote her world-renowned novels and plays about, among other things, rural and urban oppression. And Haitian literature has continued to thrive ever since.

Many of the writers you will read here are part of the flourishing contemporary scene in Haitian literature, both in Haiti and in the Haitian diaspora, including France, Canada, and the United States. Migration is such an integral part of the Haitian experience that those living outside of the country were once designated as part of a "tenth department," an ideological auxiliary to Haiti's first geographical nine. That's why this anthology includes writers from both inside and outside of Haiti, with two Haitiphile blan as well.

The writers range in age from early twenties to late sixties. Some are at the very beginning of their careers and are being published in book form for the first time. Others have been publishing in several genres for decades. However, only a handful might have considered themselves writers of noir (the mystery/detective kind) before this experience.

I can honestly say that, in spite of the difficult circumstances in Haiti right now, I have never felt a greater sense of joy working on any collective project than I have on this book. I don't want to summarize all the stories here because I want you, my dear reader, to experience the same sense of discovery I felt each time I picked one up and delved in. Seeing a book emerge before my eyes was truly a thrill and I have organized it here so that your experience somehow mirrors mine as the stories unfold. Each story is of course its own single treasure, but together they create a nuanced and complex view of Haiti and many of its neighborhoods and people.

I was nearly done with the collection when the earthquake happened on January 12, 2010, so I was afraid to reread the stories we had already selected, fearing that such a cataclysmic event, which has so reshaped Haiti's physical and psychological landscape, would somehow render them all irrelevant. I was very glad to discover, upon reading them again, that this was not at all true. If anything, each story is now, on top of everything else, a kind of preservation corner, a snapshot of places that in some cases have been irreparably altered. (The fictional places, however, remain unchanged.)

The stories that frame the collection, and one story in the middle, do deal with the earthquake. (A portion of the profits will be donated to the Lambi Fund of Haiti, a grassroots organization working to strengthen civil society in Haiti.) The book opens with Patrick Sylvain's "Odette," which explores a community's surprising reaction to an elder in the aftermath of the earthquake. In the middle we find Ibi Aanu Zoboi's "The Harem," which details an unusual arrangement for a man and his lovers. The book closes with Rodney Saint-Éloi's hallucinatory "The Blue Hill," which ends at 4:53 p.m. on January 12, 2010. The interesting thing is that many of the other bone-chilling, mind-blowing, and masterful stories in between could still take place in the Haiti of today. Noir indeed.

Edwidge Danticat
Miami, FL
October 2010

PART I

WHICH NOIR?

ODETTE

BY PATRICK SYLVAIN

Christ-Roi

T he hum quickly gave in to the sound of a hundred tumbling oil drums. Then a morbid absence of sound. Odette lay there watching the shards and splattered chunks of grapefruit marmalade dotting the white linoleum floor of her house. A few seconds seemed like an eternity. There was no other way to say it. Could time even be measured anymore, in this new silent and fractured world?

When the crash came, her five-year-old granddaughter Rose watched her with an extraordinary intensity. It was as if at that very moment the child had inherited the gift that the women in her family had been known to have for generations. The gift of double sight. The child's amber eyes narrowed and she let out a loud melodic scream that lasted the entire thirty-five seconds of the shaking. But then, like the rest of the world, she too fell silent.

Her daughter, the child's mother, had the gift as well. But she had turned her back on it, joining a Protestant church that made her believe she was haunted by ghosts. Then, over time, Odette's gift had faded. After her husband died and her daughter left, she no longer felt the desire to tell total strangers to be careful because she knew there was nothing they could do. There was fate and there was destiny. And there was nothing you could do to stop your star from diving from the heavens, if that's what it wanted to do.

As the roar reverted to another prolonged hum, she heard a constant ringing deep in her ears and felt her eyes fill with dust. When she finally heard her granddaughter's voice, it was very far and faint. As the child crawled toward her, she noticed that the girl's bony little body was moving slowly. Odette's mind and eyes faltered between light and dark. For a moment, she couldn't figure out why the child was crawling toward her; nor could she grasp why she started feeling sparks in her spine and lower legs.

By the time the child's soft, warm hands touched her face, and she noticed the girl's tear-filled eyes, a valve seemed to be cutting off power to Odette's brain. The silence and darkness were deepening, becoming shapeless. Then something seemed to stir inside her. Was she in water? Drowning? That's what it felt like. She was drowning while listening to the sound of intermittent clicking. She tried to spit each grain of dust out of her mouth as though it were water, but she could not.

Her body was playing a strange orchestra. She hadn't played classical music in the house since her daughter left to marry someone from that church—extra protection, they had convinced her daughter, against the ghosts. Leaving the child behind was part of that too. Her daughter had dreaded when that day would come for her own daughter, when the earth would seem to shake and she would pass out and wake up with her gifts. Except they had not been gifts to Odette's only child. The entire world's pains had become her own. She could not read or write or even listen to the classical music she loved without intruding voices.

"We were going to the beach," Odette heard herself say. Before the earth began to shake, she and the child were standing in the kitchen eating bread covered with grapefruit marmalade and talking about taking a trip to the beach. They both loved going to the beach, especially since the child's mother had left. Odette's daughter used to love going to the beach too. There at the beach, between swims, they danced to the blasting konpa music of the other beachgoers' boom boxes. The music, like everything else, was in their bodies. But now Odette couldn't dance to it. Instead, waves of silence filled her. Her heart was pounding faster than normal. She wanted to scream but she couldn't. She closed her eyes and felt the child's hand on her face. The child's voice still sounded far away. At moments she thought they were both still standing in the kitchen eating their sweet bread, sobbing. She closed her eyes again and clenched her teeth. Her body felt like it was being pricked by thousands of needles.

Her granddaughter's voice became clear for a second. Then Odette saw what was pinning them both to the floor. A large cement beam the size of two kitchen chairs was on her lap and on the girl's head. Her granddaughter was completely drenched with blood. It was like when they played "monster" and the child covered her entire body with a sheet. Odette wanted to tell the little girl that she loved her. She wanted to laugh and tease her about not being a convincing enough monster, but something stabbed her in her coccyx area and flushed her head once again with darkness. She envisioned herself walking on the beach with both her daughter and granddaughter while eating ripe mangoes. In her ancestral village in the southeast, they raced each other by a stream of red and violet flowers.

"We can't get to the child," she heard a voice say. It finally registered that the voices belonged to some men who were helping to pull her out from underneath the concrete.

"The child is in pieces," she heard another say.

"Continue to be brave," another said. "We're going to get you out."

While those voices were instructing her, the pain spread from the center of her back and rapidly shot up through her entire body. She was still unable to scream.

She would later remember being raised by many hands, then placed on the ground with a small cushion behind her head. When she reopened her eyes, multiple heads were standing in a dark circle over her. A car came: a black shiny 1970 Peugeot pulled by two muscular Andalusian horses. Horses? Where could horses go in a broken city? They would ride over the cobalt-blue ocean of her daughter and granddaughter's favorite beaches and their perfectly spaced coconut and palm trees.

In the tent clinic, she smelled the rubbing alcohol as they poured it on the gashes on her leg, but she felt nothing. Around her, she heard people groaning and screaming, "M ap mouri!" I'm dying! It was as if they were all swimming in a pool of fire.

When she woke up from another bout of sleep, she was in a massive white tent surrounded by doctors speaking to each other in Spanish. She remembered the bright smile of one young girl—like her Rose, she couldn't have been more than five years old—as she lifted her stumped left arm.

"Alone. Dementia," she heard someone say. "But otherwise okay."

Dust was still blanketing the kitchen where she lay. A brown angel whose white wings flapped high up in the breeze touched the back of her hand and said in a very assuring voice, "You're lucky to be alive."

After her daughter was born twenty-five years ago, driving

home from the hospital, holding the baby in her arms in the back of her husband's shiny black Peugeot, they had passed a bidonville in the middle of the city and she had thought of Hiroshima. The city she was being driven through now was like Hiroshima, the epic destruction reminding her of the World War II films her husband loved to watch. The National Palace's collapsed domes were like crushed camel humps; the National Police Headquarters compressed onto its blue and white walls. Thousands of desperate bodies were now sleeping on the streets, on bare concrete like stray dogs. Not sure where they were taking her, she felt defeated and small in the back of the open pickup. Then she remembered that she had asked to go. She had told them that she had a house, one of the few policemen still alive had volunteered to take her back to Rose, to take her home.

The entire front of the two-story terraced house had collapsed. As some of her neighbors ventured into her yard, both happy and surprised to see her, she longed for the strength to dig beneath the rubble with her bare hands to find Rose. Instead, she climbed as close as she could to where she thought the kitchen was and sat there weeping, with the scalding sun beaming down her back.

"You can't stay here alone," a neighbor said, while handing her a small packet of crushed saltine crackers. "Come."

And that's how she let herself be led to the tent city closest to her house.

In the middle of the sweltering assemblage of human bodies, she sat under a sheet held up by sticks all day and unbraided her long salt-and-pepper hair, which she then covered with a dingy red satin head-wrap that someone had given her. She had also acquired, she did not know where, a polished pine stick with intricate carvings that she tapped while humming before she went to sleep. Despite the constant chatter of her fellow evacuees, the tapping made a persistent noise in the humid hot air that seemed intrusive to some and meditative to others. Eventually, she began to inspire gossip.

The gossip was a way to both pass the time and deflect resentment, which, without an identified target, would have reattached itself to its originator. Odette thus became an unwitting target over the next several weeks, as words traveled from mouths to ears to other mouths. Her tapping and ongoing conversations with herself were rumored to be a secret code, her red satin head-wrap proof of what many had heard for years: that she was such a lougawou, a wretched person, that even her own child had abandoned her. Many could now recall her predicting some horrible event that had actually taken place. A car accident. A coup d'état. A bad hurricane season.

"Why didn't that old witch see this one coming?" they asked.

Rumor had it that Odette's only child had died from an infection and loss of blood after she'd left her mother's house and married a pastor.

"Even Jesus couldn't save the child from that old witch," they said.

People would have been happy to ask her about all of this, except Odette had not uttered an intelligible word since that horrible afternoon in January.

During the long sleepless nights of tent city life, gossip spread at a distorted speed, occasionally ricocheting past Odette's ears. She knew the pain of those who even in their search for food and water found ways to invoke her name. She started crossing herself multiple times before falling asleep.

Every once in a while, Rose would appear to Odette in her

sleep. The child would unwrap Odette's head scarf and undo her gray tresses, then would braid them again and again. At night, the neighbors watched the old woman in silhouette as though she were the heroine of a silent film.

The less hostile ones sobbed, placing their hands over their mouths, as others continued to declare: "That woman is a witch!"

"I know one when I see one."

"I've been waiting for someone else to realize it."

"I don't play games with witches."

"In my old neighborhood, they never stayed around."

The neighbor who had taken Odette to the tent city was among those who just watched and sobbed. Her young daughter, also killed in the earthquake, had been Rose's best friend until the rumors had caught up with them. That neighbor appeared now and then with a plate of rice or some water for Odette. Otherwise, Odette would have died of hunger and thirst.

As she lay down in the dark one night, Odette heard the voices discussing her outside. Most of the talk was about her flying around in the dark, her being a witch. Closing her eyes, she longed for the clamoring of crickets, for the stillness of her old house, for the embraces of her daughter and grand-daughter, for the breeziness of the beach. She had been living alone for so many years now that all this sudden company was agonizing.

An uneasy premonition was coming over her, an old sen-sation that she thought had long faded. Her hair stood up and her heart began to beat a little bit faster. As she listened to the voices, growing closer to her ears, she remembered how she had wailed helplessly when her mother was dragged into the street one night by an angry cross-wielding mob. It was the summer of 1955 and she was five years old.

Now, in a different time and place, that same fear and horror gripped her yet again. As the clamor grew louder, a wail pushed itself past her lips. The entire tent city seemed to be alive with commotion. The news that Odette, the lady lougawou, was about to be dealt with brought ecstasy to many.

A small group of stick-wielding women were already inside her makeshift tent. She felt an arm around her neck, which was followed by the tearing sound of the front of her dress and then a slap at the side of her head. All she remembered saying was: "Ki sa m te fè?" What did I do?

As the torrent of slaps continued, she wrapped both her arms around her head. Had it not been for a police pickup that was parked nearby, her body would surely have been hacked. Even in the presence of the officers, some managed to land a kick or a slap.

In the police truck, the destroyed city was not as visible, a less structured darkness now shielding the living and the dead from each other. The Andalusian horses were galloping ahead of them. Odette turned to the young police officer who sat next her to bring this to his attention, then she changed her mind. Instead, she raised her eyes to the sky, which was the brightest she had ever seen it and teeming with stars. She tried to search for her own star, but could not find it. It had forsaken her and dashed out of the heavens, it seemed, very long ago.

THE RAINBOW'S END

BY M.J. FIEVRE

Kenscoff

I'm sitting in my father's chair—a tattered and tired office chair that I've lugged to the porch. It is showing its age: scarred faux leather, armrests sprouting prickly stuffing, scents of Papa in the fabric. Half shaded by an acacia tree, I am sipping rich, dark café au lait, scattering a bit on the ground first, just like my father does, to feed our ancestors. The air is soft with breeze and sweet with roasting coffee, the few clouds in the sky moving like fishing boats out on the Caribbean Sea. The voices of the neighborhood rise and fall in spurts. Outside the prisonlike gates of my parents' house in Kenscoff, young girls balance buckets atop their heads, up and down the graveled roads. Sun-wrinkled women sell huge mangoes and homemade peanut brittle, while boys in cutoff jeans run in circles with makeshift kites or push around trucks made from plastic bottles.

Papa struts from the house. A dark beard nearly covers his entire face. This angled face is also mine. Only fear and distance make it seem less familiar. My father's hair is still wet from the shower. His I-am-home clothing is worn and comfortable: a stretched-out sweater, blue chinos, and old wool socks. The skin crawls on the back of my neck and the pit of my stomach crashes into my pelvis. My father's presence always makes me uncomfortable. He's more of a jailer than a father. I don't like his grim outlook on the world and the way he tries so hard to make a father and daughter out of us when we are in fact complete strangers.

He walks around behind me in his cramped, thin shoes, places his hands on the back of the chair, and asks, "What are you doing, Magda?"

I can't see his face now but I know his eyebrows are furrowed in curiosity. I take a deep breath, push my wild furious loathing into a soft, horrible place inside myself, and I swallow. "Thinking," I say.

He sits in the rocking chair next to me, elbows on knees, with his whiskered chin in the palms of his hands, and sighs. Then he picks up the magazine I have been reading, clutches it in his calloused and rough hands.

"I don't think a girl should be allowed to go to nightclubs until she's eighteen," he says.

I nod my head up and down, like a bobble doll, pretending to be interested.

Papa looks at me. "You don't like me much, do you?"

I raise my shoulders in annoyance. "Don't be ridiculous."

He takes a deep breath. "What if I let you go out with your friends tonight?"

Just like that. My life in Kenscoff becomes a dazzling succession of house parties, balls, gaieties, not only night after night, but also sometimes an afternoon gathering at one house followed by an evening party somewhere else. I dance, sing, and drink toasts with cheap beers. I wear trendy wide-leg jeans, white denims, belly shirts of neon colors, dresses with abstract, multicolored designs. At seventeen, I feel like I'm running my own show. I understand what it means to live at the rainbow's end and have its colors shimmer about me.

Tonight, Lakoup Nightclub is crowded, noisy, and literally vibrating with the beat of music blasting through large speakers. The air itself is alive with energy, the crowd abuzz with anticipation. I walk into the music, into the shadows, and the hot, sticky night presses against my skin until perspiration beads my upper lip. People line up three deep at the bar, in the rez-de-chaussée of the old gingerbread house. The bartender is chatting with a woman. "What is so dreadful about your hair that someone would call it dreadlocks?" she asks.

I don't know the number of gourdes required for a Coca-Cola or a Prestige beer. I let the sexy bartender get me a cocktail "on the house." I explore the dark, empty rooms upstairs. I walk out on the balcony, the den of iniquity, where a couple is smoking something with a peculiar smell. The girl laughs and reaches up. She slips her hand under the boy's blue shirt, up near the collar. Her hand is moving, rubbing the boy's neck. They're in search of privacy, but I just stand there. Then the couple leaves and I'm alone, under the stars, sipping my cocktail, watching people dancing downstairs, in the yard.

From the balcony, I can see the band in the backyard. Lead singer Michel Martelly's voice is strong and unlabored even when reaching for notes in the upper registers. I love the grainy vocal quality that lends the band a tortured but familiar sound, as if one were remembering a bad day. Martelly keeps listeners hanging on every phrase, awaiting the next pause or streak or curve.

"Hello," a voice says behind me.

There's something boyish about the man standing there—the dimples and the apple cheeks. His hair is wild and shaggy, as if the wind has been playing with it. He's probably in his late twenties, handsome, with broad shoulders and a narrow waist.

"Do you want to dance?" he asks.

He says his name is Ben and he is a lanky mulatto. As

he moves me around in a circle, Michel Martelly sings, "Yon samdi swa nan lakou Lakoup, desten fè de moun kontre." On a Saturday night, at Lakoup Nightclub, their destinies intertwined. The singer laughs and adds to the lyrics, "But he was a mad, mad man." Ben's hands leave damp spots on my back. He smells of oiled wood, and during the next dance he pulls back to look at me and says that I'm pretty. He gets me another drink.

Then we are lounging in the parking lot, his back against his beat-up Volkswagen, blowing smoke rings to the sky, watching them rise and disappear slowly. He calls me a wild grimèl. We can still hear the crunching guitar and the keyboard. They come together to create a sometimes sultry, sometimes dreamy, and sometimes raucous feel. I want to listen to Michel Martelly forever. His voice is both loud and strong and soft and vulnerable. His solos are the sound of supreme confidence: not aggressive or necessarily flashy, but casually assuring that every impulse will pay off.

"I'd like to see you again," Ben says with a grin that crinkles the laugh lines around his eyes and deepens the grooves that bracket his mouth.

We meet again at another party in Pétionville, in a two-story brick house with an iron balcony. Ben's eyes are chocolate-brown; his smile, easy and warm, makes me feel like the only person he's ever truly smiled at.

While we're dancing by the pool, a young man accidentally bumps into Ben.

"Watch it, fucker," Ben says with a flash of recognition in his eyes.

"What did you call me?" the other man asks.

I give a horrible squeal, like a kitten under a rocking chair, when the stranger pushes both Ben and me into the pool. I don't even have time to take a breath before I find myself underwater. Wild fear grabs the edges of my mind. Panic pounds loudly in my temples and twines my heart. I kick and squirm, fighting to get back to the surface. My lungs are screaming for air. I am choking. I am drowning. I gulp big mouthfuls of water; I can feel it going up to my nose and down into my lungs.

With one hand, Ben helps me out of the water. In the other hand, he's holding a gun.

He fires toward the sky. Gunshots pop like firecrackers. The air is electric—people run around in circles and scream, boys hold their girlfriends' hands. Leaving Ben behind, I plow through the madness to the side of the bar. I drop to the floor, crouching beneath the porch railing. There are too many people to see what's happening; I am caught in a spiral of chaos and movement, charging, rushing, spinning, trampling. Just a sea of people and crashing movement. There is more running, sauve qui peut, and dizziness. I press my hands against my temples as two more gunshots shatter the air.

The other guy is gone. Ben calms down. He finds me in the crowd and asks me if I'm okay. There's a dangerous flicker in his eyes.

I don't go out that much anymore because Ben seems to materialize everywhere. Besides, there's the embargo and the gas prices have skyrocketed, making it impossible to get around town. My father often spends half a day in a line to get his tank filled; no gas container allowed. I can only go to school three times a week. On school days, because of the traffic caused by the long lines, the alarm clock rings at four o'clock in the morning.

"C'est l'heure! C'est l'heure!" my mother chants each

morning as she opens the windows for the mountain air to rush in.

We fetch water from a cistern built under the house for our bath and press our clothes with a smoky charcoal iron, whose hollow interior is filled with smoldering coals. High, spoutlike openings allow for the coals to be fanned when swinging the iron back and forth vigorously.

If there's no electricity, I do my homework by candlelight. After I've studied a whole chapter on the French Revolution or read about la Négritude, there's not much to do and I'm bored out of my mind.

I don't remember giving him my phone number. But Ben calls.

We talk every night. I sit Indian-style, wringing, twirling the curly phone cord in my left hand, receiver tucked between my ear and left shoulder, until hours later it leaves hickeys on my ear. I tell him about my father. One moment Papa is normal, calm, quiet, in control, reliable; the next he is a wild-eyed stranger, screaming so loud my ears sting. His eyebrows join together in a frown line across his forehead. His thin face is stern, lips latched tight, and his black-rimmed glasses magnify his furious eyes.

"If you ever need me to kick his ass," Ben says, "I'm one phone call away."

Ben is not that bad, after all. He might be dangerous—but he's also fun. He doesn't try to hide his trying to get into my pants. We have phone sex once, or so he thinks. I am only pretending, playing Tetris silently on my Game Boy. Maybe he's faking it too.

I want to learn how to drive. Ben knows someone who knows someone else who works at the Department of Highway Control. I get my driver's license before I ever sit behind a wheel. I think that once I get the rectangular piece of colorful plastic, it will be easier to convince my parents to send me to driving school. Well, no. Papa says I am too impulsive to drive a car.

"Teach me," I tell Ben.

Mom is okay with the lessons because I told her that Ben is a math teacher chez les soeurs. Truth is: Ben doesn't exactly have a job. He was into stealing credit card numbers on the Internet for a while. Now, he admits just living off his mother's retirement money.

That same afternoon, I am in the driver's seat of his red Volkswagen. He spent the whole morning at a gas station, in an "embargo" line—his tank is full. The ashtray is polluted with cigarette butts; the floorboards have rusted out from summers at the beach.

Ben is distracted by my legs. I've been flirting with him out of boredom, wearing skimpy skirts and using words that my mother doesn't know I know.

He shows me how to turn on the engine, how to back up. I chug and lurch two or three times in reverse before we make it safely out of the driveway. I spin the buggy in a one-eighty. Dried grass from the summer's heat throws dust into the air and I narrowly miss hitting a parked pickup truck. I jump the curb, taking out several shrubs and a small tree, and then I regain control of the car.

We stop the bug and walk around it. The front bumper is wrenched downward; branches weave between it and the crammed wheel well. Ben starts pulling at the greenery and I join him. With one leg propped up on the slanted bumper so he can see some more skin, I tug on a particularly huge branch.

"I'm sorry," I say. But I don't really mean it.

Ben says I am a fast learner, and I tell him I don't want
to have driving lessons on a back road. I want the real thing,
the treacherous Kenscoff Road leading to the mountains. This
road is extremely slim and steep, with sudden turns and a ravine on both sides. There's no way to survive a fall.

I want someone to temper my urges to look for trouble. I
am expecting a *No, are you crazy?* from Ben when I mention
Kenscoff Road. That's how I usually deal with my impulsive,
crazy ideas. I state them, and a saner person rebuffs them.
Should I get a tattoo? Should I dye my hair blue? No. No. No!

But Ben says okay. So on day two, we are already on the
main road. Tires spinning. Music blasting. The freedom! The
excitement! I pop in a Bob Marley CD, crank up the volume,
and punch the accelerator to the floor. The car makes a deep-
toned hum and jolts forward with a squealing of the tires and
a cloud of dust. I scream excitedly as we speed past the huge,
honking trucks.

The first car I hit is a tap tap, a taxi full of people.

"Ben, you are in big trouble," I say.

After all, I'm only seventeen; I'm still a kid. He's the adult
here. And it's his car. Why should I care? He's the one who
was willing to let me drive.

The other driver is surprisingly unruffled, however. One
look at Ben and the stranger is flustered, nervously running
his short fingers through his hair. His eyes open wide, sending
his bushy black eyebrows to the top of his forehead. He says his
tap tap needed serious repairs even before we hit it.

The second car is a brand-new Honda. The woman looks
angry for a minute, and then she composes herself and asks us
if we've ever heard of Amway. She says there is a reason for all
this to be happening, that God wants me to become a rich girl

in Haiti. As she hands me her business card, she says, "Don't worry about the repairs."

So off we go again, down the mountains this time. We stop by my friend Nelly's house. As soon as I park, the whole front of the car collapses. Nelly's father gives Ben a hand to temporarily adjust the front of the vehicle. I let Ben take the wheel for the drive back—too much adventure for one day.

We fly up the road, kissing the embankment at speeds that test fate. Suddenly, Ben jerks the wheel to the right and sends us flying into a cow field. The headlights bob into an eternity of wheat-colored grass, the moonlight miles ahead. I can hear a million voices, like flies, buzzing at the back of my neck.

And then the engine dies.

I don't expect fear to come at me so violently. I am alone with a grown man in a deserted area. He grabs me, tries to kiss me. I want to say, *Oh no, you creep. Crank this puppy up and get me out of here or I'm . . . I'm . . . I'm walking!* But I simply ask him to stop. He doesn't; his hands are fumbling with my shirt. I can feel something in the air. Something nasty that is taking over. I have to think fast.

"I just need time," I say. "I know you're the one. I don't want to ruin it by going too fast. I've been thinking about how special this has to be."

Somehow, my hands remain steady and my voice unmarked by the fear that is overtaking me. There is something in Ben's eyes, cold and animal—something I know I will never forget. He just sits there, listening to the loud ticking of the dashboard clock, his hands locked on the wheel, his foot still on the brake pedal. The smell of burnt rubber fills the cabin.

A muscle in his cheek twitches as he drives me home. And I can read his eyes. *I know where you live.*

* * *

When the embargo ends, the partying resumes. Somehow, I manage to avoid Ben for a few months. But then he shows up at my birthday party, with the clear brown eyes and dimples that complement his bright smile. He helps Nelly out of a red BMW, and she introduces him as her new boyfriend. Ben offers a strange smile, the corners of his mouth lift, but his eyes remain dead, without the slightest twinkle in them. Finally, he shows a set of pearly white teeth and helps himself to a glass of kremas at the outdoor bar.

"Did you miss me?" he asks.

My mother pulls me aside, to a corner of the patio. "Who is he?" I can hear suspicion in her voice.

"Nelly's boyfriend, apparently."

"I see that," she says with a dismissive gesture of her right hand. "I meant, isn't he the teacher who used to drive the beat-up Volkswagen? How come he's driving a BMW now?"

I shrug. "I heard he's a cop now," then look absentmindedly at the azaleas and bougainvilleas lining the side of the house. "I don't know, Mom."

"Look at all the expensive jewelry around his neck. Smells like drug money to me."

"I don't know, Mom."

I sigh and walk toward the deejay, a really handsome young man who smiles every time he catches me watching him do his thing. The music is good—mellow and sexy, and never overpowering. At the deejay's table, I check the list of songs to be played next, smiling at the familiar faces on the dance floor. The boys wear Saturday-night smiles. The girls are in dresses and slinky tops, with their hair and makeup done to perfection. I shake hands, kiss cheeks, tousle hair, and hug. But something about Ben bugs me.

Ben and Nelly are French-kissing in a corner. Her chubby,

short, and dark-skinned body and his gangly lighter one, merging. Nelly sees me and waves her arms high above her head. I gesture back, a very bad feeling in the pit of my stomach. Well, Ben is certainly the center of attention that night. He shows his police badge around and girls giggle, beaming in adoration. Nelly hugs him proudly.

I bump into my cousin Clement who's spending a few days with us from Port-au-Prince.

"Do you know that guy over there?" he asks.

I look around, at the boys prowling and the girls flashing a lot of skin. The music is so loud I feel it vibrating in my eardrums. "What guy?"

"This guy making out with Nelly. Is his name Ben?"

I nod. "It sure is. What's up?"

"I need to talk to you. Could you give me a sec?"

I follow Clement inside my father's study. "What's up?" I say again.

"Do you actually know Ben?" he asks gravely.

"Well, we used to be friends. He taught me how to drive."

Clement scratches his ear. "Listen, I don't want to scare you or anything, but Ben is out on a bail bond."

I can hear my parents laughing in the kitchen. They drink cocktails, dark ones, often peeping through the venetian blinds to check on the "kids." "I can't believe my little girl just turned eighteen," Mom says. "It seems like only days ago when we were playing koukou, ah!"

My heart is dancing the cha-cha. "What was he arrested for?"

Clement lights up a cigarette. "A drug deal gone bad. A fight at a pool party followed by a boy's body being found in his trunk."

A pool party, huh?

The cigarette hangs loosely from his lips. He lets it dangle there until the ashes fall off by themselves into a tiny gray pile on the floor. "Damnit!" he says. "I can't believe this crooked cop is still walking around freely with his police badge."

He lets me smoke some of his cigarette, and the gray smoke curls up toward the discolored ceiling. I slump down on a sofa, hoping that Clement is mistaken. The adults in the kitchen move on to talking about politics and the situation in Port-au-Prince. About the corrupt new police who replaced the army a few weeks ago.

"Are you sure about Ben?" I ask. "I mean, you know how it works here. Could just be rumors."

"Believe me, ti cheri, I know what I'm talking about."

My heart is skidding up into my throat. I need to find Nelly. Can it be true that Ben is a murderer? I remember the pool incident. I think about his broody eyes, his listen-to-me lips.

I look everywhere. Nelly and Ben are gone. Just gone.

It's midnight. I dial Nelly's phone number. No one picks up. The deejay belts out Bob Marley, and I chug my cup of cola champagne a little harder and realize how empty it is. The music is crisp in my ears, light and airy.

One in the morning. Nothing. At two o'clock, most of the guests are gone. I try Nelly's home phone again. Nothing. While dialing, I get so many mosquito bites I take a pen and play connect-the-dots on my legs. Sleep crusts the corners of my eyes.

The last guests leave around five a.m. I finally get Nelly's mother on the phone. She says her daughter hasn't come home, and do I have any idea where she might be?

"We need to find Nelly," I tell Clement in a coarse voice after hanging up. "Maybe she's over at his house. He told me once where he lives. Would you please take me there?"

We don't exactly give it a second thought. We get into Clement's Honda. The sun is just waking up, and the wind whistles through the winged windows of the car. The cold air whips my hair as we pass houses patched with tin, cardboard, and plastic. Kenscoff smells of fresh leaves and donkey dung. The town is so quiet at this time of day that all I can hear is the jingle bells of ice-cream carts pushed by men on their way to Pétionville to sell sweet coconut popsicles. The road leading to Ben's house is narrow and crooked. My heart is burning. I am haunted by the disturbing stories about Ben, and it's nerve-racking.

Clement uses a rock to knock on the gate. We wait and listen; I think I hear the singing of psalms inside. A woman with heavy-lidded eyes and a red blouse comes out of the house. She looks at us curiously. "M ka ede w?" she asks. Can I help you?

"I'm sorry to bother you at this hour, ma'am, but we really need to see Ben," I stammer.

She asks us to follow her, and we walk inside a room where four women are praying and incense is burning with a pleasant smell. All the shades are drawn. One woman lifts her head and nods. Clement and I nod back and follow the one in red down some stairs into a basement. She knocks on a door. "Ben," she says, "there are some people here to see you."

The door opens, and the smell of marijuana rushes out along with the rank odor of alcohol and stale cigarettes. Ben emerges from the room, his lids thick, his eyes red and watery.

"Hey, Ben," I say, trying to sound casual even though I am sure my fear is visible. "How are you?"

His lips are drawn in a tight smile. His eyes are dead.

"I'm looking for Nelly," I continue. "Is she here?"

He opens the door, and there are three other guys in his

bedroom, all high on something. Two of them, their eyes set deep in their sockets, are watching TV. The third one has passed out. He is lying on a padded sofa, bathing in his own vomit, the smell of which almost makes me sick. There's a faint lamp in one corner of the room, and no sunlight gets in at all. We walk in and Ben puts his hand out, laying it on my arm. "She won't come out of the bathroom," he says.

His hand is raw on my skin. The darkness in his voice makes me shiver. His expression is unreadable. How did I ever find him cute? I notice a gun on his desk. The danger in this room is sharp enough to make the air around us crackle.

"Seems like you had quite a party here," Clement says with a detached voice. How can he sound so relaxed?

I knock softly on the bathroom door. "Nelly, are you in there?"

No answer. Clement gives me a quick glance over his shoulder. I knock again. "Nelly, it's Magda. Please open the door."

Ben pulls me near. His hand caresses my shoulder, slides down my back, and comes to rest beneath my armpit, at the swell of my breast. "I'm sure she's okay."

I hear someone's faint crying. Oh God! What did he do to her? Then the door cracks open, and Nelly sticks her head out. Her dark hair hangs across her forehead in messy strands. She comes out of the bathroom and hugs me. Her eyes are dark, hooded.

"We'll be going now," Clement says then.

Nelly turns away from me to look at the men. Fear whisks across her face. Ben is tracing his finger along a scar on his chin. "No problem, man," he says.

He doesn't appear anything like the man I met months before. His good looks are gone. There is a stiffness to his face.

He has an empty stare. When he kisses Nelly on the lips, she doesn't kiss him back. Ben's cheeks harden and his neck tendons engorge. There's this dangerous look in his eyes again. The one I've seen in cats' eyes while they play with their prey.

We make a quick exit to the car. I am about to get into the vehicle when a wave of nausea rolls over me too fast for me to feel it coming. I dry heave for several long moments. When the nausea finally abates, my temples are pounding, and the sunlight suddenly seems too bright. I pull myself inside the car, taking deep breaths to calm down.

On the cusp of morning, we ride into the sunrise, past the big old two-story houses with porch swings and flower beds along the front walks, the beautiful old flamboyant trees that line the quiet streets and hold on to their bloody leaves.

"I was afraid he was going to rape me," Nelly says. "That's why I wouldn't come out of the bathroom."

"I was afraid he was going to kill me," I say. "But I couldn't just leave you there."

The bumpy Kenscoff Road is quiet, and the damp air raises goose bumps on my skin as I look ahead into the breaking clouds, warm colors coming in to soften the sky—pinks and golds that blossom against the horizon like jungle flowers.

But as I suck in my breath, I can't taste the sunrise. I'm looking over my shoulder. Because Ben knows where I live.

THE FINGER
BY GARY VICTOR
Port-au-Prince

Translated by Nicole Ball

W ith an agility that revealed an extensive amount of experience, Dread Lanfè leaned on his hands and, after a perfect pull-up, hoisted himself to the top of the wall that enclosed the property. Then he checked out the surroundings with eagle eyes. The premises were deserted. Except for a dog barking next door, there was nothing to disturb the silence. As soon as he was sure the way was clear, he put the fingers of his right hand in his mouth and made a high hoot that sounded exactly like the screech of an owl. Right away, his two accomplices, each carrying a canvas bag, popped out of the night. They climbed up the wall too. Dread Lanfè slung a .38 Uzi across his shoulder and walked quickly to the door indicated by the servant who served as informer for the job. Dread Lanfè stood still a moment to make absolutely sure the way was clear. The two German shepherds that might have stirred up the neighborhood had died a few minutes before, after they had swallowed—the pigs!—two pounds of meat spiced up with homemade poison. It was Grizon's turn to act now. He was a former Tonton Macoute turned political activist, like Dread Lanfè. Grizon was famously expert at picking locks: he could force open the most recalcitrant doors, and it took him less than three minutes to open this one.

Dread Lanfè, his Uzi in hand, entered a dilapidated room

with walls blackened by smoke. The scents of oil, spices, and spoiled food floated in the air. Pots and plates were piled in a jumble on shelves. A faucet was letting out a thin flow of water that was running in the darkness with a sinister hiss. He gestured to Grizon to close the door, then gave him the order to remain in the room and cover him. He liked to talk like the military, copy the way they acted and put on their look of mean dogs, to show that he was no petty thug but a political activist about to be integrated into the police force by the dictator—in exile at the moment—with the rank of inspector. If he had become a full-time thief it was because the bourgeoisie and the expat intellectuals had ganged up with the Americans and the French to kidnap the leader. He fully intended to come out of this rich house loaded with major loot. Eight kids to put through school, one wife, and three mistresses, among them the luscious Italian who loved his enormous member so much. He really had to move his ass now. Gone were the checks and suitcases stuffed with money coming from public agencies, the afternoons spent with all the activists who met to smoke grass, snort coke, and talk politics.

While brooding over these dark thoughts, Dread Lanfè walked gingerly up the stairs leading to the bedroom where Fanfayon, the owner of the place, and his wife were sleeping. Dread Lanfè always picked his victims with care, gathering all necessary information about them ahead of time. Certain mistakes had to be avoided at all cost. After you had taken enormous risks, you could either return with an empty trunk or go after a big shot who'd been a supporter of the former dictator. Fanfayon was one of those. He owned several gambling houses, two supermarkets, a money laundering enterprise, and a dozen or so pawnshops in Port-au-Prince. The money made in the gambling houses was transferred to his bedroom safe at night. Dread Lanfè trusted his informer. Sure of himself, he burst into the bedroom, followed by Fat Alfred, his other accomplice. In the wink of an eye they had Fanfayon, still sluggish from sleep, under control. The businessman's wife screamed. Fat Alfred made her stop by hitting her on the head with an iron bar. The woman collapsed, unconscious, her face all bloody.

"The money!" Dread Lanfè bellowed, the tip of his .38 pressed against Fanfayon's temple. "Give me the money or I'll scatter your brain all over this room!"

Fanfayon rolled his frightened eyes. He stammered something and let out a cry of pain when an impatient Dread Lanfè kicked him in the groin. He doubled over, gasping. Dread Lanfè quickly brought up his knee. The noise made by the impact, the blood gushing out—he enjoyed it all. Fanfayon remained slumped on the floor. He was holding his belly and moaning.

"Give me the money!" barked Dread Lanfè again.

Fat Alfred forced Fanfayon to stand up and dragged him violently to the safe located between a dressing table and a bulky mahogany wardrobe.

"Open it!" screamed Dread Lanfè. "I've got no time to waste."

"There's no money here," Fanfayon managed to say between sobs. "I swear it on my mother's head."

"Liar!" hissed Dread Lanfè, kicking him hard. "If you don't open the safe, I'll kill you."

Whimpering, Fanfayon put his hand forward to dial the combination. Dread Lanfè was following the businessman's movements with distrust, his finger on the trigger of the .38. When Fanfayon opened the safe, Dread Lanfè went back at his victim with renewed ferocity, hitting him with a kind of blind rage. Fat Alfred, meanwhile, was frantically looking through the safe. "Dread Lanfè, there's no money!" he yelled. "What do you mean there's no money?" Dread Lanfè cried, turning away from Fanfayon, who lay unconscious on the floor.

He shoved his accomplice back and stuck his head inside the safe. He had to face the facts and it didn't take long. The safe held uninteresting, worthless papers, a passport with an American visa stamped in it, and small change. Eyes bloodshot, Dread Lanfè grabbed Fanfayon, who was no longer moving. Dread Lanfè didn't know how to perform artificial resuscitation so he turned to Madame Fanfayon. But Fat Alfred had killed her on the spot with that iron bar to the head. Dread Lanfè and his accomplice combed the place desperately, one room after the other, in search of some nook where a sizeable sum of money might have been stashed. Finally, he realized that this was not going to bring in much and came back to the bedroom. Fanfayon was still breathing. Dread Lanfè finished him off with a quick bullet to the temple. He had to get out of there quickly, he thought, but then noticed the ring his victim was wearing on his left forefinger. It was a solid gold piece of jewelry that glowed in the dim light as if it were phosphorescent. Dread Lanfè examined it with interest. He was mesmerized by the two snakes elaborately carved on the precious metal. Fanfayon was certainly a servant of a lwa who favored him with wealth and protection. As he couldn't manage to get the ring off the finger, Dread Lanfè angrily cut off the appendage with the knife that had already cut so many. He put the finger in his shirt pocket before signaling to Fat Alfred that it was time to leave the premises. The neighbors might have been alerted by the shot. They vanished into the night as furtively as they had come.

* * *

Depressed, Dread Lanfè didn't go home. He had another plan in mind. He decided that this was a bad-luck night, and he shouldn't do another job. He went to Paola's, his Italian mistress. She worked for an NGO and was always proud to show him off—him, Dread Lanfè, like a trophy you fought hard to win. He was fond of Paola even though he knew she didn't care too much about the dire poverty of the people in the city where she'd come to work. Her apparent commitment was hiding something else. Some deeper discontent. A loneliness her culture had planted in her. Poverty, death ever-present, black bodies gleaming with sweat. All those niggers wanted was to gobble up white women and that made her panties wet—she, who had been frigid before. When she met Dread Lanfè, it was love at first sight, an explosion. The man had the reputation of being a criminal. He was tall, ugly, wild, and most of all, blessed with a member (a publicly known fact) that made all the other niggers in town envious. When Dread Lanfè put his hand on her, she could visualize mud and blood, and that propelled her right down the track to orgasm. And Dread Lanfè told himself that Paola was his safety net in this fucked-up country. Perhaps some day she would take off with him and they'd go live under other skies. That's why he felt he had to concentrate on her, always keep himself in condition to satisfy her well.

So he knocked on Paola's door. As soon as she knew it was him, she yanked the door open. She didn't even give him time to undress. She wanted him to take her right there and then, in the living room. Dread Lanfè lifted her up with all his strength, propped her against a shelf, crushing china, pictures, statuettes in the process, like the brute he was. The anger he felt about the botched job at Fanfayon's increased his energy tenfold. Paola nearly fainted after her orgasm. Dread Lanfè, following the ritual they had worked out together, made her come back to reality with a pair of slaps.

"Let's go to bed," she stammered.

"Give me a little powder first," ordered Dread Lanfè. She complied. After they had both snorted their dose of coke, they felt like the world was at their feet. Paola quickly fell into a deep sleep. Dread Lanfè then remembered that he had Fanfayon's finger in his shirt pocket. He couldn't fall asleep with a dead man's finger on him. He got up, took the finger, tried once more to take the ring off it, but didn't succeed. That ring could very well bring him a nice bundle of dollars. Dread Lanfè knew how to recognize gold. He put the finger on the dressing table, in a china glass. Paola would see the finger when she woke up. Lanfè didn't care. It would only add to his charm. He tossed his shirt over on a chair and came back to lie down next to her. He tumbled into a heavy sleep, disturbed by the impression that a foreign body was crawling over his chest. He knew it was the finger when he felt the ring rubbing against his skin. He screamed and sat up on the bed, gasping, his body drenched in sweat. Thinking that maybe some horrible creature had slipped in next to him, he jumped out of bed. But he couldn't find anything suspicious. The finger was still on the dressing table. He managed to convince himself that it was just cocaine playing tricks with his mind.

"What's the matter?" asked Paola somewhere between sleep and wakefulness.

"Nothing," he muttered. "A bad dream."

"Come back to bed. Come closer to me."

Dread Lanfè went back to bed. He held her tight, seeking comfort and safety in the warmth of her body, safety that only his mother, a peasant woman from Artibonite, could give him when he was a child. He was unable to go back to sleep. The nightmare just caught him like that, while he was still awake. He felt the finger on his thigh, climbing up, lingering over his navel. Dread Lanfè got rid of the intruder with an abrupt swing of his hand. He heard the finger falling on the floor and immediately trying to climb back onto the bed. Terrified, he jumped up and rushed to the dressing table. The finger had disappeared. Terror took hold of him like a gust of wind carrying a dry leaf away. He grabbed the machine gun he had placed underneath the dressing table. In the semidarkness of the bedroom, Dread Lanfè heard the finger climbing on a chair. Like a madman, he opened fire, unleashing an infernal racket. Paola woke up screaming, just as the finger jumped on Dread Lanfè and clung to his chest like a devilish bloodsucker. Without meaning to, Dread Lanfè pulled the trigger of the machine gun again. A hail of bullets brought Paola down. He dropped the gun in an attempt to snatch the finger from his chest. A demonic laughter rang in his ears. The finger was growing, transforming into a hideous, slimy creature with a cold and scaly body, a body that was coiling around his. Dread Lanfè tried to shout. He died without even realizing it.

When the police, alerted by the neighbors, burst into the bedroom, Dread Lanfè was lying on the floor, his body all dislocated. Paola was naked on the bed, her corpse riddled with bullets. The magistrate had not yet arrived for the report. The inspector who was leading the police squad gave the order to cover the foreign woman with a sheet. The officer crossed himself in front of Dread Lanfè's body. He knew him well, for he had met him many times at the dictator's place. While searching the room for possible booty, he discovered the finger on the dressing table, hidden behind a bottle of perfume. The ring immediately caught his eye. Surreptitiously, he grabbed it and slipped it quietly into his uniform pocket. The inspector knew a fence who always gave him a good deal. He didn't pay attention to the finger, which was already on the move.

PARADISE INN
BY KETTLY MARS
Gokal

Translated by David Ball

I t was pitch-black out when I reached the town of Gokal. We were in the rainy season and the humidity grabbed me by the throat through the open window of my car. All I could see were a few little houses shrouded in darkness and an occasional dog prowling around. I was looking for the Paradise Inn.

At the very end of the main street, to my left, I could see a light. A house was floating in the surrounding darkness like an ocean liner cruising through the sea at night. A rectangular one-story concrete building in no particular style, a few yards back from the main street. No garden in front, just a few agaves growing in the midst of the gravel. A loud neon sign was blinking mauve letters inside an orange circle: *Paradise Inn*. What a pretentious name for such a godforsaken place.

A rather unexpected apparition in this isolated spot. No one in the street, not the least glimmer in the windows of the other houses. The policeman inside me was already asking himself questions. From the moment I'd arrived in Gokal I'd been feeling vaguely uneasy. But I wasn't going to worry myself with suspicions when I saw the place where I was going to live. I was lucky to come upon this kind of establishment in this dismal town in the northwest, the most unprepossessing corner of the island. Plus, it was all lit up and apparently comfortable. I'd see about the rest tomorrow. My stiff muscles were begging me to find them a decent bed.

I left my things in the car, put my weapon around my waist, straightened the kepi on my head, and headed in. I would go back and get my bag after checking in.

The main entry door opened onto a big hall that served as a lobby and cafeteria. A shiver went across my scalp as soon as I stepped inside—the cool temperature contrasted so violently with the stifling heat outdoors. An oldies tune was coming from a radio that I couldn't locate. I looked around the place. In the back, to the left, there was the reception desk, separated from the rest of the room by a curtain of multicolored glass beads swaying under the breeze from the ceiling fan. I walked over to the reception desk. Nobody was there. I could sense some movement in the room behind the desk, which was also lit up. A half dozen small square tables, each surrounded by four chairs, took up the space used for the restaurant. They were covered with red tablecloths and decorated with glass pitchers containing bouquets of plastic flowers. Some of the tables still had scraps of food, dirty dishes, and glasses on them. I thought I could make out the clicking of knives and forks, but that must have come from the kitchen. The service left something to be desired: still nobody around. At the rear of the dining room, a staircase lit by a dark red light led to the floor above.

I shook the bell on the table. A few moments later, a woman came out of the back room. She was wearing a wide white dress that went all the way down to her ankles. A multicolored madras scarf was knotted around her head, hiding the top of her forehead and her ears. Her careful makeup gave her an incongruous appearance: such stylishness within these lonely walls was certainly unexpected. A solid gold Virgin hung from a massive chain around her neck and danced as she breathed. She was beautiful despite her plumpness, which weighed down her features and figure. An artificial smile stretched her lips and I admired a perfect row of teeth. The kind of black beauty who is hardly affected by time. She must have been about fifty.

The smile suddenly vanished from my hostess's face. "Good evening, sir?"

"Good evening, madame! Umm . . . I'm looking for a room for the night, perhaps for a few nights . . . That depends . . . I was . . ."

"Ah! You must be the new chief of police for Gokal?"

"Err . . . Yes, I am. But how do you know that, madame?"

She hesitated a moment, and then answered with a cold smile: "Oh, you know, Gokal is just a small town, no bigger than the palm of one's hand, and news travels fast. There never were a lot of people here, and they leave, one after the other, every day. Everybody knows everybody else, everybody knows what's happening or what's going to happen. And the uniform you're wearing confirmed what I thought. Policemen don't wander around this place just for fun."

She scored a point there. I didn't press it, and asked her to register me for a week at Paradise Inn. Her only answer was to hand me a key.

"Don't you need to know my name, my address? Don't I need to give you a deposit? How much is the room?"

I was dumfounded by my hostess's reply. She gave a deep sigh and looked me straight in the eye while she said this, all in one breath: "You are Commissaire Vanel, born in Jérémie on September 28, 1968. Appointed to the police as a level two officer August 15, 1990, at the Port-au-Prince Academy. Bachelor. After your first year of service, you won a scholarship to Japan, where you went through twelve months of intensive training in the investigation of drug trafficking and related money laundering. Back in Haiti, you were a detective for eight years in the anti-gang division, and you were then appointed assistant to the head of the Criminal Investigation Department. In the capital, you live at 39 rue Bouvier. You know, Commissaire Vanel," added the woman with no particular emotion, "I have the register of the Paradise Inn in my head. Don't worry about it. As for the price of the room, you will be perfectly satisfied. Trust me."

Oddly enough, I didn't feel like arguing. The place was now so cold it was freezing my very core, paralyzing my reactions. Despite how surprised I was by the declarations of the woman standing before me, I could only think of getting a bite to eat and sinking into a bed. Tomorrow I could review the situation, look around the place, find police headquarters, and begin to adjust, so to speak.

I asked my hostess if she could have dinner brought to me in my room. She confirmed this. I took the key she gave me; it had the number 6 on it.

She had a last recommendation for me: "In the dining room, you must always sit at table number 6. It is reserved for you. At night, try not to make too much noise, so as not to disturb people in the other rooms."

I was surprised at these precautions, since I hadn't seen a soul in the place. I went out to get my bag and locked the car.

Room 6 had minimal furniture. A double bed that seemed fairly comfortable. A table with a reading lamp on it. Opposite the bed, there were armchairs on either side of a small round table. I found a few hangers in the freestanding wooden closet decorated with a long mirror. The bathroom was just as plain. A narrow shower, a sink, and a toilet. The towel was clean and the soap had not been opened. I took a shower; hot water flowed from the faucet. This hotel was surprising me at every turn. I felt better after the shower. A pleasant torpor was invading my muscles and brain. I was surely going to fall asleep soon. The situation seemed less dramatic than I thought it would be. In my mind I was thanking my old friend Froset, who used to be my partner in my years as a detective. I had been stunned by the news of my imminent transfer to Gokal and called him up. Practical as ever, he'd given me the name of the Paradise Inn. It was known in high places. Froset had rapidly climbed the ladder because of his excellent service record and was now part of the high command. I wasn't too worried, because Froset would surely not let me rot for a long time in this hole. Of course, when the top brass appoints you to a new place, they don't care how you get there nor even where you'll live.

I put on a loose undershirt and clean underpants. Then I took my cell phone to call my brother in Port-au-Prince and tell him I'd arrived safely. The screen of the phone showed the signal wasn't getting through; there was no way to communicate. Not too surprising—that often happens in out-of-the-way parts of the country. I'd try later.

Someone knocked at the door. I took my weapon out of its holster and, holding it at arm's length, opened the door halfway. A young woman stood there with a dinner tray. The mauve light from the corridor darkened her very black skin still more. All I could see of her was her white smock, her eyes, and her teeth. I waved her in and she set the tray down on the round table. In the light of the room, I could see she was a very young girl, no more than sixteen or seventeen. An oval face and big eyes that looked right through me. Her lips were thick and well defined: a mouth that ate up her face. Her kinky hair showed from underneath her scarf. Her breasts, firm as unripe fruit, pushed out at a little blouse cut off at the navel. A long filmy skirt covered her ankles. No jewel decorated her wild beauty. Once the tray was set down, I expected her to leave. But she didn't. I looked at her more closely. She reminded me of someone—but who? Oh, yes! The woman at the reception desk. My landlady must have looked like this girl forty years ago. The presence of this adolescent disconcerted me. The aroma of the consommé stirred my hunger and reminded me that I'd had my last meal more than twelve hours ago. I swallowed with difficulty and finally sat down at the table to eat. She retreated and stood in a corner of the room, watching me stealthily. The soup was thick and tasty.

"The lady downstairs is your mother?" I asked the girl.

She nodded.

"What's your name?"

"Josiane."

"Your nickname is Jo?"

She smiled, and this gesture hollowed out two wonderful dimples that hung on to her smile.

"Sometimes."

I kept on asking: "You've been working here for a long time?"

"Yes . . . I mean, no . . . I help my mother out from time to time."

"Do you often serve guests in their rooms?"

"Yes."

"Aren't you at all afraid?"

"No . . . The guests are always nice to me. And then, before long they become harmless."

I didn't get the meaning of that remark. I was wondering if this child was really all right in the head.

"What do you mean, harmless?"

"Umm . . . Yeah, after a few days here, all they usually think about is resting. Yes, that's what I mean. Are you going to stay in the hotel a long time?"

"I don't know yet. Why?"

"You're leaving tomorrow?"

For every answer, she was now asking me another question. What a funny girl. I thought I could detect a small note of alarm in her voice. Her eyes were staring at my face with touching attention and her question almost resembled a prayer. No, I really didn't understand the coded language of this sweet child. I continued to doubt her mental capacities. Living year-round in this desolate environment, serving all kinds of guests in their rooms, could shake up a young mind.

"No, not tomorrow, Josiane. I'm here on assignment, unfortunately."

Josiane sighed and turned her eyes away. The situation was becoming stranger and stranger. I continued to eat, thinking all the while. The atmosphere of this place had weighed on me as soon as I arrived. I kept trying to reason with myself, but I couldn't quite get rid of that feeling. And now, this girl in my room. I picked up the glass of rum on the rocks from the tray and took a good swallow. Here I was, Commissaire Vanel, a career police officer, awarded medals by the high command, shut up in a strange hotel room in the middle of nowhere with a girl with exciting breasts and a deranged mind. When I got the envelope with the official seal on it yesterday—the envelope of my disgrace—I had absolutely no idea what was waiting for me.

The same torpor I'd felt after my shower took over again. My limbs were growing heavy, my joints seemed made of cotton. I finished eating and drank the rest of my rum. I thought

Josiane was going to clear the table and I went over to the bed. When I sat down, she walked right up to me, very close. Now I was surprised by the passivity of her features. She was acting like an automaton. Deliberately, this child-woman was indicating that the time had come to stop the little game of Q&A. She was putting herself at my disposal.

A violent perfume was coming up from her armpits and provoking chain reactions under my skin. She was standing directly in front of me with her nipples brushing my face. She took my head by the nape of the neck and pressed my face between her breasts. I was progressively losing consciousness.

Thoughts of prudence did flash through my mind—she must surely be a minor—but no argument in the world could stand up against the tide that was sweeping me away. I wanted to touch her, my fingers were burning to caress her dream of a body, but she stopped my hands every time. She wanted to be the only one in charge.

"You want me," she whispered. Her desire was of no importance; perhaps she felt none at all. All I had to do was let her do what she wanted. Was this service included in the price of the room? My eyelids were getting heavier and heavier, and as I threw back my head, the big mirror on the wardrobe showed me the picture of a child kneeling as if in prayer before my erect virility.

I woke up relatively early. Roosters were still crowing. From my room I could see the main entrance. My car was in the same spot. The brilliant sunshine reflecting off the stones of the street burned my eyes. The trees were rare and stunted in this place. There was something like a bit of life animating the main street. Doors on the side streets opened and a few people with dull looks on their faces were leaving their homes.

I freshened up and put on a pair of jeans and a green T-shirt. I didn't think it necessary to wear my uniform. First I wanted to take an inventory of the place, more or less, and transmit my report to the high command. I wanted to call Roland again, but my cell still wasn't getting any signal; it remained strangely dead.

I got the idea of taking a discreet little tour around the property. The uneasiness I had felt the night before was persisting. I wanted to get a better idea of the Paradise Inn. I slipped my .38 under my belt. My room, number 6, gave onto the stairway at the end of a long corridor that connected the different accommodations. I tiptoed by them. When I reached the first landing, I opened the little door that closed off the corridor. It opened onto another series of steps leading to the ground floor at the back of the house. Might as well learn what was happening down below, stage left.

I came upon a vast courtyard. The place seemed dead; everything was covered by a thin layer of dust. The courtyard faced a garden overgrown with brambles. Empty pans were waiting around the dry basin of a fountain. I couldn't see anyone but I remained vigilant. I would have preferred to see people: the silence and desolation of the spot were giving me the shivers. I heard a noise and my heart started pounding wildly. In my whole career as a policeman, it was really the first time I'd been that scared inspecting a place. I couldn't foresee what kind of enemy I was going to be faced with. The lady upstairs had turned on the radio. Suddenly I realized that the whole time I'd been there, I hadn't heard the humming of a generator. I glanced at the roof. No solar panels. They couldn't have a system that worked on batteries when there was no current to recharge them. So? And yet everything seemed to work on electricity at the Paradise Inn.

The backyard of the hotel was uninhabited. No staff, no life, no smell. I continued my tour, hugging the walls as I walked along. I opened a door. It made an eerie sound, amplified by the emptiness of the place. A bedroom with closed windows bathed in a red half-light. I didn't go in, but I looked around. Cobwebs hanging from the ceiling. The place smelled stuffy. There were many mirrors hanging on the walls, in all dimensions. Most of them were covered with big, dark veils. I made out the shape of a motionless body in a large bed, and I could hear regular breathing.

Josiane was lying in the middle of a mess of dried flowers, veiled mirrors, and spiderwebs. Her perfume reached me despite the strong smell of mold. I was chilled to the bone. What was Josiane doing in this sinister setting? How could people live in a place without leaving any trace of life? Who were these people?

I moved on. Two other rooms had the same dusty, abandoned appearance—what used to be a kitchen and a pantry in brown ceramic tile. I thought I'd seen enough.

Yet I still didn't know what to make of my tour of inspection. It was all muddled up in my mind. What conclusion could I draw from what I'd seen? Everything seemed frozen, fossilized. What energy was feeding this façade of life?

The lady at the reception desk greeted me as coldly as before. She suggested fried eggs and boiled bananas for breakfast. I agreed. The room was empty. No employee was bustling about to serve up the meal. My landlady appeared to do it all herself. I walked over to a table—number 5. I stumbled on something that seemed to be a foot stretched out right next to the table, but I couldn't get a good look. I stumbled again and tried to pull out a chair to sit down, but it resisted. I looked around. What do you know? The receptionist was watching me from behind her desk. Then I remembered what she had told me and walked back to table 6, rather embarrassed. I sat down with no problem. I had to keep my eyes open. Something very fishy was happening here. I was facing extremely tough enemies. Instinctively, I felt for the gun stuck between my skin and belt.

When my hostess brought over my breakfast, I decided to have a little conversation with her.

"I saw your daughter last night," I said.

There was no strong reaction from her. She looked me right in the eye as she answered, "Oh, yes. Were you happy with her services?"

The impudence of the question threw me for a loop. I wasn't expecting such audacity from the woman. I answered, as naturally as possible, "Yes, she does her work very well. But doesn't she help you with the service? I noticed you don't have much of a staff."

The woman smiled. An ironic smile that stung me to the quick. "Josiane only works in the evening. She takes care of room service. She has to save her energy for certain guests. Tell me, Commissaire Vanel, aren't you satisfied with our service so far? The room doesn't suit you?"

"Uhh, yes. I have no complaints."

"So don't worry about a thing. The staff here is competent and efficient. But I do thank you for your interest, Commissaire Vanel."

I decided not to continue the conversation. I had just received a lesson in authority, in all due form. The woman was chilling. She left me powerless.

I was hungry and ate greedily.

Like the previous evening, I noticed leftovers on the other tables, but no guests. The customers of the Paradise Inn were as discreet as could be. By the time coffee came (which was very sweet, strong, and hot), I felt myself overwhelmed by the same weariness as the night before. If this went on, I'd just laze around in bed. The air of the hotel must have soporific vapors, for I couldn't explain the lifelessness of my limbs and my will. I had to force myself to get up and head out to my car. It was time to take a drive around the town and locate the police station.

The two right tires of the jeep were flat and the vehicle was leaning to one side. This was hardly surprising: the road I'd gone down the night before could disable a tank on treads. I had to find someone who could repair the tires. There are always one or two people like that on the main street of every small provincial town. If I took the street back from the hotel, I'd surely find someone to help me. I walked for a good fifteen minutes. The whole town of Gokal was composed of one main street lined with little low houses with wooden lace cornices, all of them in disrepair and saturated with the surrounding gray dust. The road gave onto a little public square that I'd crossed the night before without realizing it. In the middle of this space rose the only tree worthy of the name, and around it was a church, a general store whose shelves seemed empty, and a few other houses in the same style as the main street. A little farther on, slightly behind the square, an open space must have been used as an outdoor market. The darker ground in this place suggested that the sale of charcoal must still support the dying economy of the town. I couldn't see any sign of a police station. Didn't the high command know that nothing—but nothing—happened in Gokal? On my way I only met a child carrying a bucket of water on his head, two old men sitting under the covered passageway of a rickety house, and a crippled woman squatting in a doorway.

No able-bodied man in view. The situation seemed bad.

I was sweating profusely. The best thing to do was to go back to the hotel and ask my hostess for help. I didn't like the idea. I felt I was at this woman's mercy. But she had to know the resources of the town.

I found her sitting at the reception desk. "Look," I immediately went up to her, "I'm sorry to bother you, madame, but I really need you to help me."

"How may I help you, Commissaire Vanel?"

Once again I felt like a child who'd been caught out, scrutinized by an adult. What was happening to me? Normally I was the strong one. I was the one who asked the questions, doubted, pushed, intimidated people. I was the police officer, the expert sleuth. I represented authority. People were afraid of me. I knew all the methods of persuasion. What was happening to me? Why did this woman have such a strong hold over me?

I forced myself to go on. "Well, here's the situation: I have two flat tires. So I have to find a repairman. I'm also looking for the local police station. My transfer happened pretty fast and I haven't had time to bring myself up to speed on the town of Gokal."

The lady seemed embarrassed, like someone who had to give someone else a piece of bad news. She fidgeted on her chair, leaned her head to one side, then to the other. Finally she said: "There are no tire repairmen here, Commissaire Vanel. As you must have noticed, there are no cars in Gokal."

"No cars?"

"None."

"But what about the customers who live in your hotel? And market days?"

She made an effort to continue the conversation, which clearly annoyed her. I was reduced to a child bombarding an irritated adult with questions.

"The hotel's guests are very special. Most of them are people who've come here to rest, men who want to get away from the craziness of city life. Among them there are a few policemen, like you. Once they've come here, they send their cars back so they can enjoy their isolation more fully. They rarely leave their rooms. As for the market, every Tuesday a few trucks do come to pick up the bags of charcoal that people in the country around here carry in by donkey. And that's all the traffic there is."

I couldn't believe my ears. How could the high command send me to a place like this? Why me, an elite police officer? Little by little, I was beginning to realize that I had been exiled, abandoned. I thought over my last conversation with Froset just before I jumped into my car to come to this wretched town. Come to think of it, he hadn't seemed particularly surprised by the news of my transfer. I was too happy about the hotel recommendation to pay attention to his lack of interest in my situation. And yet I regarded him as a brother. Once I had risked my own life to save his, during a clash with a bunch of gangsters. He used to tell everybody he was eternally grateful to me. With him in the high command, I felt I had some protection.

What was it he'd asked me on the phone? Oh, yes! He wanted to know what cases I was working on. Why had he asked me this question at that exact moment? And without thinking, I spontaneously told him I was working all alone on a big drug trafficking case involving someone close to the high command and that, after weeks of hard work, I was on the point of discovering this person's identity. My investigation wasn't taking place on the ground, but on the administrative level. I was trying to trace a network of fake customs documents to the top. Froset hadn't said anything, but now I recalled that he'd seemed embarrassed as he peered at me for a few seconds. Then he suggested that I shouldn't tell anyone about the results of my investigation. I could take it up again when my stay in Gokal was over. After that, he reassured me somewhat by telling me my posting there surely wouldn't last long—three months at most. Then he'd back my investigation with everything he had. Now the connection between the investigation and my transfer stared me in the face. I'd let myself be fooled, like a beginner. Instead of coming out here, I should have headed for the border at a hundred miles an hour. You always think things like this only happen to other people. I was like a rat caught in an invisible net.

These ideas were whirling through my head. I had to lean on the desk for a moment to continue the conversation.

"Uhhh . . . can I use a phone, madame? My cell hasn't worked since I got here last night."

"Sorry, commissaire. The hotel phone hasn't worked for ages."

"Oh! So I'll go phone from the police station."

"There is no police station here."

"You're telling me there's no police station here?"

"Yes, that's exactly what I said, Commissaire Vanel. Ever since President Belony's administration, at the time when the town of Gokal was part of the Villefranche district, there has never been a representative of the law here."

A question came to mind immediately: "But how do you know that, madame? President Belony's administration goes back more than a century."

This time she lost some of her composure. Her eyes

clouded over and she stumbled on her words as she answered. "My parents told me. I am from here, you know, Commissaire Vanel."

Her way of punctuating every sentence with a "Commissaire Vanel" was getting on my nerves. But I decided to keep calm. This woman was the only one who could help me. Josiane was floating between intermediate worlds in an amnesiac room. I kept asking questions.

"Where else can I find a phone?"

"The closest telephone switchboard is in the city of Papay, about an hour away by car," she answered sharply. My despair must have been evident on my face, because she softened up and said, "Come on, Commissaire Vanel, don't get all worried. Things will be okay. I'll serve you a good cup of coffee and you'll see things more serenely."

I walked over to table 6, surprised at my own obedience. The sensation of not being alone in the room bothered me for a moment, but I got rid of the feeling very quickly. My brain was being heated up by too many questions and too many sensations at once.

After some coffee, I did feel better, much better. My skin, my limbs, and my muscles pleasantly relaxed. All my worries seemed light to me. I was filled with a sweet sense of well-being. I watched the hotel owner move around and she seemed to float as she walked. I had a gentle smile on my face.

I spent the rest of the morning in bed. The effort of the morning's investigation had drained me. I felt a strange new sensation: my body was being emptied of its substance. I was drifting, carried along by a languor that only my bed could soothe. First I had to get rid of my fatigue, I thought. Once I was back in shape, I could get things under control and consider the situation. My first goal would be to fix my tires and find a phone. The only family I had was my younger brother Roland, with whom I shared an apartment. He wasn't in the capital at the time I left. I had left him a note to tell him what was going on. I had to call him, reassure him. I also had to call the high command, tell them about my situation, and wait for orders. But nothing seemed urgent to me now. I might as well take advantage of my forced vacation. After all, I had a hard life. To have a career as a police officer in a corrupt environment meant coming close to death all the time. Colleagues and friends kept dropping around me every day. Sometimes I had the feeling I was fighting shadows. The law watched impotently as convicts got out after just a few days in jail. Only the high command made real decisions. A thankless, risky job. This rest might actually be good for me.

I caught myself waiting for the night, waiting for Josiane. If she came back she would give some sense to my situation. She would make me forget my powerlessness, just as she had the first time. I spent the afternoon in my bed, sleeping. From time to time I would wake up with a start, feeling the presence of shadows moving around in the room, but I would immediately fall back into a deep sleep.

Josiane returned at nightfall. She knocked on the door; I was expecting her. I had dragged myself out of my comatose sleep half an hour earlier, and a cold shower had cleared up my mind. When I looked at myself in the bathroom mirror, the sight of my emaciated face gave me a shock. I looked as if I'd lost at least twenty pounds. I could hardly recognize myself. But I didn't attach much importance to this discovery. Probably an optical illusion. All fresh and perfumed, I was chomping at the bit, hoping Josiane would come. When I opened the door for her, the hinges squeaked with a familiar sound. She stood in the hall lit by the bulb with purple reflec-tions, wearing the same clothes as the night before. The same aroma of beef consommé got me in the guts. The same ice cubes were clinking at the bottom of the same glass of rum. A strong feeling of déjà vu weighed down on me: I felt as though I had lived through this scene hundreds of times. What day of the week was it? How long had I been in this place? I had to make a great effort to place myself. My God, what was happening to me? From time to time, I simply lost my train of thought.

Josiane watched me eat. She was spying on me from under the thick fringe of her eyelashes. I thought again of the girl I'd seen asleep in the room with a décor from beyond the grave. I could see her breasts again, the hollow of her belly. Once again, after dinner, I felt almost faint. I was drifting sweetly, wearily along. I thought only of Josiane's body, so very pres-ent in the room. All my questions sank into oblivion. The rhythm of my blood was slowing. My movements were getting all bogged down. I had only one desire: to give myself up to Josiane's skillful youth.

And yet when she put her hand on me, a last burst of conscience propelled me to my feet. I was sinking, calmly dis-appearing into quicksand. They'd sent me here to destroy me. Paradise Inn would be my final destination. But it wasn't too late to escape. I had to get out of here right away, on foot if need be, this very night. I'd surely find a truck driver on the highway who would take me to the next town. My survival instinct was telling me to react, to shake off this torpor that was inexorably condemning me to oblivion.

I caught Josiane's wrist and twisted it until a little cry of pain burst from her lips. I badgered her with questions.

"Who are you? Who is your mother? Who do you put up

in this hotel? Where are the other guests? Who are you working for?"

She was turning blue with pain under my grip. It hurt me
to manhandle her, but I had to save my skin first. She gasped
out: "I don't know. I don't know anything. I only work here.
Ow! You're hurting me."

I felt like slapping her. All compassion left my soul. I just
kept squeezing her wrist harder.

"I won't let you go until you answer all my questions. Got
it, you little bitch? Who are you, you and your mother?"

She was groaning with pain but said nothing. I squeezed
her wrist harder still and kept on pushing her with questions.

"Who does the cooking, and the wash, and the cleaning
up here? Why is the rest of the house dead? What is hidden
behind all that?"

Josiane's silence was incredibly irritating. I was foaming
with rage. This little woman thought she could manipulate
me through sex, lead me to the scaffold by my prick. I was going to teach her a lesson she'd never forget. I let go of her wrist
and slapped her very hard. I thought I'd broken every bone in
my hand. Her head was wobbling, she looked like a puppet.
She fell to her knees and I kept badgering her.

"Where do you get the electricity from? I haven't heard a
generator and I don't see any other system, how do you make
electricity? Answer me, for Christ's sake, or I'll strangle you!"

Kneeling on the floor, she tried to look into my eyes.
Maybe she thought she'd move me. Her lower lip was already
swollen; blood was gushing out of a crack in it. At last she
spoke. It was hard to understand her words.

"I'm telling you, I swear. I don't know anything . . . My
mother takes care of everything!"

A tear flowed down her cheek. I wanted to continue my

questioning. I raised my hand to hit her again, but my energy was rapidly disappearing. I was out of breath, my heart was about to burst in my chest, as if I'd run a hundred miles. I had exhausted my last stock of energy. I was being paralyzed by a will stronger than my own. My arm fell to my side. All I could do was drag myself to bed and sit down. Josiane realized I couldn't budge; she understood my exhaustion. She kept on crying softy as she spoke to me. I could hardly make out her words, which seemed to drift over to me from so far away.

"I don't know the people who live here. They're all men but you can't see them. They're sent here by the high command. The electricity that powers the hotel comes from draining their energy and willpower. They don't last long. That's all I know. You'll become like them too, until you're just a breath. You never should have set foot in this place. Never."

That's all I heard. I couldn't hold my body up anymore. I sank back into the pillows and passed out.

I felt better in the morning, although still very weak. When I looked at myself in the mirror, all I could see was a silhouette, a blurry image. My car was no longer in front of the hotel. On a hunch, I searched for my weapon in the chest of drawers where I was sure I'd left it the night before, next to my police badge. They had disappeared too. I smiled. I couldn't care less about all that anymore. I didn't give a good goddamn. It really relaxed me to not worry about a thing. All I was thinking about was having a good breakfast in the dining room on the ground floor, at my table, number 6. And above all, enjoying a big cup of that good, strong, scalding coffee my dear hostess had served me the day before.

I was calmly eating breakfast at table 6. Banana peels and crumbs of bread littered the other tables around me. But the guests still could not be seen. Through the window, I saw my brother Roland arriving. He parked his car in front of the hotel with a big squeal of the tires. He seemed worried. He rang the little bell and spoke to the manager as soon as she appeared. I heard my name. I realized my brother was giving her my physical description. He raised his arms to indicate my height, and with both hands he outlined my width. My hostess shook her head and looked truly regretful. No. No. She hadn't seen a police captain around here for ages. She said she was sincerely very sorry not to be able to help Roland. And I watched the scene from my table, sipping my coffee, totally indifferent. The high command had sealed my fate. Another life was beginning for me. I thought Roland would see me but his gaze just passed over me as I sat there, no more than ten yards away from him. He stood still for a moment, hesitating. Then he thanked the lady and walked away.

WHICH ONE?

BY Evelyne Trouillot

Lalue

Translated by David Ball

T he great-aunt in Brooklyn had promised to come get one of them, but which one? And take her in under her own roof, in her four-bedroom apartment—a godsend in New York! In a neighborhood that was getting less and less shabby: now the whites were trying to force her out.

"They can't make me leave. They can move in with their sidewalk cafés, their little 'boutiques' with those French names they pronounce in their terrible accent. No way I'm leaving here!" declared the aunt in Brooklyn.

"Her apartment takes the place of a husband," her niece Beatrice confided. "A submissive husband who doesn't answer back, stays clean, and doesn't have wandering hands. Who could ask for more? Four bedrooms is a luxury in New York!"

The bathroom next to her bedroom was graced with an enormous bathtub on ornately decorated feet. She had it put in after visiting the house of a friend audacious enough to tell the aunt that not having a bathroom connected to the master bedroom revealed a standard of living that was borderline primitive. The Brooklyn aunt allowed no one she knew to school her, be they relatives or friends. After all, ever since she came to the States she'd worked for a rich family on Long Island, Italian Jews with a taste for the good things in life and the ability to turn their money into more money. So nouveau riche Haitians thinking they could spin yarns to her—that really takes the cake! At her last yearly visit, Beatrice had gone into long raptures about the Italian tile in the bathroom and the bouquets of artificial flowers decorating the master bedroom. The second bedroom was reserved for the few rare relatives and friends bold enough to face the aunt's sharp tongue for more than a few hours. After all, she was a hardened spinster set in her opinions and prejudices. The third bedroom was transformed into a sewing workshop where the aunt made cushions and curtains in velvet materials she thought were fancy because her employers were crazy about them. For the moment, the fourth room, the smallest, was full of old furniture and knickknacks. It served as both a storehouse and a treasure trove. This was the shambles she counted on fixing up to take in one of her grandnieces, one of the daughters of her nephew Aramis. But which one?

When Beatrice talked about the whims of her Brooklyn aunt, both of us would listen with a mixture of dread, fascination, and envy for that other world of perpetual wealth and light. But also with the vague fear that TB (Tante de Brooklyn), which we only called her behind her back, of course, might learn of our conversations in which we made fun of her. Still, they were so much fun and so therapeutic that we never got tired of them. We mothers. After all, it was the great-aunt who regularly wired us money and had sent for her nephew Aramis, the one who was carrying on the family name. The one who looked the most like his late father—and the one who had gotten us both pregnant roughly two days (or maybe a few hours) apart. Who knows? In any case, our daughters were born on the same day, at full term and almost at the same time. Right in the middle of an Easter Sunday, like a double, sunny act of defiance. Aramis had told his aunt about it right away. From her Brooklyn apartment, the great-aunt had used her privilege as an elder, settled in the States for more than three decades, to name the babies: Marie Catarina and Marie Carlotta, Italian names embellished with the name of the mother of God in the good old Haitian Catholic tradition. We had not protested because these imposed first names were associated with the father. For Aramis Salnave—with his aunt's approval and an endearing smile from his sister—had legally recognized both children. I wonder what the clerk at City Hall thought when he saw the same date of birth and the names of two different mothers.

Which one of us had first succumbed to Aramis's charms? He's as seductive as the most handsome of the musketeers, Beatrice would repeat, always with the same pensive, nostalgic expression for that brother who'd left too soon, and also for a time when such literary allusions did not necessarily have to be explained. She would look at us almost despairingly when we didn't react. And yet from the very first day Aramis told me about the character to whom he owed his name, I got all excited despite myself, and without ever telling him, read and reread whole passages in the copy of the novel he'd lent me, carefully covered in plastic. His father, Hébert Salnave, had unlimited admiration for Alexandre Dumas and gave this name to his only son. Beatrice and her younger brother had grown up reading, listening to, and telling the stories of the three musketeers. Aramis knew his namesake's lines by heart and would quote them in the course of many conversations. He could easily narrate a whole episode if the person he was talking to seemed a bit lost. With a childish smile on his lips, he had charmed me with his cloak-and-dagger stories that were so far removed from our world that I was enchanted despite myself. I should have known this plunge into fantasy would cost me dear, I should have listened to my instinct, which told me to watch out.

He moved his hands when he spoke, like an enchanter whose only material to work with was his body. A beautiful body. Long, long, from his forehead to his slim, muscular legs. He walked like someone in a hurry, but with that relaxed, elegant air that attracted my eyes right away. Did the other mother also instantly feel fire spreading beneath her skin like lit paper before it's burned up by a flame? I could kick myself even today for not being able to resist that need, for having wanted the burning encounter of our two skins at any cost. Despite my instinctive distrust of sweet-talking men, despite my persistent refusal to believe that life was granting me a re-prieve. Even when I learned that he'd wooed another woman in the same month, with the same success, all he had to do was touch me and I was conquered anew, impatient to feel the delicious bite of his body again and again. Even while deep inside me, a child was already growing.

Yet my twenty-five years of existence had not really en-titled me to become somebody's mother. According to the family legend, after the departure of the man who had non-chalantly declared that the earth already had enough people on it, my mother, who was six months pregnant, let herself die. For five years. I still remember her lackluster, teary face and a childhood spent bucking up against that ever-present maternal sorrow. A world of constant privation, of sighs. Never enough food to satisfy you completely, restrained laughter, and shrunken, stifling spaces. No affection. My good grades in high school confirmed my conviction that education wasn't much use when poverty and bad luck were aligned against you. There I was with my diplomas under my arm, an arid mouth, and a long, gray, dirty avenue in front of me. You had to use people and things—before you were used yourself, and then discarded. That was my motto for survival. Aramis challenged it with a hearty laugh.

When Aramis told me he was leaving, he once again sang the praises and expressed his affection for his aunt in Brooklyn, the one who'd always promised the son of her deceased brother she would bring him to New York for good, on a student visa. Since the papers were ready, he was to leave as soon as possible. As for Beatrice, she had no desire to immigrate to the States. Comfortable in her role as a middle-aged childless widow, she did not want to start life over outside of the country. But Aramis always seemed like he was about to take off and fly. He was always looking for an excuse to change worlds. Put him anywhere at all, he always preferred elsewhere.

He left us mothers, each one with a baby less than a month old in her arms. He left without any sign of emotion except for a teary half-smile and his eyes drunk with anticipation. He left us with our sudden disillusions; the fury of targeting each other. He left us with the rage of tearing each other's memories away, along with any affection we might have felt for him. He left us to devour with our fingernails the breasts he had touched, the skin he had stroked, the folds of the arms where he'd buried his lips.

It finally took an international phone call from that four-bedroom apartment in Brooklyn to restore order and calm between Carrefour Feuilles and Delmas, between all those streets Aramis had walked down to go from one neighborhood to another and get into our homes, and into us, with promises and smiles and words so sweet that believing them was pure pleasure.

If I get the slightest whiff of a quarrel, I'll stop the money trans-fers. No more presents for the little girls, no more anything. Bea-trice transmitted the implacable message from the Brooklyn aunt with a touch of commiseration in her voice. Beatrice, with unavowed fantasies in her eyes and her bitter, frustrated hands. I pitied her a little, for her eyes often searched us for a spark of the fire that the merest mention of her brother's name would light up, turning us into two wild beasts. Peace reigned in her house, at 15 rue Paultre, where she remained in her secure solitude and refused the rare men who were brave enough to dare measure themselves against the frozen perfec-tion of her deceased husband.

"Why don't you move in here?" she finally asked us both. A skillful way to watch our every move and distribute her gifts according to our behavior. "I think that solution would please TB."

When did we mothers learn to tolerate each other? When the memory of Aramis's caresses was too distant to give his body any human substance? When the sweet heaviness of his sex faded away under the weight of unforgiving daily life? Searching for something to eat every day, looking for a job, picking up your dignity and shoving it under your hunger. In vain. Starting over again the next day. Holding back your surges of rage and walking up and down the streets of Port-au-Prince, trying not to deposit your fear onto them. Taking your desire to hit someone and transforming it into a caress over a baby's soft skin.

We couldn't reject Beatrice's invitation. She was giving us a neutral, comfortable space between our two wretched lives. Saving us from the envious mockery of our families, giving more legitimacy to our offspring. At 15 rue Paultre, in this wild, monstrous city, we found a stopover where we could shelter our shared disappointment. With Aramis gone, we found ourselves abandoned in exactly the same way. All the more so, as he quickly became too sick to talk on the phone and his destructive silence blanketed our memories with distrust. News came to us through Beatrice, who talked regularly with the great-aunt.

A few months after Aramis left, a family acquaintance brought some photos that showed us an emaciated, almost unrecognizable figure. Which of us turned her eyes away first? A hideous grin had replaced the seductive smile of the man whose lips had imposed their law on my body. His clothing floated around his tense, stiff arms and legs, as if the fabric refused to have any contact with his dried-out skin. A quickly metastasized cancer killed him a short time later. He'd sworn he would come for me as soon as he got his green card. Maybe he'd also promised the same thing to the other one? My hopes, already so slim, were utterly crushed.

Beatrice flew to Brooklyn for the funeral, armed with the tourist visa she was always careful to renew. She brought back a videocassette for each of us as an inheritance.

"My aunt thinks the children will probably want to watch it later," she said.

We mothers followed the religious ceremony on the screen, more curious to see TB's face than anything else. A very short, very plump little woman, hardly five feet tall without the high heels she wore—quite elegantly, in fact. Her face hidden behind a black veil, Italian style, of course. I was unable to watch the whole recording and I stopped before the burial. All those dark silhouettes gave me the impression of a black-and-white film, the kind impossible to understand, where the action never quite ends and you have to guess at so many things. Except I could already assume I hadn't been given a good role in this film. I closed my eyes. I wonder if the other mother kept watching to the end.

Beatrice then informed us of the great-aunt's decision to have one of the little girls brought to New York. To adopt her legally. Surprisingly, TB had hung onto her Haitian passport even though she'd only set foot on her native soil three times in thirty-two years—for her father's funeral, her mother's funeral, and then the double funeral of Beatrice and Aramis's parents, who had died in a car accident. She'd said goodbye to this unhealthy country, a perpetual insult to her delicate senses, definitely a danger for her eyes, which had been recently operated on to remove hard, thick cataracts. So, she was going to come here to adopt her nephew's child.

"With her, it's family first," Beatrice affirmed again. She had been entrusted with the task of setting the administrative procedures in motion as soon as possible. We mothers both had the same question on our lips and in our eyes. Which one of them? Faced with our anxiety, Beatrice's enthusiasm collapsed. Her voice fell silent between words as if she could suddenly see all the complications that lay ahead. "She says she hasn't made up her mind yet."

Late in the afternoon after the babies' bath, we would sit on the stoop with them. But most often, when Beatrice got back from her job as a civil servant in the General Tax Office, she would volunteer to take her nieces out for some fresh air. "Go for a little walk, go see some friends, I'll take care of the girls." She seemed to avoid talking to us individually. In her eyes we were merely the two mothers, the women who had borne the fruits of Aramis's love. Her affection for her brother stripped us of our identities. Just as she would say "the little girls" when she spoke about our daughters. Always referring to them in the plural, relegating them to the position of a falsely twinlike appendage of their father and thus doubly erasing us, the mothers.

The neighbors would come by for a little chat, depending on the day of the week and the time, to get their fill of gossip and more details of that tragic story of the deceased brother, the little orphans, and the impoverished mothers who were taken into the home out of Christian charity by their child- rens' paternal great-aunt, a good person despite her difficult personality. Passersby who didn't know the hidden side of their births would always react. The girls are the spitting image of Aramis, they would say. You can't tell them apart. Real twins. Man, do those little girls look alike. It's incredible! Doesn't God work wonders? Isn't that the truth! Beatrice would agree complacently. Often we would dress them the same way. It was inevitable, after all, as most of their clothes and linen— towels, washcloths, bibs, pajamas, onesies, tank tops, T-shirts, caps—arrived from Brooklyn in pairs. Only the loveys came with a very slight difference, and all that did was emphasize their similarity: two stuffed rabbits, one pink with white ears and the other white with pink ears. Compared to the display of clothes from America, with their smell of talcum powder and lavender (TB sent over laundry products and toiletries too), the few modest items of clothing we bought stood out immediately, like the poor relatives that we were.

Which of us set off the latest skirmishes? Waiting for the final selection fed the hostility between us. Our hesitant complicity rapidly crumbled away under the weight of tight-lipped com- ments and suspicious glances. A muted battle began, all the more unnerving as it was hidden under civil appearances so as not to provoke the wrath of the Brooklyn aunt. A dress inadvertently stained, a door banging a shoulder a little too hard—unfortunate accidents followed by hasty apologies. Beatrice took note of our new attitude with an astonished, disappointed look. She who'd never had a child, never known the pangs of hunger that wake you up at dawn and don't give a damn about the beauty of the rising sun. She who had always lived in the banal security of her job as a government employee, with her grandaunt's support for those needs people call superfluous, but which give life some color. With the ability to go far away if ever poverty drew too near 15 rue Paultre. To take off for Brooklyn and live with the great-aunt, work like her with Italian Jews or plain Jews, or work somewhere else. Beatrice who had probably never desired someone hard enough to trample on her fears and hold on only to the intimate smell, elusive and fleeting, of skin between her fingers. Hold on to it at any cost, for otherwise everything is pointless. And see it disappear in time nonetheless. Despite all my attempts to hold on to memories, all I had now was this baby, so much like her father and the other little girl, just as vulnerable as she was. Which one of them would reap the benefits of the aunt's hospitality?

"I'll always be there to help," Beatrice would declare tersely when the tension reached a climax in the house, making the walls seem as thick as a tomb. "My aunt can't adopt both of them. She's not young anymore, but the other little girl will stay here with me, if you like. Don't worry, they'll both be taken care of."

I could see my hopes and frustrations reflected in the other one's hunched shoulders. Our anxiety broke the silence. Even Beatrice couldn't escape from it. The two little girls were becoming individuals who were still largely indistinguishable, but who each had her own fate. The one who'd stay here in our country and the other who would go live with the Brooklyn aunt in her big four-bedroom apartment. Oh, not right away of course, but in a few months or perhaps a year. All the papers had to be in order and the aunt had to reduce the number of hours she worked for her Jewish-Italian bosses, to get her early retirement and do all that was needed to take care of the child. Just as soon as the lawyer filled out the adoption request form, the administrative process would begin. And already, when she pressed the girls to her chest, Beatrice would whisper into the ear of one or the other of them with a misty look in her eyes: "Well, sweetie, are you the one who's going to leave me? So it'll be you, my little sweetheart?" And she would shower both of them with kisses.

Sometimes I could feel the other mother's despair overwhelm her, and her moist eyes would make me even angrier. Apparently, she didn't understand that when you're used to getting hit, one part of you hangs onto the leather of the strap and you absolutely must not flinch when it grazes your skin. On the contrary, you get your back up, you brace yourself and you wait for what's coming, with your arms ready to pick up the broken pieces. And yet sometimes, in a flash, I could see the same dry, desperate determination in her eyes, which too often looked faded. Under her fragile appearances, was she, too, hiding rage strong enough to turn life upside down and give her little girl a chance?

And then one day Beatrice announced that in accordance with the aunt's orders, she had scheduled an appointment with the lawyer to begin the proceedings. That TB was going to inform us of her decision very soon. As she saw us jerk in alarm, Beatrice quickly added that she didn't know what the decision was. She would learn which of the little girls would be adopted at the same time we did. I managed to keep a poker face but I could feel my heart beating as if it wanted to jump from my chest and howl out its helplessness. The other could no longer hide her panic. Her fragility irritated me more and more. I would have liked her to be tough and unshakable like me—a formidable enemy, not a doll, easily smashed. Sometimes she would lean on the table as if she couldn't bear life any longer, with her baby on her hip. We often carried our little ones that way, like a bump on our side that wriggled and gurgled from time to time.

When the little girls' glances met, I wondered whether each one thought she saw her own reflection turning toward her. Of course, we could tell them apart, the other mother and I. I'd pick mine up and right away I could feel her little arms and legs clenching my body in total abandon, and in spite of myself I would lose some of my cynicism. How could I resist those tiny fingers clinging to my hair?

"Actually, you two resemble each other too," Beatrice declared. "That's why the little girls look like twins. My brother liked that type of woman. Ethereal, and a bit distant, taciturn. Both orphaned at an early age. Both frail, and mysterious," she added with a knowing smile. As if we reminded her of a character in those romance novels she was always devouring. It's true that we looked a bit alike, the other mother and I. We were the same age, both of us slender women with distant gazes. But I had discovered real differences very quickly. Through the other one's dull eyes, I could see the trembling of a woman asking for friendship. Physically, too, she would sway from time to time like a rootless plant shrinking under the heat of the sun. Sometimes Beatrice would give her a worried look. "I'll take you to the doctor if this keeps up." Egalitarian to the very end, she wanted to include me in the consultation. Or maybe it was one of the great-aunt's criteria. A medical evaluation of the two mothers before the definitive choice.

* * *

We were informed of the decision two days before the other mother had her first heart attack, four days before her death. As if her organism refused to assimilate the magnitude of the new situation. The announcement that the great-aunt would pay for the funeral quieted the discontented grumbling of the parents of the deceased far more than the verdict of the doctor who had hurriedly been called in. The young woman's heart had collapsed. From New York, TB demanded an autopsy, furious at the fate that had interfered with her plans. But the family—cousins and an old uncle who seemed greedy and self-serving—were against it. No way they were going to cut apart their relative's body. All they needed was a few thousand extra gourdes to do what had to be done.

The money was quickly paid, and an old woman came in with her panoply of leaves and bottles blackened by years of use. She shut herself up with the body to ward off any ill-intentioned attempt to get hold of the corpse after burial. The guilty party or parties would be punished. With the old mambo's expertise, it would not be possible to turn their cousin into a zombie. The rumors of evil actions went on for a few days and then went to feed the store of tales to be told.

The great-aunt was more indignant than ever at the country that once again proved how little it could be trusted. Young or old, people were dying like flies. But God moves in mysterious ways. For this death—so unfortunate and unexpected—confirmed her decision: more than ever, the little orphan needed all the help she could get. As for Beatrice, she repeated to all the visitors that before the other mother died, her aunt had a dream in which Aramis whispered which one of the two little girls to adopt. The Salnave family had always boasted of very strong spiritual connections with deceased relatives.

Meanwhile, they gave the little orphan to me, the surviving mother. Still stunned by the rapidity of my action and
its consequences, I cradled her with my own daughter. I had
hatched my plan hastily, no doubt, but it was pretty smart. I
couldn't believe I was really carrying it out. All I had done, in
fact, was take advantage of a given situation and wait for nature to take its course. After the very first visit to the doctor,
even before the great-aunt announced her decision, Beatrice
had confided that the other mother had a heart condition
and had to be spared any strong emotion. The doctor had
prescribed medicine and a special diet. Her lifestyle had to
change to limit risk factors. Beatrice repeated the entire doctor's jargon to me with a worried look. I listened with the
appropriate expression on my face, without playing it up too
much, already thinking of ways to exploit this illness, a gift
from heaven. I needed to *increase* the "risk factors," because
the other one had to disappear for my plan to succeed. If I
didn't watch out for my daughter's interests, who would? That
was the least I could do for this child. She hadn't asked me for
anything and I had brought her into the world. It was fine to
say that the two little girls would be cared for, but how could I
not dream of that expansive horizon offered to the one who'd
be taken in by the great-aunt? How could I not want to pre-
vent my child from taking that long, sterile road I had gone
down, the permanent anxiety of never knowing what tomorrow will bring, the feeling of walking with your arms dangling
helplessly at your side in a perpetual state of frustration and
rage?

I didn't go to the other mother's funeral. I stayed with the
two babies. On that day, I said goodbye to my daughter.

It was so easy to substitute one for the other, to comb my

baby's hair the way the other mother combed hers, to switch the few articles of their clothing that were different, to put one stuffed rabbit in place of the other. It never would have worked if the other mother were still alive. She would have seen through the swindle right away. But I didn't touch her that night. I could have activated the process, hastened the end. I did nothing of the kind. I let fate decide what would happen next. Who knows? They might have found her still alive at dawn.

That night, I'd been awakened by a thump and a child's whimpers. Instinctively—a child's sigh now had the power to dictate my actions—I turned my head to the cradle. My daughter was sleeping peacefully. I walked through the doorway between the two bedrooms.

The other mother was writhing on her bed. I took care of the baby first, gave her back her pacifier, before turning to the shrunken form on the rumpled bed. That's when I noticed her pale, literally twisted face. With one hand on her left breast and her features ugly with pain, she was inhaling noisily, a wild sound wrenched from her guts. The Bible she read every evening before she went to sleep was lying on the floor. My first reaction was to look for her medication; the pills Beatrice had brought back from the pharmacy, and put one under her tongue as the doctor ordered. Then I held back. Why would I do that? I gently covered the sleeping child in her cradle and patted her little raised bottom. I had nothing against that little girl. She was my own baby's sister, and besides, she was indispensable for my plan. Before leaving the room, I turned my head to the other mother. It seemed to me she was trying to raise her hand in my direction. I could hear her increasingly awful gasps, like calls for help stuck in the bottom of her throat, unable to reach the voice. For a second, her eyes—two frightened butterflies, prisoners of silence and pain—rested upon me. I turned mine slowly away.

In the bedroom at the other end of the hall, Beatrice wouldn't get up before dawn. I went back to bed and waited for daylight.

When she returned from the funeral, Beatrice took out Marie Carlotta's birth certificate. "Now this child has no father and no mother, but luckily she has aunts who love her very much and will take care of her. While I'm waiting for her to go to the great-aunt's, I'll take good care of her. Tomorrow I have an appointment with the lawyer."

I leaned over the two little girls lying on their backs in their playpen and picked one of them up. I kissed my daughter and gave her to Beatrice.

Ever since then I've been living in agony, an agony I deliberately chose. I had to learn to accept the brutal and unexpected pain of separation. Every gesture has become an open wound that gets larger, adds onto the other wounds, accumulating like a blazing fire that can't be put out. When I put her in Beatrice's arms, she was so very attentive to the little "orphan." I hugged the other baby and felt tears well up in my eyes, stinging my flesh. Hearing my daughter cry, knowing that the sound of my voice and the closeness of my body could calm her down, yet not budging, was agonizing. Letting Beatrice take care of her until her final departure, even more so.

I would have liked the process to go faster, the great-aunt to come over, sign the necessary papers, and leave with my daughter. That way I wouldn't have her before my eyes every minute of the day, treating her like someone else's child, watching her separating a bit more from me and turning to Beatrice, with the survival instinct natural to human beings.

There was no turning back now, and despite it all I did rejoice that my trick had succeeded. My daughter would have a much better life. She would have all the opportunities I didn't dare dream of anymore. One day, I saw Beatrice looking at me while I was watching the child asleep in her cradle, with the other one's daughter snuggled up against me. Did this childless widow understand my deception? Did she suspect that for once I had taken my destiny into my own hands, amending her aunt's decision?

It's too bad that, since then, every time my arms close around the one I kept, I can feel pieces of my heart disintegrating, then coming together again as I wait for the day that my daughter will leave me.

TWENTY DOLLARS

BY MADISON SMARTT BELL

Morne du Cap

I n the twilight of his last sliver of dream, Magloire saw VEN
DOLA, not as a single slip of green but all the bills fanned
out in a diadem and glowing with an incandescent light,
like a crown set on the head of Christ Resurrected. Indeed,
the dollar bills crowned his own head but at the same time
they appeared far away, so that he could not reach or grasp
them. In this slippery zone between sleep and waking he often received counsel of his spirits, and now he believed that
Èzili Je Wouj was promising him he might conquer such a sum
in the course of the day: twenty U.S. dollars—too small an
amount to resolve his difficulties, thus not so large as to be
unattainable.

He woke completely now, to cockcrow and the wispy
sound of a palm leaf broom, sweeping the yard beyond the
door. It was still almost completely dark. Anise's sleeping
breath flowed onto his forearm. She had turned toward him
on the thin pallet where both of them slept. Were she awake
she would not have done it. The whisper of air stirred something in him which he hurried to suppress, sitting up on the
pallet and wiping his face with the back of his wrist. When
he was a little younger, still in his teens, Magloire had been
counseled by Doctor Oliver to wear a kapòt during all acts of
love; such was the sort of foolishness that a well-meaning blan
would conceive. He, Magloire, enjoyed only natural actions

and undertook no actions that were not natural; therefore, he could seldom bring himself to wear a condom and by extension had not lain with his wife, as a man with a woman, for longer than two months. Besides, Anise would be irritable if he woke her now.

In a market basket near the door, draped with colored netting like a Christmas parcel, their son Léonty breathed easily in sleep. He was nearly two years old and had to curl his legs under him to fit into the basket, but he needed the protection of the net because mosquito bites had caused his fever; mosquitoes were still whining in the close humid air of the room, though the light was growing quickly. Magloire turned back the net for a moment to look at his son's face. It seemed to him that the fever had passed, though he had not been able to find money to buy medicine.

In the yard outside the back door there was clean water in the white enamel bowl. Magloire used a little of it to wash and brush his teeth. The whispering of the broom had stopped and he straightened up to see his mother standing over a cluster of scrawny hens, holding a scant handful of cracked corn in one hand, irresolutely.

Presently she scattered half for the hens and returned the rest to the slack cloth bag. Her deep-set eyes passed over him without stopping. Magloire knew that later in the day she would pound the remainder of the corn and mix it with a greater quantity of dirt to make small cakes—not very nourishing but able for a little while to block the most cutting pangs of hunger. Some passersby might purchase them. If he could, he would buy green coffee beans at market and a little charcoal so that his mother might roast the beans in her iron caldron and pound them in her mortar if the customer desired. There was some profit to be made preparing coffee.

The bare-swept area of their yard climbed sharply up the jagged backside of Morne du Cap. On the high ground, propped on stones beneath a stand of bamboo, were two gas generators Magloire had taken for repair. He was trained as mechanic, electrician, plumber, refrigerator repairman, and could also drive trucks, guide tourists, and pilot small boats (in one case all the way to Miami). But lately no one could be found to purchase any of these skills. The two generators ran smoothly now but their owners would not pay to recover them, so Magloire was simply holding them hostage. This situation reminded him of a story he had heard from the capital: some zenglendo had summoned a man to shine their shoes, then kidnapped him when he was done, though the most they could raise for a ransom was twenty dollars.

VEN DOLA. Shaking off the thought of the kidnapping, he walked through the house, pulled on a shirt, and came out onto the street. Through the alley that cut down to the waterfront, the rising sun blazed off the surface of the harbor. From the neighboring bar curled a stale odor of last night's frying. Magloire's stomach fisted. Squinting a little in the brilliance of the light, he walked through the alley to the edge of the breakwater and stood breathing in the clean salt air. Men called to each other from a couple of small boats going out to fish. Rope creaked against a makeshift mast as a sail bellied full, and from behind him Magloire could hear the steady hollow thump of his mother's mortar. It was said that one should take ten deep breaths each day before the sea.

Doctor Oliver drifted to a halt in the public square before the cathedral, a madman standing bare-headed under the scorching noonday sun. Once there had been shade trees in this place, but those were plowed under in some renovation and now there was nothing but bare flagstones and the statues of the national heroes, the metal ones looking as if they might melt. There were no people about on the square though a few had pressed themselves into tiny pools of shadow under the lintels of the church across the way.

In the southwest corner of the square was a new monument Doctor Oliver had not seen before, a different style from the venerable statues: three curving husks of polished aluminum, grouped together and standing about man-high. When he approached he saw there were inscriptions on the inner curves; the sculpture was arranged so that he had to step inside the grouping to try to read them. The effect was obscurely menacing, like standing inside some sort of iron maiden that had not yet been completely shut. Doctor Oliver did not feel well. He needed to take off his teardrop sunglasses to read and the burst of reflected light worsened his headache, which might have been brought on by sun or by early stages of narcotic withdrawal. The inscriptions were in Creole, which he had trouble puzzling out; he was more functional in French.

Gradually he absorbed the idea that each silvery husk memorialized a martyr of the Revolution who had died on this spot. Doctor Oliver recognized their three names from histories he had read. One had been burned at the stake and the other two broken on the wheel. This information seemed to be borne to him by some sort of voice-over narration, but surely that could not be real. Yet there was a Creole phrase being repeated in an angry monotone: *Blan! Pa gade dokiman m!* And a person saying it, a long scarecrow who'd detached himself from a niche of shade at the corner of the church and was walking toward Doctor Oliver in a jittery stride, obsessively repeating the words the doctor now understood to mean, *Foreigner! Don't look at my documents!*

Doctor Oliver put his sunglasses back on but that did not make him feel any safer. He felt dizzy and sick and unsure of himself. Normally this part of town was perfectly safe, but there were always exceptional days. The week before, an election had gone wrong somehow and since then demonstrators had sealed off the approaches to the town with burning barricades. Though those phenomena existed comfortably far away from the central square, the aggression hurling itself his way now seemed to partake of the same spirit. Doctor Oliver opened his dry mouth and found he could not frame a placating phrase in the right language.

Then someone else had put a hand under his elbow and was steering him gently away, and at the same time speaking to the other man with the calm fluency Doctor Oliver had been unable to summon: *Oke monchè, nou prale, nou pa gen pwoblèm ak sa wi?*

They turned a corner and there was shade. Immediately Doctor Oliver felt a little better. With his free hand he checked the nearly empty pill bottle in his pants pocket. He was in the company of Charles Morgan, a white American like himself, known to the locals as Charlie Chapo. Their soft tongues elided the "r" and took the crunch out of the consonants, turning Charlie into Shawlie.

"You don't want to be out in this with no hat," Charlie Chapo was telling him now. They passed the grilled gateway of the Hotel International. Charlie's battered Montero was parked across the street, and in the heavy dust on the back window someone had scrawled the name *MAGLOIRE.* An air conditioner rumbled in a window of the hotel restaurant and Doctor Oliver automatically moved toward the door, but Charlie nudged him past, to the "popular" bar beside it, which catered to the less prosperous locals and had no air-conditioning.

"You'll get pneumonia in that cold," Charlie said, "come in here first," and he assisted Doctor Oliver when he tripped on the step into the popular bar, which was, unusually, stone empty. Charlie rapped on a hatch in the side wall and some-one passed two bottles of beer through it, releasing a puff of frigid air before the hatch slapped shut.

Charlie Chapo took off his hat, which was the reason for his sobriquet, and set it on the chest-high counter where both men leaned. It was a nondescript straw hat of the sort the peasants wore, shaped like a Panama and as finely woven, with heavy sweat stains at the brow. Beneath the hat Charlie had, as always, a red bandanna covering his head and tightly knotted at the nape of his neck. The ensemble made it look as if he were affecting Indiana Jones, though if asked Char-lie would say that he'd adopted the rig from pictures of the colonial planters and that it worked very well to protect his head—from heat and sun, presumably, though Doctor Oliver also knew that the red head-rag meant something or other among practitioners of Vodou, of whom Charlie Chapo was rumored to be one. At the embassy they sneered that he had "gone native," which struck Doctor Oliver as peculiarly quaint in the twenty-first century, a line out of Somerset Maugham.

"What's the good word?" Doctor Oliver said.

Charlie Chapo released a dusty chuckle. "We're not dead yet." He drank from his bottle of Prestige and snapped a lighter to a Comme Il Faut cigarette. "Nou lèd men nou la!"

"Have you been out of town?"

"Not possible, monchè. The soulèvman's still up and running."

At this, Doctor Oliver's withdrawal pangs got sharper. "I thought those things were only supposed to last a day."

"Supposed to," Charlie said. There was no electricity in

the bar, which was shadowy as a cave. Charlie stepped to tip ash through the blazing doorway and took a quick look up and down the street. "Full moon's coming," he said. "They'll start the ceremonies on Morne Calvaire. That might shut it down if it was local but word is those guys on the barricades came up from Port-au-Prince."

"Who's running them?"

Charlie shrugged. "There's a hundred stories."

"That guy who was after me on the square," Doctor Oliver began. "He was, I don't know, more possessive than usual." *Possessed* was another word that came to him. As if the whole person was owned, invaded, by the phrase he kept repeating.

"There's some strange stuff swirling around today." Charlie leaned forward, pushing his sunglasses up above the dust-crusted rim of his red bandanna, exposing to Doctor Oliver his tired eyes. "They killed La Reine D'Ayiti, did you know that? In the Place Montarcher."

"What?" Place Montarcher was a smaller square, only a few blocks uphill from the cathedral. Nothing bad happened there. "In daylight? Who?"

Charlie Chapo was nodding slowly. "I meant to tell you that. Chimè."

That, Doctor Oliver knew, was the current word for zenglendo or bandits or occasionally lawless persons who might sometimes engage in political thuggery, abruptly materializing, then fading away. Those on the barricades were chimè as well. The literal translation was "chimera."

"They cut her heart out," Charlie added.

"Jesus. Why?"

There was a flash behind the bar, where a server had silently appeared, his eyes widening white in the shadows at what Charlie had said.

"Scare the bejabbers out of everybody." Charlie shrugged.

He had known her, Doctor Oliver realized, this harmless madwoman who'd styled herself the Queen of Haiti and did the stroll from Place Montarcher to the Boulevard de la Mer, capturing whomever she could in tight lassoes of her crazy talk.

"There's always a sort of big energy buildup," Charlie Chapo was saying. "Between Pentecost and Trinity—and it releases in the ceremonies. Normally it should. A thing like this, though . . . it can all start going in the wrong direction."

"I need to get out of here," Doctor Oliver said. The demonstrations had cut him off from the airport, which was probably out of service anyway; he was meant to have flown to the States three days before.

"Right," said Charlie, "it's inconvenient for me too."

Doctor Oliver touched the bottle in his pocket. Two pills left and why was he saving them? So there would be that much between him and the void. He resolved to speak about this to Charlie Chapo, who was sometimes something of a fixer.

"Charles. I need to . . ." A delicate matter. "Um. Refill a prescription."

Charlie was looking at him slantwise. "For what?"

"Um." Too much delicacy and he would not be understood. "Well, it's Dilaudid. But I can substitute! OxyContin, Percocet even . . ."

"Or heroin would do."

"Yes," replied Doctor Oliver, naked now, and almost unashamed. "It would."

But Charlie Chapo was shaking his head. "There's coke around," he said. "There's even crack, believe it or not . . . but what you're after—it's not obvious."

"At the hospital maybe?"

He felt Charlie Chapo withdraw a little, though his body had not moved. "You do the medical missions, right? So you know, they never have enough painkillers for . . ."

. . . *nonrecreational users*, Doctor Oliver thought, his shame bitter now.

"I've got a couple of cats to kill," Charlie said. "I think you shouldn't be kicking around by yourself—not today. Magloire's looking for you, maybe he can help."

"Oh," said Doctor Oliver, remembering the name scrawled in the dust. It gave him a faintly reassuring sense of connectedness. "I thought he was looking for you."

"I don't have anything for him, though. All this traka— I'm light in the pocket." Charlie Chapo put his hat back on and winked as he stood up. "I'll check you tonight at the hotel." In the burning doorway he turned back again. "Watch yourself, will you? Drug jail here's not funny."

Surely no one could be in greater pain than this, Doctor Oliver kept thinking as he followed Magloire in an aimless stroll around the town. His organs were shriveling in withdrawal, his brain withering on its stem. The sensation worsened when Magloire persuaded him to buy a hat—a gaudy monstrosity designed for some nonexistent tourist. But the sunstroke warded off by the hat left him prey to all the rest of it. They were then in the thick of the crowded market streets with people pressing into them on all sides, picking their way to avoid stepping on wares spread over the gummy ground and Magloire's eyes staring hungrily at everything. Among the market women strode a coat hanger of a man who shook a plastic jug of filthy yellowish oil in one hand crying "Lwil, lwil, lwil" like a crow. Seeing that Doctor Oliver was faint, Magloire procured a ladder-back chair for him, but sitting down in the midst of the crush was not helpful and Magloire led him out of the market, up the hill where the streets were calmer. They passed the gateway of the Hôpital Justinien, and paused to look at the whitewashed trunks of the corridor of palms receding to the stairway, but they did not go in.

Doctor Oliver held himself up with a fist wrapped around an iron spear of the hospital gate. Somewhere in all the moil of frantic exchange there must be something to answer his need. Or else he would simply have to kick. He had done it before, but here? Not here. It seemed to him that somewhere the heart of La Reine d'Ayiti must be impaled on a fence-spear like the one he grasped, deflated, tightening, the blood blackening to the iron as it dried.

Magloire walked him back to the hotel, where Doctor Oliver invited him in for a beer. He had also purchased Magloire a paper plate of spaghetti in the market, but so far had not offered him any money. They had walked around the market for an hour without Magloire being able to buy anything that he needed, and although the figure of VEN DOLA was burning in the center of his forehead, like the mark of Cain, Doctor Oliver never seemed to notice. Magloire could not bear to describe it now, as they sat in the shade of the bar above the hotel pool and sipped their beers.

"It is very difficult to earn twenty dollars," Magloire said, constructing the sentence carefully out of bits of French he still had from school. Doctor Oliver did not appear to hear or understand, just lurked behind his sunglasses as though blind.

"To make twenty dollars," Magloire tried again, "requires a great many transactions in the head."

"Twenty dollars?" Doctor Oliver raised his head.

"Twenty dollars! Yes, yes." Magloire felt hopeful, then excited. Twenty dollars—the doctor had spoken the words. The resonance of two voices saying the same phrase produced a sudden harmony between them.

Now Doctor Oliver felt the confidence that had failed him before, in the light of all Charlie Chapo had said, to explain his requirements to Magloire in his own rickety French from school, and yes, Magloire was nodding and agreeing, though at the same time lapsing into Creole as he leaned forward to confirm the understanding, "Nenpòt sa w bezwen map jwenn li, wi!"

"What?" said Doctor Oliver

"Anytheen you wann, I get!" Magloire said in English, then, as if it were a code they shared, "Fòk nan pwen poum pa jwenn."

Magloire went back to the market quickly, his head illuminated with a pleasant ruby light. He had two minds, or more than two, and had just shifted from one to another. A certain mind had been molded by the bon frères of Saint Jean Bosco who had taught him his trades. This mind could calculate, plan ahead, and undertake the interminable transactions needed to acquire ven dola (in this case)—it was like the mind of a blan, he thought, or even of a Haitian filozòf, for some Haitians were educated to the point that they no longer heard the spirits, or if they did they were afraid.

But now, as he sailed through the market streets, his mind was washed clean of all that arithmetic that had burdened it earlier, for Doctor Oliver had simply answered his prayer—without knowing it he had obeyed the will of Èzili Je Wouj, not because he knew her or served her the way Magloire did, but because he was a good man of the right instincts who could let himself be moved to restore order to the universe by folding a twenty-dollar bill into the warm pale palm of Magloire's hand. Tout pou nan amoni, Magloire was practically singing to himself as he fractured Doctor Oliver's deuce into larger soft piles of Haitian currency, the bills limp and fragrant with a fruity, sweaty smell and so blackened from passage from hand to hand they were entirely illegible. He purchased small but double rations of charcoal, oil, rice, and dried beans, and canned milk for the children, then green coffee beans for his mother and a handful of ibuprofen tablets for himself—his head had hurt a good deal earlier from the all the transactions scrambling in it. At another stand he bought two red candles and a ball of black string. There were then left four hexagonal coins; enough for a basket of green oranges.

He divided his purchases into two sacks and the smaller of these he locked in a cupboard when he returned home, putting the iron key into his pocket. Anise looked at him sourly as he did so, for she knew very well what that was about. When he gave her the condensed milk for the boy she brightened, then asked him sharply about the medicine, but he pointed out that it was no longer needed, for the boy was well, happy today, teasing the chickens out in the yard, and then he gave Anise the oranges. As for his mother, when she received the charcoal and coffee she smiled at him with all her four remaining teeth.

Magloire had to hasten now, *fast*, the red light in his head compelled him, over the unpaved road that wrapped around the outside edge of Morne du Cap beyond the dwellings of the town, then splashing across the beach where the tide was coming in, as the sun, still blazing hot, tilted just a little toward the west. Hopping from boulder to boulder around the next point, he climbed into the walls of Fort Picolet, which in the time of the heroes two hundred years before had been the scene of a great battle between indigènes on shore and the French warships. Now the fort was full of spirits, and there were other sèvitè there pursuing their own missions. Magloire paused to draw breath and looked down the black stone spikes of côte de fer, where two or three youths were scribbling on school paper, just above the spring of Èzili Freda, but it was Èzili Je Wouj who would catch and deliver his desires. He climbed a little further, till he was facing her grotto. There he lit a red candle for her, and left a complex little bundle of black string, a figure eight bound to itself with a tightly wrapped waist, like the waist of a wasp that might sting.

Descending, his head began to hurt again, perhaps because of the heat and sun, which now flashed directly into his face from the mirroring sea. He had already taken two ibuprofen. Could they have failed so soon? If he had more money he would buy sunglasses like those Doctor Oliver always wore. The luminous red glow of Èzili Je Wouj was fading from his brain, and a grimmer something else began to replace it. The boys above the spring were smiling at him and showing him their scraps of paper, on which they had been scrawling phrases over and over until the papers grew dark and confused as a jungle at midnight and finally became a perfect graphite-shining black.

These were Vodou passports the boys had made, and they wanted Magloire to purchase them, or maybe just admire them. His other mind was forcing itself back, the one with the calculations. The tide had certainly come in now and he would undoubtedly get wet when he crossed the shoal. He could not wait, so procuring dry trousers would be added to his mountain of difficulties. When he looked at the blackened papers the boys were showing him, his whole brain felt scribbled over in just the same way. In a headachy flash he perceived for the first time the flaw in his situation: he had spent the whole twenty dollars without obtaining what Doctor Oliver wanted. Indeed, he no longer had a clear notion what that thing was.

Doctor Oliver spent the hottest part of the afternoon in his hotel room, half-watching coverage of the demonstrations on Haitian national television. When he woke the screen had gone blank and the day was almost over. He put on his shirt and ambled out barefoot. Charlie Chapo's dust-covered truck was parked in the hotel lot, so he was unsurprised to find the man himself in the bar, drinking a large glass of the excellent local rum, except that it was rare for him to drink hard liquor. Charlie had taken off both his hat and his head rag and the remnants of his extremely dirty hair were sticking up. Doctor Oliver sat down and ordered the same.

"Bwa debèn," Charlie was muttering fixedly, as if it were a mantra of some kind. "Bwa debèn."

"What?" said Doctor Oliver, as jovially as he could. Charlie Chapo started as if he had not previously been aware of the doctor's presence.

"Ebony wood." His left hand had begun folding his red head cloth into ever smaller triangles. "It used to be code for slave cargo, back in the day when they had to smuggle them. Of course, whatever real ebony there might have been here was slashed out and ripped off and sent to Europe along with the gold and the coffee and sugar and hope, till there's nothing left but bare rock most places, and women making dirt cakes instead of corn bread. That's us, monchè! We find a place as close to Paradise as this universe allows, that's what we do to it. Sa kab fèm rele Mèt Kalfou mwen!"

"What?" Doctor Oliver repeated. His sense of incomprehension had now taken on an ominous cast. Charlie Chapo was pumping that triangle of red cloth very hard in his left fist and Doctor Oliver felt obscurely that this action might cause something bad to happen.

"Oh," said Charlie, looking at his left hand as if it belonged to somebody else. "I mean, do things the way I shouldn't. Sorry . . ." He shook out the bandanna with his right hand and wiped his forehead with it. It was getting dark quickly. Bats skimmed the surface of the pool and a cocotier by the railing shivered its long fronds in the breeze. In the far distance they could both see the series of flaming barricades that cut the town off from the airport and the road down to the capital. Doctor Oliver's apprehensive feelings intensified as he touched the vial in his pocket where his two remaining pills still clicked. He considered that Charlie Chapo might possibly have taken care of his problem personally if he'd wanted, instead of fobbing him off on Magloire. Charlie Chapo was occasionally assumed to be a drug dealer himself because he had no other obvious portfolio. His presence in Haiti was one of the many anomalies from which the whole country sometimes seemed to be constructed.

"My people can't get in and I can't get out," Charlie Chapo was saying. "It just gums everything all up—and for nothing, that's what gets me sometimes. You know a bad day here can be—"

"Very bad." Doctor Oliver felt the truth of this in his spleen at the moment he said it.

"And you know, I hate it that they killed that poor woman. I just don't— All right, there's no less point in that than in anything, but it really didn't have to be her."

Charlie Chapo drained his rum glass and shook himself all over, then turned on Doctor Oliver a lopsided smile. "I just need to clean out my head is all." There was something in the way he said it that made the doctor think he could lift off the top of his skull and rinse out the inside and replace it. "Do you mind if I use your shower?"

"Go for it," Doctor Oliver said. "There's even soap. It's from Taiwan."

By the time Charlie returned to the table, it was completely dark. The barefoot servants had lit the lamps, and the fires on the barricades seemed much further off—as did the dark portents of Charlie's earlier words. On the strength of Magloire's quick visit, Doctor Oliver had dry-swallowed one of his two remaining pills and he now felt quite agreeably insulated from . . . what had it been?

"*Without fear of the nighted wyvern*," he pronounced in a fat mellow tone, as Charlie hove up to the table, still raking water out of his thin hair with his fingers.

"Something cheered you up," Charlie said, raising an eyebrow as he sat down.

"I ordered for us," Doctor Oliver said, and at that moment a waiter began setting down platters of poulè kreyòl and banann peze. They ate without talking very much, which was the custom of the country. Or, rather, Doctor Oliver pushed his food around his plate, since the drug he had taken destroyed his appetite. As the dishes were cleared, he ordered them postprandial glasses of the marvelous rum. Just beyond the hotel's outward rippling of light, drums had begun a rich insistent rhythm. The ceremonies Charlie had mentioned would be gunning up now, not far away.

"Thanks for putting me onto Magloire."

"He take care of you?" Charlie seemed pleased.

Doctor Oliver reached for the envelope in his shirt pocket, then stopped. "He said something to me: *Fòk nan pwen*." He couldn't remember the rest of the phrase. "I didn't get it."

"Magloire said that?" Charlie's eyes had narrowed. "That's Bizango, basically. Vodou for most people here is Ginen, which is a whole lot like charismatic Christianity from all I've seen of it, but there's this other thing that goes on, a kind of inversion of it, I mean. Left-handed."

The word *sinister* surfaced in Oliver's mind, like a paper flower blooming in a glass. Charlie Chapo's left hand pumped on the tightly folded triangle of red.

"I mean," Charlie Chapo was saying, "from the ougan's point of view, well, yeah, Ginen is all sweetness and light, but it's hard to get paid for that, see? So most of them work with the left hand too, that's how they put it. For people who'd sell their mother or eat their own children to get what they want, sometimes . . ."

"What do they want?"

"Power. Sex. Money. Power." Charlie shrugged. "Same as you, right? It's not like these are the only people in the world who'll throw a lot away for immediate gratification. In the long run it's not such a good idea, because they have to bind their spirits to make them deliver like that, and the spirits can be pretty angry once they get loose. But in the short term, fòk nan pwen pou'm pa jwen."

"That's it," said Doctor Oliver. "What does it mean?"

"There'd have to not be any for me to not get some." Charlie frowned. "Let me see what he got for you."

The jab of anxiety Doctor Oliver felt was, thanks to his pill, no worse than being prodded with a hair. He pulled the small red and gilt envelope from his shirt pocket.

"Huh," said Charlie Chapo. "That's a ghost-money envelope. I get them in Chinatown and use them to give money to people down here. Well, no reason Magloire wouldn't have a few."

When Charlie Chapo opened the envelope and curled his index finger into it, Doctor Oliver felt a stronger stab: somebody's messing with my dope. Charlie Chapo rubbed a generous amount of white powder between his thumb and forefinger. "I don't know," he said, and dragged his finger through a drop of water on the table. A smear like white paint appeared on the wood of the tabletop.

"I wouldn't run this up my nose." Charlie caught Oliver's eye. "It's lime, I think."

"What, quick lime?"

"No, no! They're not trying to hurt you. It's like chalk, basically. They use it for whitewash." Charlie closed the envelope and flicked it across the table like a paper football. "What did you pay for it?"

"Twenty U.S."

"Right," said Charlie. "Kind of suspiciously cheap, don't you think?" He looked out the ring of local light toward the fires on the barricades. "I dunno, though, in '97 I could have bought an assault rifle for that in the capital. Twenty dollars."

"Ever wish you had?" Doctor Oliver managed to ask, from the depths of the chill now locked around his heart.

"Sometimes, yeah," Charlie said. "But you know, if you've got one of those things, the odds go up somebody will get killed with it." He turned his head back into the circle of lamplight. "Don't feel so bad—you can try again tomorrow."

"Why not?" Doctor Oliver said. "Why not feel bad?"

"What I love about this country is that magical thinking actually does work here. But it's got to have a little something to work with, you see? Like Magloire—in better circumstances he'd be a completely honest person. As it is, he has to cut a corner sometimes."

The drums had grown louder and there was chanting now

too. Charlie Chapo turned his head into the wind that came constantly off the bay, flipped up his red bandanna, and knotted it tight to the nape of his neck. He's going to leave me, Doctor Oliver thought. Charlie leaned toward him across the table. "Understand, Magloire wanted you to have what you wanted. His desire is for you to have what you need. And for him to have what he needs and . . . so somebody has to spin straw into gold. If the charm had worked like he wanted it to, you'd come out with the coin instead of the dried leaf. As it is . . ." Standing, Charlie clapped Doctor Oliver on the shoulder. "Thanks for dinner. And the shower. And what the hell, it's only twenty bucks."

After his delivery to Doctor Oliver, Magloire returned to the street where his mother lived with Anise and his son. Anise sat on a low stool holding the child on her knee and stirring an iron pot which released a rich smell of diri kole ak pwa. Beyond, in the darkness, his mother roasted coffee; a rim of red coal outlined the bottom curve of her cauldron. His mouth watered at the smell of the rice and beans, but although Anise was using provisions he had provided, he did not mean to share the meal. By the grace of Doctor Oliver he had already eaten quite well once today and that was better than he often managed. Also, it was easy enough to unlock the cabinet and slip away with the second bag while Anise was busy over the food.

With the neck of the loose cloth bag in his hand, he stood on the Boulevard de la Mer and watched the bone-white moon rising from the sea. His thoughts scattered, to the point he was not completely in one of his minds or another. Some men along the breakwater were fishing, each with a hook and a line rolled around a chip of wood, and a couple of students had clustered under the electric lamps to study their homework. Behind and above him, beyond the lights of Doctor Oliver's hotel perched on its eminence, the drumming tightened, intensified, and there was a lone voice singing.

Kwi nan lan men m ap mande . . .
Se pa pou mwen pòv m ap mande charite
Se relasyon Ginen m ap chache . . .

With cup in hand, I'm begging . . .
Not just for poor old me
I'm begging for a way to Ginen . . .

Magloire turned from the waterfront and climbed an ascending street. This little pocket of the old colonial town compressed a number of disparate things together as if in the heel of a sock: a middle-sized hilltop church was quite near the onfò where the ceremony was, and not far from that was the fancy hotel for blan, and not far from that was the very modest quarter where Magloire's mother lived with Anise and the grandchild. A ravine and the steepness of the mountain beyond it had forestalled any further construction to the north from colonial times until quite recently, but now Magloire was picking his way across the ravine toward the shantytown that had mushroomed on the other side.

He had built the little clay house for Douslina with his own hands and it was stronger than most others, made properly with raclage under the clay, a real tin roof, and a concrete floor. True, Douslina had demanded it when she reported herself pregnant by Magloire a second time, yet he was proud to have accomplished the house, and her children were healthier than the son Anise had given him. The sweetness of Lina was that dous he'd woven to her name, and now when she saw what he had brought and came to him, surrendering all her warm weight against his body, Magloire felt stronger and more intelligent and capable than before, and he felt that all the paradoxes of his life had for a moment integrated: the constant puckering sourness of Anise completing a sphere with this sweetness now.

One of Douslina's hands explored the bag and another was interested in Magloire's other possibilities (the children were asleep, she said), but he pulled a little away from her, muttering *Fòk mwen ale* as he turned his face toward the drumming, the choruses that answered the lead singer now— it was well to remain pure, or at least somewhat pure, until he had thanked the lwas for their generosity; furthermore, it would not be practical for Douslina to have another child, or anyone else Magloire was responsible to feed.

He kissed and left her somewhat regretfully, but that feeling faded as he grew nearer to the drums, merging with threads of other people going there. The moon was so bright it was easy enough to see his way, and in the ring of the onfò there was electric light now, along with a sound system that projected the voices out over the church and across the bay. The pathways to the central area were labyrinthine, twisting among houses pinned to the steep flank of the mountain, but Magloire's movement became automatic with the drumming. He greeted his acquaintances without seeing them. On the periphery women sold fried food, soft drinks, raw cane rum, and even cold beer, but Magloire had no money left and did not care. Bleachers had been built around the oval floor of the onfò, which by day was sometimes used for cockfighting. Magloire slipped through and moved toward the altar, a crazy tall structure in tiers like a wedding cake and with many real layer cakes offered upon it, along with holy cards and novenas and Vodou passports and candles and padlocks and mouchwa tèt and grubby illegible bills of money and the less valuable hexagonal yellowish coins. VEN DOLA. In his comings and goings all day, Magloire had encountered various creditors who'd heard of his spending money in the market, whom he could only tell *Demen, demen*, tomorrow and tomorrow, as his last centime had been spent on the red candle he affixed now to the corner of the altar and the looped black string he set beside it: at once a gesture of gratitude for the VEN DOLA he had received today and a sort of fox trap he hoped might snare him another VEN DOLA tomorrow.

He could give way now. The whole walk to the onfò he had been feeling a pulse rising between the cords at the back of his neck, responding to the drumbeat, the red magic rising from the back of his brain toward the front so that soon the Maji Wouj would submerge him completely: this was good. As he moved toward the concentration of dancers under the drums, Magloire caught a glimpse of Charlie Chapo on the periphery—Charlie had in fact discarded his chapo and wore only his red mouchwa tèt, to show the spirits he courted the red magic too. He stood at the edge of the dancing, turning his torso lightly at the waist and letting his slack arms sway like cooked spaghetti. In the glance they exchanged, Magloire understood that Charlie Chapo desired what possessed Magloire and that he would not get it. Magloire went altogether under the drums.

Charles Morgan, le-dit Charlie Chapo, was a connoisseur of many cultures and had experience of more than one pathway to the trance state that preceded full possession. Tonight he was combining several techniques—a scrap of qi gong, a bit of yoga, a subroutine of self-hypnosis—all in hope of bucking the ego out of his being for a time. He had planed down his consciousness till it was as frail as the weave of his worn-out hat, but he could not get all the way through membrane. Not tonight. A couple of times the thing had happened to him by itself, and while it terrified him then, he still desired and tried for it even though he knew how wrong-headed and futile it was to think that he could get there by trying.

Monkey-mind had a hold on him tonight. He let his monkey watch the show. As it would do before a crisis, the drumming knotted up as the dancers tightened themselves under the drums; the dancers mostly women now, except for one male onsi clad in white, working his way blindly toward the center, holding out a white candle with its yellowish flame and a white enamel cup of water. Charlie let himself sway like a tree in the wind. A respectable-looking woman standing just ahead of him let out a quiet sigh and slumped back into the arms he'd reflexively raised to catch her. As easily as that. It was a peripheral event; the dancing and drumming were still binding tighter. Charlie supported the woman from her armpits; her limp arms spread wide, like the arms of Christ on the cross. Presently others came and bore her away.

Charlie had just been relieved of his burden when the clenched fist of dancing cracked open under the drums. Two women who'd been dancing very close flung back, repelled from each other; one screaming harshly and tearing at her head. Charlie didn't know what had happened to the onsi with his candle and cup, but between the two possessed women appeared Magloire; the women falling away from him like two halves of a hatching egg. Strangely, Magloire now seemed to be cradling the nub of red candle Charlie had earlier seen him place on the altar. That was Magloire's body certainly, the deep eyes ringed with red, then white, but the person

Charlie knew as Magloire was nowhere behind those eyes, not now. He had gone elsewhere, and Charlie, knowing that he could not follow, swelled up with jealousy and loneliness; at the same time, however, there was a moment of sympathy, for he knew in a backward fashion the same thing Magloire had known of him before, thinking, *If only I could see, could be, the face of a living god.*

Abandoned, Doctor Oliver sat by the railing above the hotel pool, lapping at a stale beer. There was a three-way discord between the soft konpa playing in the bar, the drumming and chanting and occasionally shrieking from the onfò, and the more aggressive dance music booming from a club at sea level down below. He watched the moon climb higher in the sky above black waves, perfectly round and full and alien and cruel. This moon cared nothing for him or for his predicament. A number of starved dogs quarreled in the dark streets below the battlements of the hotel; he felt sure they would devour him if they could. That man, that man in the square today, had believed that Doctor Oliver was stealing something from him with his eyes.

Behind his eyelids he could feel the pullulating of the marketplace where he had been that day with Magloire, the interminable screaming of need and exchange and over it all that harsh voice crying in its monotone, "Oil, oil, oil." Grease the wheel. How abjectly everything seemed to cooperate in its own spoliation, quite as Charlie Chapo had said. The scene was miniaturized in his mind's eye as if he saw it through a backward telescope, and he did appreciate how very small of him it was to imagine that this whole swarming nation existed only to serve his need. Still, they had robbed him. He had been robbed. He'd been robbed and he wanted to kill someone.

PART II

NOIR CROSSROADS

CLAIRE OF THE SEA LIGHT

BY EDWIDGE DANTICAT

Ville Rose

The morning Claire Limyè Lanmè Faustin turned seven, a rogue wave, measuring, by some visual accounts, between ten and twenty feet high, was seen in the ocean outside of Ville Rose. Claire's father, Gaspard, was one of a few people to notice the wave as he untied the twin sisal ropes that bound his fishing boat to a large rock on the beach. He first heard a low rumbling, like that of distant thunder, then saw a wall of water rise from the depths of the ocean, a giant blue-green tongue, trying, it seemed, to lick the sky.

Just as quickly as it had swelled, the wave crashed in, collapsing on itself, sending hardly a ripple toward the beach where Gaspard was standing, in shock. Thrust above the crest of the wave then pinned down beneath its trough, a small dinghy vanished. Its owner was a man who for years Gaspard had greeted as they hurried past each other, at dawn, on their way out to sea. In an instant Gaspard's neighbor and friend was gone and so was any sign that anything out of the ordinary had taken place.

That sweltering morning Gaspard had slept in, contemplating the impossible decision he'd always known he'd one day have to make: to whom, finally, to give his daughter.

"Woke up earlier and I would have been there," he tearfully told his sweet-faced little girl after watching the boat disappear.

Molasses-toned with bulging penny-colored eyes, Claire was still lying on the foam-board cot in their single-room shack, her thin night dress soaking in the back with sweat, as she dreamed of something she wouldn't be able to recall when she was fully conscious. Upon waking, she wrapped her long bony arms around her father's neck, just as she had when she was even littler, pressing her nose against his tear-dampened cheek. Some years before, her father had told her what had happened on her very first day on earth, that giving birth to her, her mother had died. So her birthday was also a day of death, and the rogue wave and the dead fishermen proved that it had never ceased to be. Even so, before her father had spoken that morning, Claire had hoped that he might have come to wish her a happy birthday, but she knew that he might also be saying goodbye.

The day Claire Limyè Lanmè turned six, Ville Rose's new mayor decided to host a massive victory party in the seaside town. However, before the party, he gave a long and tiresome speech from one of the stone steps of the town hall, which overlooked a flamboyant-filled piazza, where hundreds of residents stood elbow to elbow in the May afternoon sun. The mayor's speech was badly organized, and even more badly delivered, and the mayor, a tall balding man, soaked, with his sweaty fingers, the nearly twenty typewritten pages the speech was written on, even while occasionally pulling a handkerchief out of the breast pocket of his armpit-stained linen suit to wipe his brows. Claire was wearing her pink muslin birthday dress, her thick, woolly hair neatly plaited and covered with tiny bow-shaped barrettes. She sat on her father's shoulders while he stood on the edge of the crowd, close to the giant speakers that made Claire feel the mayor's words rattling through her bones. Still, she could hear a familiar voice shout above it all that it seemed as though the speech had been written by a primary school boy.

"Don't all political speeches sound like that?" her father replied, inspiring a coy smile from the woman he had snaked through the crowd to stand next to. The woman was in her early thirties but, because she was short and round with an oval girlish face, looked a lot younger. She owned one of Ville Rose's most popular fabric shops, where Claire's mother, a seamstress for the town undertaker, used to buy cloth. After Claire's mother died, whenever Gaspard went in to buy a piece of cloth to have a dress made for his daughter, the woman would always refuse payment by saying, "Fòk youn voye je sou lòt." We must look after one another.

Only when the fabric vendor stroked Claire's knees during the mayor's speech, occasionally glancing at her then quickly returning her gaze to the mayor's clammy face, did Claire realize that this was the woman her father had been trying to give her to for years.

The mayor had commissioned from a local artist a giant portrait of himself, looking younger and more lithe and athletic than he had ever been. That portrait, reproduced on what seemed like a massive bedsheet, draped the front of the town hall and other official buildings.

"Thank you for putting your trust in me," the mayor was winding down nearly an hour after he'd begun speaking.

Gaspard cupped his hands over his mouth, joining his fists into a funnel that led into the woman's delicate seashell-shaped right ear: "Next time we'll put even less trust in you."

Later that evening, the fabric vendor showed up at the seaside shack to have another look at Claire. Gaspard had insisted that Claire pat her hair down with an old bristle brush and that she straighten out the creases and wrinkles in the pink muslin dress that he'd made her keep wearing all day. Standing in the middle of the shack, the woman asked Claire to twirl by the light of a bell-shaped kerosene lamp on the small table where the girl and her father usually ate their meals. The walls of the shack were covered with flaking, yellowing newspapers glued to the wood long ago with limestone and manioc paste. From where she was standing, Claire could not see her own stretched-out shadow, which always made her feel taller, and thus older.

While twirling for the lady, Claire wondered whether her father had already been made the usual promises, that she would not be whipped, that she would be kept clean, that she would be well fed, that she would be sent to school, that she would be taken to a clinic when she was sick. All this perhaps in exchange for some cleaning both at home and at the shop. The woman had no living children so there would be no older kids to tease and beat her.

"You would be staying with a nice lady," her father had told her on the way to the mayor's speech that afternoon. "It would be like an adoption. You'd be a doll for her to dress up, the little girl she lost."

But as soon as Claire stopped twirling, the woman turned to her father, her long shiny fake hair blocking half of her copper face.

"My girl was older," she said.

Gaspard's eyes dropped from the woman's fancy hairpiece to her pricey open-toed sandals and bright red toenails. "She'll grow," he replied.

"I can't afford to wait for her to grow." The woman headed for the narrow doorway.

"No problem," her father said, following her out.

Claire allowed them the breezy darkness outside and moved closer to one of the moths circling the kerosene lamp. "Why would you want to give your child to me?" she heard the woman ask her father over the loud sound of the evening waves.

"I am going away," he said, "pou chèche lavi, to look for a better life."

"Ohmm," the woman groaned a warning, like an impossible word, a word she had no idea how to say. "Why would you want your child to be a rèstavèk?"

"This is what would happen anyway," her father said, "with less kind people than you if I suddenly died. I don't have any more family here."

Her father put an end to the woman's questioning by making a joke about the mayor's victory and how many bad speeches Gaspard would be forced to suffer through if he remained in town. This made the woman's jingly laugh sound as though it were coming out of her nose. Reaching closer to the kerosene lamp, Claire expertly captured a spotted tiger moth between her palms, not sure whom she wanted to imagine it to be, the fabric vendor or her father.

The good news, though, was that this would be the only day her father would do this for a year. The rest of the year, he'd act as though he would always keep her, letting life go on as usual. During the week, she'd go to the Protestant preschool where she had received a charity scholarship, requiring her father to only pay a few Haitian dollars a month. At night, she would sit by the lamp and try not to be distracted by the moths as she recited the alphabet out loud. He would enjoy the singsong and her hard work and would miss it during her holidays from school. The rest of the time, he would go out to sea at the crack of dawn and always come back with something for her to eat. He'd talk about going to work in construction or the fishing trade in the neighboring Dominican Republic, but he would always make it sound as though it was something the two of them could do together, not something he'd have to abandon her to do. But as soon as her birthday would come, he would begin talking about it again, chèche lavi, going away to make a life for himself, placing her with someone, finding her a family. His and his dead wife's relatives, whom they'd left behind in the hills, had it even harder than he did. Rather than a nearly barren sea, they had the dry eroded earth to contend with and already too many mouths to feed. If he died they would take the girl, but only because they had no choice, because that's what families do, because fòk youn voye je sou lòt. We must all look after one another. He didn't want to leave anything to chance.

That night after the fabric vendor left, colorful sparks rose up and filled the night sky before fading and plummeting into the sea. With cannonlike explosions, the mayor was celebrating his victory with fireworks. Still lying on her foam mattress as her father snored on his across the room, Claire couldn't help but feel like she was the one who'd won.

The day Claire Limyè Lanmè turned five was a Sunday, so she and Gaspard walked to the beach in the morning, watching a sandy pool that had formed, where a group of children splashed inside a ring of brown water then plunged into the sea to rinse themselves. Claire wore the pink muslin sundress, which Gaspard had ordered made for her in the same color and style but a slightly smaller size the year before. The afternoon air felt sticky on her skin as though they were trapped in one of the many humid air pockets where the sea breeze met the stifling heat of the town. Moving away from the beach,

Gaspard motioned toward town. Even before they turned their backs to the sea, Claire knew that, just like the previous year, they'd be visiting her mother's grave.

The main road was crowded with pedestrians either dodging or hailing moto taxis and tap taps. Gaspard held his nose up and sniffed the air, breathing in the scent of soft tar on an asphalted stretch. Raising his arm to respond to the occasional greeting, he kept walking at a steady clip, daring her to keep up. Passing a Vodou temple with pictures of Catholic saints doubling as lwas, he pointed out, just as he had many times, the glowing face of a pale Mater Dolorosa and said, "The goddess of love, Èzili Freda, your mother liked her."

Claire had never seen a picture of her mother. There were simply none. If not for the class portrait at the Protestant school, which her father had not purchased, there would be no pictures of her either.

Leaving the main road behind, they cut through a narrow dirt track with wooden houses enclosed by tall cactus fences. Claire trailed behind her father as he followed the smell of wet pine and burnt sugar in the air. A muddied rubber-booted man returning from the cane fields with an overburdened mule called out to them, "Paying a visit to the dead Mesye Gaspard and Manzè Claire?"

Gaspard nodded, as he did to everyone else who greeted him from then on.

The burial site was next to a cane field so vast that Claire couldn't even see where it ended. Standing on the edge of the twenty or so cement crosses rising out of the hilly terra cotta earth, she forgot at first which one was her mother's. Her father bent down and, using the end of his shirt, wiped a light coat of red mud off the letters of her mother's name. She could only read the letters because she had just learned to write her name at school. Her mother's name had also been Claire, Claire Narcis. Her father had decided to call her Claire Limyè Lanmè, Claire of the sea light, after her mother died.

Squatting there with one knee lodged in the moist earth, Gaspard spat on the end of his shirt, but could not produce enough saliva to further clean his wife's headstone.

"Need some from you too," he told his daughter, who at first hesitated then playfully obliged, digging deep into the back of her throat with adultlike grunts.

Next to her mother's was a year-old grave with a polished gray cross that was smaller than the others. On the cross was a metal wreath, painted in pale blue and white with a brown angel carved on the front. It was the grave of a child.

This was one of many times that Claire wished she knew how to read and write more than her own name. Her father didn't even know that much, so she couldn't ask him to read the name for her, to tell her who the child was that her mother was now looking after in death.

Once her father was done wiping her mother's headstone, covering the entire front of his shirt with the red earth, he sat down on the stone slab that in Claire's mind kept her mother forever pinned to the earth.

Gaspard was mumbling, talking to himself as he sat there, seeming strangely at home among the dead, until he saw the fabric vendor.

The woman was wearing a white lace dress with a polka dot scarf wrapped around her head.

"I knew she would come today," he said, quickly standing up.

Grabbing Claire's hand, he pulled her forward, blocking the woman's way. The woman peeked over his shoulder at the child's grave with the angel wreath on top.

"Do you remember my daughter?" her father asked while nervously patting Claire's shoulder.

"Please let me remember mine," the woman said.

The day Claire Limyè Lanmè Faustin turned four, the fabric vendor's seven-year-old daughter, Rose, was riding in the back of a moto taxi with her teenage caretaker, when a private car rear-ended the motorcycle and sent Rose flying fifteen feet into the air, forcing her to land, headfirst, on the ground. Rose was plump, like her mother, and her hair was perfectly coiffed. The mother did it herself in playful and colorful designs, carving simple flower and butterfly shapes into the girl's scalp. Those, like Gaspard, who witnessed the accident, swore that when Rose's body ascended from the rear of the motorcycle, she almost seemed to be flying out of her primary school uniform—an azure pleated skirt and spotless white shirt with white tennis shoes and lace-topped ankle socks—raising both her hands and actually flapping them before she hit the ground.

It was not the first time Gaspard had seen an accident like this. This was a small and sometimes unlucky town and the narrow, mostly unpaved streets were crowded with motorcycles and cars. But none of the previous accidents had been so personally disheartening. He had expected Rose to scream at some point—just as the mothers and other spectators had rushed up to the spot, cradled their heads in their hands, and screamed—but the girl had not even made one sound.

The moto taxi had nearly reached the mother's fabric shop when the accident happened, so it did not take long for word to reach the fabric vendor, who even before she was told the details was bent over and retching, looking only at the ground as she made her way through the stalled traffic toward where her child was lying, bloody and still, in the dust.

Gaspard had not seen such grief since the public high school in town had collapsed some years back, killing eighty-nine of the two hundred and twelve pupils enrolled there. The day of the moto taxi accident, however, the fabric vendor was the sole owner of that tragedy. The driver and Rose's caretaker were miraculously fine, like those students and teachers who had merely crawled out of the rubble of the collapsed high school building some years back.

Gaspard was grateful that his daughter, after having visited her mother's grave that morning, was safe with a neighbor, momentarily away from cars and motorcycles, at the beach. Still, in that moment he missed his daughter more than he had at any other time since she was born. He missed her so badly that he even felt jealous of the way the fabric vendor was holding her daughter. At least she'd looked after her own child during the girl's entire short life, he thought. But he was a man. What did he know about raising a little girl? He would always need caretakers he couldn't afford, neighbors from whom he'd have to beg favors, women he could either pay or sleep with, so they would "mother" his child. And even those most motherly acts, like bathing and dressing and plaiting hair, did not include embraces, like the type this woman was lavishing on a blood-soaked corpse. It took watching another child die in her mother's arms to make him realize how very much he'd miss Claire when he finally gave her away for good.

The day Claire Limyè Lanmè turned three, she was returned to her father from the countryside where she had been living with her mother's relatives since she was two days old. His wife's death had been so startling and abrupt that seeing his daughter's face had not only saddened but terrified Gaspard.

To most people, his daughter was a revenan, a ghost, a not quite fully whole person who had entered the world just as her mother was leaving it. And if these types of children are not closely watched, they can easily follow their mothers into the other world. The only way to save them is to immediately sever them from the place where they are born. Otherwise they will always spend too much time chasing a shadow they can never reach. All this was once believed about children like Claire. San manman, motherless, was the way you described someone who was lost, brutal and cruel. Fantom, ghost, was another. People without mothers, it was believed, were capable of anything.

Aside from all of this, as soon as the umbilical cord was cut, there was the immediate problem of feeding the baby. The midwife had dressed her in a light yellow embroidered jumper from the layette his wife had spent months sewing. Gaspard had picked up the baby, wrapped her in a matching blanket his wife had also made. The midwife had rushed into town looking for some formula or possibly a wet nurse. But Claire was a silent, easy child. It was as though she already knew that she had no mother and could not afford to be picky.

During those first moments with his daughter, there were times when he had visions for which he detested himself, fantasies about letting her starve to death. He'd even considered dropping her in the sea, but these were things he was dreaming for her because he could not do them to himself. He could not poison himself like he so desperately wanted. He couldn't hazard the possibility of leaving his child totally parentless, of having her end up in a brothel or on the streets.

While he was fantasizing about his daughter's death, he was also worried that a mosquito might bite her and that she might get malaria or dengue fever. He feared for himself too.

He feared getting hit by a car, or being struck with a terrible disease that would separate them forever. So when the midwife did not return, he wrapped the blanket more tightly around his daughter and took her into town at dusk.

Walking by the town's largest fabric shop, he saw the fabric vendor standing by her night watchman as he locked the tall metal gates. Next to her, her fidgety three-year-old daughter Rose was tugging at her skirt. Claire began to cry and the fabric vendor turned to see where the cry was coming from. Before her eyes could rest on them, Gaspard was already walking toward the gate.

"Madame," he said, unsure now what his next words should be.

He could already see on the fabric vendor's cheerless face that she knew what had happened. Most of the women in town must have heard by now that his wife had bled to death toward the end of her labor, and nowhere does news spread faster than in Ville Rose.

The fabric vendor was still nursing her pudgy three-year-old—the town's namesake—who was tugging at her skirt. This was so unusual for such a busy woman of her societal standing that everyone knew about it.

She asked her night watchman to unlock the gate, motioned for him to wait for her outside and for Gaspard to follow her inside. She pushed open another door, then flipped on a series of lightbulbs dangling over the fabric-filled shelves and standing spools of cloth. There was a long wooden bench in the waiting area and she motioned for her now sleepy-looking daughter to sit there before she and Gaspard did as well. Signaling Gaspard to bring Claire closer, she unbuttoned her loose hibiscus print blouse.

Claire Limyè Lanmè latched on quickly and emptied both

the fabric vendor's breasts while Rose, the woman's daughter, looked awestruck and grief-stricken as though she had not been aware until that moment that this was something her mother could do for anyone but her.

Gaspard thought he might bring Claire to the fabric vendor every day, but after smiling and cooing at the baby and stroking her tiny elbow, the woman's face tightened as she handed his daughter back to him, giving him the scowl one might imagine she reserved for her credit-seeking customers.

Pointing to the sleepy three-year-old sitting next to her, the fabric vendor said, "My child needs my milk."

He did not say it, but he was thinking that his child and hers were now milk sisters. The fabric vendor had offered his baby her breasts. He could now freely ask her to be his child's godmother. She certainly had the means. She had a big house in the hills overlooking the beach and a cook and a yardman to see after her every need. The only thing Gaspard didn't like about her was her reputed loose ways, her rumored love for several men at once, her renowned insatiable longing for other people's husbands. Still, because she had money and the shop, and because her father had once been the justice of the peace of the town, she had also inherited her own private pew at the cathedral down the street from the fabric shop. Gaspard's wife had come to the shop often, sometimes to buy fabric for the undertaker she sewed for and other times to barter her hand-embroidered little girls' dresses. Gaspard now wondered if his wife and the fabric vendor had ever spoken at length. Did they ever talk as more than client and customer? As potential young mothers?

While he stood there, near the shop's entrance, rocking the contented baby in his arms, he thought that if he waited long enough the woman might change her mind and let his daughter come again to nurse. Instead, she reached into her skirt pocket and fished out a few bills and pushed them toward him.

"Do you have any other family?" the fabric vendor asked, while stroking her own daughter's perfect hair. "A sister?" Before he could answer, she added, "If you don't have a sister, you should send her to your wife's people."

He hadn't thought of that. He hadn't thought much in that direction at all. The child had taken the mother away. Now there would be no mother. That's all he'd been able to concentrate on for more than a few minutes. She was right, though. He could not do it himself. He couldn't even feed her.

"Do you have a place to lay her body, your wife?" she asked, steadying her fidgeting daughter's hands in hers. "You can, if you like, make use of a burial site in the cemetery where I have some open land."

When he left the parlor, he walked back home, with the child, where the frantic midwife was waiting with the bottles and powder and purified water, which along with the funeral expenses would wipe out most of his dead wife's savings.

"You went out with this san manman child after dusk?" the midwife chided.

The next day, when his wife's sister arrived for the funeral, he simply gave the baby to her along with the little money he had left. He was relieved not to have to worry about her for a while.

He worked harder, spent more time at sea so that he'd have enough to send for her care, but he never visited her, nor did he ask for her to be brought to him for visits. But as her third birthday approached, he felt he was ready to see her again. So he asked that she arrive on her birthday. And she did, looking long and thin and just like her mother. He had a pink ruffled muslin dress sewn for her that he would have replicated in a larger size each year. Her mother had made her one just like it, imagining that she would wear it for her first birthday. He had sent her off with it, not knowing whether they'd even put it on her. He wished now that his wife had been prescient about her own death, like so many people's relatives claim to have seen them be. She had never told him what he might do with their daughter should anything happen to her.

The night of Claire Limyè Lanmè Faustin's seventh birthday, there was an informal vigil on the beach for the rogue wave victim, Gaspard's fisherman friend, who was now considered lost at sea. Even though a full moon gleamed overhead, Gaspard and a few of the other fishermen had made a bonfire, and over the fisherman's widow's occasional wails they sat on the warm sand and drank kleren, played cards and dominoes, and told stories, just as they would at an official wake.

Dozens of townspeople came by the beach, bringing, as was the custom, small amounts of money to the fisherman's widow. The town's mayor came too, fearful that the way the fisherman died might be the very first sign of something more potentially and geographically tragic and widespread in the days and weeks to come.

At some point in the evening, Gaspard had lost sight of his daughter. He had occasionally looked up from his drink and seen her holding hands in a circle with a group of girls playing won or dashing behind the shacks on the beach for hide-and-seek. But he hadn't seen her for some time, and the crowd of townspeople had grown thick.

Rising from the sand near the bonfire, he felt unsteady

on his feet as the alcohol seeped through him. He was unable to even string together the words to properly ask the people he staggered into whether or not they had seen his daughter.

Suddenly he spotted her, sitting alone next to a woman. It was a woman he knew, except he had never seen her like this. Her hair was wrapped in a silver net, above some giant plastic rollers, and she was wearing a satin night dress the same shade as the moon. She had slippers on her feet, fuzzy red ones that looked like they might stink if they got wet. It was the fabric vendor, and she was in deep conversation with his timid-looking daughter.

This pleased him, made him happy, but it also made his drunk and nearly broken heart start beating faster. What could the woman be telling his daughter? he wondered. And why here? Why now?

He was too afraid to approach them and would have been happy to stand there with the kleren bottle dangling from his hand, except the fabric vendor noticed him and waved him over with the flailing sleeve of her fragile-looking nightgown.

She and his daughter were sitting on some large boulders that must have been picked up from somewhere else and put there for them. He sat on the sand and leaned closer so that he might hear them above the chattering well-wishers.

"Condolences for your friend," the fabric vendor said.

His daughter turned her face away each time one of them glanced at her.

"Yes," the fabric vendor blurted out emphatically, as though they were toward the end of a very long conversation. "I'll take her. Tonight."

Claire kept her eyes on the sand, but he could see a tear

instantly slide down the side of her face. He wanted to reach for her, bury his nose in her face the way she liked to needle hers into his when he was distracted or sad.

"Why now? Why tonight?" he managed to say.

"It's now or never." The woman reached down to wipe the sliding tear, but the girl quickly moved her face. "I need another way to remember this day." She brought her hands together in a fold in her night dress, between her knees. "Now or never." She then clumsily lowered her hands to the girl's back and attempted to stroke it.

Claire's body was shaking as she watched the pile of driftwood and dried sticks that made up the puttering bonfire, which was meant to be as much a farewell as a beacon to bring the lost fisherman home.

"Claire Limyè Lanmè," Gaspard called out to her.

Claire did not turn her face.

He had one final story to tell her before she was no longer his, but the kleren and the light-headed feeling it gave him were suppressing his words.

One night before he knew his wife was pregnant, they went out to sea together for some night fishing. Rowing quietly for some time, they circled the same small area before his dinghy stalled as if it had reached a wall. He was afraid that they might be stuck on a reef, but he managed to push back. Peering into the moonlit surface of the sea, his wife had removed her pleated sundress until she was sitting there in only her plain white cotton panties, her protruding belly aimed like an arrow at the void.

"Non," Gaspard said, quickly noticing her slightly larger belly and breasts and realizing what she was trying to show him. But before he could say anything else, she slipped both her legs over the hull and slid into the sea, her body parting the waters, pulling her forward as she sunk her head into the wet darkness then raised it up and out again.

She was gliding away from him to even deeper water. He rowed toward her, now frantically shouting, "Claire, reken, sharks. There could be sharks."

"There will be if you keep calling them by name," she said, and laughed a deep, breathless laugh.

As he caught up with her, his face relaxed. Then they saw what she had swum out to see. Surrounding her was a dazzling glow. It was as though her patch of the sea was being lit from below. She was, from her perfectly round breasts down, in the middle of a large school of tiny silver fish, which were ignoring her and feeding on equally gleaming specks floating on the water's surface.

He stopped rowing and remained outside of it, watching her and pondering the news she had silently delivered to him, in awe. Then it was the sea he was watching. The bioluminescence amazed him. But soon, his panic returning, he started shouting her name again.

"Claire, come in now, Claire!"

She backed away from the fish, splitting the school in half as she paddled toward the boat. And for a moment she reminded him of Lasirèn, the long-haired, long-bodied brown goddess of the sea. With an angelic face like a bronzed Lady of Charity, Lasirèn's vision was, it was believed, the last thing most fishermen saw before they died at sea, her arms the first thing they slipped into, even before their bodies hit the water. In his dinghy, like many others, he had a mirror and comb, a bugle and conch shell, which comprised a small shrine to attract Lasirèn's protection.

When his wife reached the boat, he reached over and offered her his hand and she took it and climbed back in, even as the silver fish vanished, returning the sea surface to a charcoal gray.

Wiping the saltwater from her dripping face with her fingers, she whispered, "Limyè Lanmè. Limyè Lanmè." Sea light. Then she cleared her throat and in a louder voice added, "Claire like me. Limyè Lanmè. Limyè Lanmè." Claire of the sea light.

"You will not change her name," Gaspard heard himself tell the fabric vendor.

The fabric vendor shook her head no.

"You will not let her ride moto taxis."

"Non." Both the woman's hands immediately rose to her chest, as though she had been stabbed there. "I would never do that again."

Even after all these years of wooing the fabric vendor for his daughter, he never expected it to actually happen so fast. But there was no turning back. From now on his Claire would be the fabric vendor's daughter.

"Before you leave the country, there are papers," the woman was saying.

Gaspard would later try to figure out where Claire got the courage to raise her skinny arms at that moment. He had underestimated her attachment to her few belongings and had assumed that she wouldn't want them, but she did, and once her raised hand was acknowledged with a nod from both him and the fabric vendor, she pointed to their home and whispered, "Bagay yo," the things. Not *her* things, but *the* things, as though nothing in the world was truly hers.

Gaspard understood immediately, but it took the fabric vendor some time to decipher the gesture.

I hope this woman comes to know my daughter's ways quickly, Gaspard thought, as he watched the girl slowly walk, more like an upward crawl, toward the house. Claire weaved in and out of the groups of other children on the beach, ignoring their calls to play as she moved by, her long arms frozen at her side. Gaspard saw her reach the wobbly door of the shack before she walked inside.

She did not have that many things, Gaspard thought, only two bright green jumpers and two white blouses for school, the birthday dress she was wearing, her night dress which was really an adult T-shirt, her notebook and reading primer, and the foam mattress and patchwork blanket on which she slept. Maybe he should go and help her with them. She wouldn't be able to carry everything by herself. Certainly not all the way to the fabric vendor's house. He would have to accompany them. It would be the right thing to do. Maybe the woman wouldn't even want those things in her house. Maryse. The fabric vendor's name was Maryse. Now he could think it again. Now he could even say it. He could at least call her Madame Maryse. His daughter was now Madame Maryse's daughter.

Madame Maryse was fidgeting a bit, shifting the weight of her round frame from one fuzzy red–covered foot to another. She looked at some of the townspeople clustered on the beach, then turned her gaze back to the door where the girl had entered the shack, then glanced back toward the water where many of her neighbors were sitting by the dimming bonfire with the fisherman's widow who was still sobbing and rocking her face in her hands.

Gaspard followed Madame Maryse's gaze and remembered how during the first three years of his daughter's life, he used to dream of his girl, a little baby lying in his arms at night. Then in the morning, while he was on the water, he would imagine seeing her baby face bobbing in and out of the gentle wake of his fishing boat. He would instantly fear that she had joined her mother in death and would anxiously wait for the news of it to make its way to him, but it never did. She remained as alive as he was, and he was even more afraid of the possibility of seeing her in the flesh, as fearful as he was that she might have the face she had inherited, her mother's. He never dreamed of his wife, though. That part of it, something in him kept locked away out of sadness and guilt. He had been absent when his wife had died and his child was born. He had been hoping to get one last series of catches before his daughter came. He had been at sea.

The crowd on the beach was beginning to thin out. People were slowly drifting away, heading back toward town. He felt sad that he had nothing more to say to this woman who was offering his daughter a new life, this woman who from now on his daughter would call mother. He had once fantasized that he would marry her, but he knew that even with her preferences for questionable men she would still consider him inferior, socially beneath her. And now there she was, growing impatient as his daughter refused to come out of his house.

"How much is she bringing with her?" she asked.

"I'll get her," he said.

He felt the woman's solid and perhaps judgmental gaze on his back as he headed for the house. He was doing his best not to stumble, but each time the soles of his feet dug into the cooling sand, he was certain he would fall over.

Gaspard could immediately tell when he entered the shack that his daughter was not there. Several fast-moving creatures darted into further darkness as he inspected the foam mattress his daughter usually slept on. It was covered with its usual patchwork blanket, untouched since she had carefully pulled it tight and tucked the corners under that morning. Hanging from a wire hanger nailed to the wall were her school uniforms. He picked up the kerosene lamp by the door and, using it to light his way, searched all four corners of the room.

When he didn't find her, he ran out to the beach and screamed her name. Madame Maryse rushed to his side, saw the look of panic on his face, and joined in the shouting of Claire's name. Others did too, walking off in different directions until they had searched the entire moonlit stretch of the beach. Some even walked to the edge of the water, calling Claire's name into the horizon.

When after some time Claire did not surface, many of Gaspard's neighbors walked over to him and took turns telling him some variation of, *Maybe the girl fell asleep somewhere. She will surely be home by morning.*

The fisherman's widow came to embrace him, her grief momentarily stalled by his. Her face was swollen from crying and the mourning scarf around her coarse black hair slid toward the back of her very long neck. She was his wife's age, the age his wife would have been now, too young to bear such a burdensome grief, yet too old to start over.

The fisherman's widow, like many of the others, thought that Claire might have gone to town and encouraged those heading there to continue their search. Gaspard, however, was certain that Claire would return soon and wanted to be at home when she did. Madame Maryse decided to follow those who were headed home. Squeezing Gaspard's shoulder, she said, "She doesn't understand, perhaps. She'll be back."

Using the boulder his daughter had sat on to rest his drunken and spinning head, Gaspard lay down on the sand and with his eyes glued to the scattered stars, he promised the heavens that he would never try to give her away again.

Most of the townspeople had left, except for a few young

men who had nowhere to sleep and were grateful for the company all the commotion had afforded them. They and a few other stragglers set up for the night, arranging their sleeping bags and sisal mats and bedsheets in a protective circle around Gaspard.

Every once in a while, one of them would walk to Gaspard's shack and peek inside, checking for Claire. They did this without asking Gaspard if they should and timed themselves so that they checked every half hour or so, when it seemed Gaspard might want to go and check himself. The entire night was spent like this, until worry, exhaustion, and drink overcame Gaspard and he finally slept.

The next morning, Gaspard woke up at the usual time that he would have been heading out to sea. The air was gray and growing lighter and the young men were still asleep. Gaspard's head ached, his temples still throbbing. He staggered to the house and checked all the corners once more. Claire had not returned.

It suddenly occurred to him where his daughter might be. His heart was pounding and he was nearly breathless as he half walked and half ran through town. The early mass was beginning at the cathedral as the bell chimed the six a.m. hour. A large crowd of sick people had already gathered in front of the town hospital, hoping to be seen at the clinic that day. The streets were already crowded with cars and moto taxis ferrying people to and from the outdoor markets. He felt the gazes of people on his face as he raced past them, too quickly for them to say hello and for him to respond. He could barely breathe as he sped by the cane field toward the burial site.

At first he did not see her, lying on her side, coiled up like a baby on the dew-soaked red earth. Her head was resting on a large stone, half leaning against the farthest tip of her mother's grave. She was still wearing her pink muslin birthday dress and a quarter of her face now seemed buried in the ground, showing that she had been there for some time, possibly all night long. Bending over, he placed his cheek next to her nose. He thought he felt a warm stream of breath against the cool earth, but it was his not hers. Reaching down, he pulled her into his arms and pressed her against his chest.

"Claire Limyè Lanmè?" he said, wanting to finish a thought, but not sure which.

Her eyes were wide open but she was not looking at him. She was looking somewhere off in a distance, past him. He swayed his hand back and forth in front of her face, but she did not blink. Her arms and legs were limp the way they were before she woke up from a very deep sleep.

"Claire Limyè Lanmè?" he said again. He felt her damp dress, and when he saw the blood that ran from the side of her face onto her shoulder, it did not startle him. She had pounded her head against the ground several times, it seemed, before one side of her forehead gave way in the form of a crack that had seeped with blood and further reddened the earth around her.

THE HAREM

BY IBI AANU ZOBOI

Delmas

The women called him Robby. A flash of his gorgeous smile, his fake Rolex watch, and a flick of his shoulder-length dreads would get him a phone number. Only after a few date nights, when he'd join them in bed, would they know his full name: Jean-Robert Dieujuste. But he insisted that they mustn't ever call him that. To most of Pétionville's young and fabulous, he was Robby, the smooth-talking Haitian sensation whose café-au-lait complexion and designer-looking clothes made the women fight each other, as he would oftentimes relay to his childhood friend, coworker, and roommate Antonio, better known as Toni.

"Ah, you get too involved, Robby," Toni said to his friend one morning when he came home from an all-night rendezvous. Toni was sprawled out on the bed smoking a joint. He picked up a few pieces of Robby's dirty clothes from the floor and threw them at him. "These women are not looking for love. It should be easy. But no, you are the one going goo-goo-ga-ga for them."

Robby sucked his teeth, took a pull from his friend's joint, and dropped himself on his ever-rumpled and unmade bed. "Did you see Caroline last night? Did you see the way she looked in that dress, man?"

"Yes, and you got to take off that dress and take care of some business, right? I don't understand why you're always crying *She doesn't love me, she makes me leave.*"

"Well, what do you think is wrong with her?" Robby asked.

"She doesn't ask me to stay like Tanya or Minouche."

"Maybe it's because she knows you're loving two, three other women at the same time."

"You should talk!"

"Believe me, I know I am a vagabond," said Toni. "That's the difference between you and me. I admit it. But you don't. You want to be in love, but this is about sex. If a woman meets you in a club and gives you her number and brings you home, then she just wants sex and everybody's happy and you can go home. But you want to stay and have breakfast, lunch, and dinner, and then marriage and children—with all of them!"

Toni got up, buttoned his shirt, and pulled on a navy blazer. He was headed out to his job at the telephone company, in the same office where Robby worked. Toni clasped his watch, brushed his wavy, close-cropped hair, and splashed some co logne on his face. He took one last look in the mirror between their beds before turning back to Robby. "Going to work today or what?"

"I worked Saturday," Robby said. "I'm taking two days off."

"It's Tuesday, you already took two days off."

"Sunday we're closed, so it doesn't count."

"What's the matter, Caroline wore you out?" Toni walked out of their shared bedroom and into the adjacent small kitchen. In an instant he was out the door.

Robby lay down on the bed, exhausted. Caroline had indeed worn him out. He inhaled deeply at the thought of her cocoa skin and long dark hair. Robby would have never approached her if it weren't for Toni's encouragement. Caroline was ten years his senior, and she preferred her men young and hip. She had spent her early adult years traveling the world and dating men twice her age. Older suitors now bored her.

She'd been promised her own villa in Italy, an apartment in Midtown Manhattan, a beach house in Tobago. But home had summoned her to repair the failing family business and maintain the magnificent chateau that towered over Port-au-Prince. After hours of intense lovemaking, Robby would stand on the second-floor balcony and search for the little two-room house he and Toni shared.

Caroline made love as if she had never made love before, as if she were searching for something buried deep inside her. Robby liked the hair-pulling, the delicate biting, and the throaty calling of his name. But he resented being shooed away afterward as if he were a pest. Once, after an evening together, she even left some money on the table, which made him yell at her.

Tanya showed him a lot more respect, but she was not as passionate as Caroline. She was still young, with a tender body and pliable mind—but courageous nonetheless. It was she who had approached him on the dance floor at a nightclub, turning her back and grinding against his body. After they made love, she would always get him a glass of water, wash herself and comb her hair, and head to her aunt's makeshift neighborhood restaurant to bring him back a plate of food. She was quiet afterward and let him sleep. She did not badger him with questions. Robby always slept with her warm body pressed against his. With her, he felt comforted and soothed. Not like the hot-headed Minouche.

Minouche would open the door wearing only a tank top and miniskirt and begin cursing him out for not answering his cell phone for three days. He'd promised each of them that he'd never let more than three days go by without seeing them. But he couldn't promise long conversations on the phone in between those visits.

Whispers of the possibility of marriage were enough to ease Minouche's suspicions. While he was submissive with Caroline and gentle with Tanya, he was his wildest with Minouche. She would yell and cuss and threaten to leave him and return to her ex-husband, whom she claimed was wooing her again. She'd grab his cell phone and search for other women's numbers. That's when Robby would pull her from behind and cup her large breasts in his hand and suck the damp, salty skin of her neck. She'd soften in his arms and cry, and demand that he tell her he loved her. He imagined marriage to Minouche being full of drawn-out arguments, but it would all be worth it for the makeup sex.

Robby turned his face to the warm morning sun beaming from the small window beside his bed. The sounds of the cars and trucks on the busy road outside the house quickly lulled him to sleep. He envisioned the beautiful faces of all three women: Caroline with her long eyelashes, ruby-red lips, perfect white teeth, and dark, distant eyes; Tanya's smooth brown complexion, close-set eyes, and long, braided hair extensions; Minouche's dimpled plump cheeks, too-thin eyebrows, and cute button nose.

Robby sighed, rubbing his hands over his crotch while thinking of his night with Caroline. But it was Minouche's often tense and angry body he longed for. He hadn't seen her since Friday night and soon she would be calling. For now, he would sleep, resting as if he were in each or all of their arms, with their lips pressed against his ears telling him how much they loved him. But Toni was right, he was the one who most often declared his love. In the end, he could see himself married to all three of them. He loved them all.

Robby awoke from his sleep with a jolt, as if something had

yanked him up from the bed. He was sweating; the room was unusually hot. There were sounds of children's laughter outside the window, letting him know that it was late afternoon and the neighbors' kids were home from school. He was starving. Unlike Caroline, Tanya would have certainly made sure that he got something to eat the night before. Tanya often told him that she wanted no other woman to feed him. She said this with what seemed like genuine concern and not in the jealous way that Minouche would. She wanted him to eat good meals from either her own kitchen or from her aunt's restaurant where the stewed cashews and the chicken were legend.

Robby wanted to catch Tanya right when she was leaving work so he wouldn't be bothered with having to say hello to her uncle, whom she worked for in a small office behind his mechanic's shop downtown. The old man expected Robby to ask for his niece's hand in marriage any day.

Sporting a freshly pressed pair of khaki pants, a striped short-sleeve rugby shirt, and Italian leather shoes, Robby strolled down the busy street outside his house in Delmas. He took his sweet time, seductively whistling his favorite konpa tunes at some of the women passing by. Only once did he stop a lady whose breasts were nearly spilling out over the neckline of her T-shirt. She didn't own a cell phone so Robby gave her his number instead, even though her shoes were cheap and her fingernails were dirty. Robby would never dare bring a woman like that around Toni or his other friends. After being with Tanya and Caroline, his standards were higher. Minouche was the least sophisticated, but at least she took care of herself with weekly manicures and pedicures. Whomever he chose to marry when he was good and ready, he would also have to be able to introduce, with pride, to his mother.

Robby smiled at the thought of his mother. She had called him on New Year's Day to remind him to come visit her in Léogâne for a big bowl of soup joumou. He got his bowl of soup joumou with nice big chunks of beef and fresh warm bread, but it was from Tanya's aunt and not from his mother. It was just past four o'clock and Tanya would certainly be happy to see him. She wouldn't have to get into her uncle's jeep as he made all his stops at his friends' houses. It was noisy as usual in Delmas. The scent of grilling chicken from a new outdoor barbecue place enticed him, but he would wait to eat with Tanya. The air was thick, and unusually still. Not even a subtle breeze blew in from the ocean to remove the daily stench. He looked up at the sky, now a paling blue, the sun a dim yellow. His eyes wandered across the road toward a woman he thought looked like Minouche. He stopped, his brows furrowed. He tied his dreads into a knot, smoothed his beard, adjusted his shirt, and made his way across the street to encounter Minouche's accusations that he was obviously going to see another woman because he wasn't at work.

It wasn't until he was nearly halfway across the street, having been almost run down by a speeding tap tap, that he realized the shapely woman was not Minouche after all. He was still in the middle of the street when the ground began to shift, and it was as if a huge truck or maybe a train, like the ones that used to carry sugarcane from Léogâne to Port-au-Prince during his childhood, was approaching. He looked up and down the street, trying to figure out from which direction the truck or train was coming so he could move. But when the balcony of the nearby auto parts store collapsed onto the pedestrians and merchants below, he stayed put. He crouched down to the ground, not knowing what else to hold on to, because the ground was moving. The cars and trucks stopped.

The people ran in every direction. Then the buildings, the cement, maybe even the sky and clouds and sun, were falling! He knelt, covering his head with both his arms, and clenched fists as a few small things landed on his back. He began to pray, realizing that this must be it—la fin du monde, that final judgment day that the old man who often sat on an overturned bucket down the road from his house was always preaching about to passersby. He'd been to the Protestant church with Tanya, Catholic mass with Minouche, a Sunday luncheon hosted by a foreign missionary organization at a fancy hotel with Caroline, but never in any of those instances did he give his life to Tanya and the old man's Jesus, take Minouche's Holy Communion, or give one cent to charity for the peasants in the countryside, as both Caroline and his mother often urged him to.

He sobbed, slowly raising his head and opening his eyes to see a cloud enveloping him. The screaming pierced his ears. He looked up at the sky, still a pale blue with a dim yellow sun, and waited for it to part, for a beam of white light to descend like some sort of ladder—something, anything, to justify the thunderous sounds. But the heavens were too peaceful. Then it must be hell, he thought. Slowly rising to his feet, he was unable to see more than a few inches in front of him. He looked down at the ground and glimpsed a crack in the road. Everything beneath him was too white. Maybe this was heaven, he speculated. But people were screaming and there was still that horrible sound as if the world itself was crumbling.

Tremblement de terre, he heard the people say after what seemed like hours of walking aimlessly through the streets of Port-au-Prince. It had only been an hour but Robby took slow, calculating steps. He had been coughing and swallowing dust, had felt a stinging pain on his back near his left shoulder and touched it to see that it was bleeding, though not profusely. He kept walking, even when he heard someone screaming to him for help. He just looked at the bodies beneath the fallen rubble, some reaching for anyone or anything, others unmoving. Toni was at the phone company where they both worked. The top floor housed the office where he, Toni, and the secretary, who was also Toni's on-and-off girlfriend, worked along with two salesmen, Marlo and Donaldson. As he stood at the intersection where the building should have been, cars and trucks—some speeding, some slow-moving—dodged him and hundreds of other people who were suddenly crammed at every corner of every street. Maybe Toni, Carole, Marlo, and Donaldson had managed to run out. Maybe Toni had stepped away to get something to eat. His friend whom he had known all his life was smart, witty, and quick on his feet. He should have had enough sense to get out.

The building had completely crumbled. Robby searched for the door, a window, any opening he could squeeze through to find his friends. But then the ground shook again and he sped away from the rubble to the middle of the intersection. A woman came running toward him, screaming, grabbing him and burying her head in his chest. He did not hold or comfort her. It surprised him that he had absolutely no desire to press his body against hers, to caress her hair and tell her, *Everything's going to be okay, chérie.*

Instead, he pushed the woman away and turned in the other direction to find Tanya. Had he not kept her tender body and warm smile on his mind, he would've never gotten to her. The men shouted at him, demanding that he come help move rubble off a friend, a mother, a child. He moved around the dead on the ground. He walked in the middle of the street where tap taps, cars, trucks either cruised slowly by, surveying the fallen buildings, or sped past to get to a hospital, any hospital.

Had Robby not felt the stinging pain near his shoulder, the slow movement of his legs, he would've sworn that this was death. He stopped at an intersection that was barely recognizable. The landmarks, the signs, the stationary street vendors were all gone. He stood, turning in a full circle to survey what had become of this little portion of Port-au-Prince. He peered up toward the hills. The houses in the distance looked like an avalanche of concrete.

Robby stopped in front of the auto parts store Tanya's uncle owned and saw a group of men lifting pieces of concrete from the caved-in entrance. The cinder-block archway where he always stood waiting for Tanya to emerge from the tiny office in the back of the open yard was buried beneath piles of rubble fallen from adjacent buildings. Tanya's uncle, according to a spared neighbor, had been seen running back into the office, probably to alert Tanya when the ground started to move.

Robby had no idea where he found the strength to lift a fallen piece of concrete the size of a small child with his bare hands. He thrust his body into a narrow opening that led to the yard. He thought that above the screaming and praying that had become the new background noise of the city, he heard some people cheer. He could not get Tanya out of his mind. If she were under there, he would not leave until he had pulled her out. He blindly moved large chunks of concrete and long strings of rebar aside, estimating with his hands and feet the approximate location of the tiny office where Tanya might be trapped. Finally, he saw what he thought were Tanya's beautiful legs peeking out from beneath a huge piece of wood from the doorway of the tiny office.

Robby clawed at more concrete and wood and managed to loosen the load on top of Tanya's chest. Hauling the creaking wood aside allowed him to see an arm, then another. The impact of the fall had torn apart most of her clothes. Her flesh was sunken in places that, as well as he knew her body, he no longer recognized. Her face had been chipped apart by the debris as well, her features, her beautiful nose and mouth, all flattened into one, as though she had been kneaded by some gruesome baker's hands.

Some more men were crawling on top of the rubble nearby. They were calling for Tanya's uncle Serge and Manuel, one of the other mechanics.

Neither one answered.

"The building next door might collapse on top of this one," one of the men said, as he turned around to leave. "You should get out of here."

"Tanya!" He began calling her name, even though he knew she could not answer.

The screams he was hearing now were from farther away, out in the distance and not in the rubble beneath him.

He quickly went back to digging, lifting more cement from Tanya's sunken torso. Her entire compressed body was now loose. He grabbed her and tried to lift her up, but she was limp and her body gave way, sinking back into the hole from which he had just plucked her. He tried again, grabbing her harder this time, not being as gentle. He lifted her with all his might over his healthy shoulder. She was soaked with blood and the movement released a cloud of bloody dust over his body and into his face, throwing him into a coughing fit that made his body convulse and nearly forced him to drop her.

He found an opening that both their bodies could fit through and exited the rubble. As he struggled down the crowded and dusty street, a woman holding an open Bible moved up beside him, placing a hand on Tanya's body. His shoulder ached from Tanya's weight, his thirst was unbearable from the heat and dust, and he shooed the praying woman away.

He had never thought of it this way before, but he now considered it a good thing that Tanya, Minouche, and Caroline, even with their various societal standings, all lived rather close to each other, and to him. The walk to his house from Tanya's uncle's mechanic shop took nearly a half hour with her body over his shoulder—it would've been much quicker had she not been so heavy. His house was one of the few on his block that were cracked, but had not fallen. He ignored the long gashes in the cement and headed inside.

It was only after he lay Tanya's body down on his bed that he allowed himself to focus his full attention on what might have happened to Caroline and Minouche. Had they died as well? Was he the only person in their maddening puzzle who was still alive?

He'd been so cautious all along, trying his best not to fall in love with any of them. But he loved them all and now might lose them all, along with his mother in Léogâne, his city of birth. Who knew how widespread this thing was? It might come again, with the same vengeance, this time in the middle of the night while he was having a one-person wake for Tanya. It would be unfair, Robby thought, that his dear Caroline and Minouche would be out there longing for his embrace, when it was only Tanya that he had saved.

Toni was right. (Oh, had Toni perished too?) It would have been better if he'd never fallen in love with the three women. He was now feeling a stinging pain on the shoulder which had carried Tanya all that way. It was the least of his problems, though. Hell, he knew, was just outside his window. The screaming and praying continued in the distance as night fell. Tanya was snugly tucked in when he stepped outside. The brokenness of the world around him shocked him for a moment. In the brief time he had spent inside, sitting at Tanya's side, he had forgotten what it looked like now. How long would it be before he was used to it? Before he would look at it as though it had always been there, a normal part of the new landscape of the city he'd escaped to from the provinces when he was a teenager and had loved ever since? He would look for Minouche first. He imagined her smile and her plump, dimpled cheeks. He imagined her cursing him out for not coming sooner.

He didn't know whom or what to thank when he spotted Minouche sitting on a plastic crate right in front of her partially collapsed house. She was surrounded by a group of dusty and bloodied women and children, crying. Many of her companions were hurt, others praying and singing. Minouche had her face in her hands, sobbing.

Robby braced himself for a slap in the face, but instead Minouche held both arms in the air toward him, like a child greeting a parent. Her left foot was crushed so badly she could not stand on it. He kissed her dry lips and caressed her dusty face. Even with the smell of blood and death all around, he kissed her neck, pressed his chest against hers.

"Hospital," she whispered, grinding her teeth in agony. "Robby, please."

"I'm taking you home," he said. "With me."

It now occurred to him that none of these women had ever seen his home. He had been at times ashamed of the cramped space and at times afraid they would take his willingness to bring them there as a sign of total surrender.

His shoulder throbbed with pain, but he allowed Minouche to place an arm around him to brace herself as she hopped on her good foot. When she cursed Robby for not being strong enough to carry her, he hailed down a pickup truck filled with people—some limp, lifeless, others staring blankly into the night air.

Maybe he was crazy for bringing her here, he thought as they entered his and Toni's room. He could hear more singing and praying through the window that had earlier allowed children's laughter to wake him. He helped Minouche onto Toni's bed as she moaned in pain then mumbled something—another curse or demand. The whole world may be wanting a hospital or doctor, but his Minouche was safer here; he could care for her better than any doctor or nurse. He kissed her forehead once more and placed a single finger on her lips. She groaned in pain as he wrapped a towel around her bloody foot. She could barely ask for water.

He found some in the tiny kitchen and put a cup to her lips. She did not sip, she just let the water drip past her lips onto the pillow. He lay next to her for a moment, pulling her body close to his. Then he checked on Tanya, kissing her softly on the forehead as well. She was already cold and clammy, rigor mortis having set in. Both his girls were so peaceful. If indeed the devil had raised the earth, then it was here in his nearly unscathed bedroom that God lived. But Caroline was still out there. Unprotected by him, unsafe.

Minouche squeezed his arm, signaling for him not to go. She didn't appear to notice Tanya in the next bed. Or maybe she was in too much pain to care. He kissed both their foreheads again. Minouche was getting warm, either from the heat or from an infection. Her body was shivering too. He wondered whether she'd be alive when he returned.

Outside, he managed to climb into a packed tap tap heading up the hill. It was full of people praying, crying, and cursing at their cell phones for not working. There was a body sprawled out on the floor by their feet. Robby avoided their eyes and the arguments about what had happened and thought of only Caroline's face and how she looked in that dress the night before.

Caroline never stayed in her NGO's office past two. Robby hoped that she had been safely nestled in her large, sturdy home. He jumped out of the tap tap at the foothill leading up to her minimansion.

Out of habit, he dialed her number on his cell phone, but of course there was no reception. At the still-standing high metal gates, he called out her name, but she did not answer. There were no lights on in the house, or anywhere for that matter, and everyone seemed to be in the streets. Her car was not in the driveway.

He remembered how she'd sometimes call him in the evening. If he didn't answer because he was with Tanya or Minouche, she wouldn't care. She'd tell him that he was free to do as he wished. He was more attractive to her, she told him, because she had to compete for him.

If Robby was indeed the ghost he was starting to believe himself to be, then he would have been brought back to life by the lilting sound of Caroline's voice. Then he turned around to see her running toward him through a crowd of her neighbors gathered in small groups holding bedsheets and pillows, as if preparing to lay down in the middle of the street for the night. She hugged and kissed him, and he picked her up and swung her around.

"How are you?" she asked.

"Come back to my place," he said immediately, while staring at her made-up face, neatly combed hair, and clean blouse.

"Your place? Robby, I can't even go back into my own house," she replied, dusting off his clothes with her hands.

Someone, another man, called her name in the distance.

"I'm coming!" Caroline shouted back to him.

"Who's that?" Robby asked.

"Victor. He's a friend," she said, not looking into his eyes. "Some of us are going to sleep in his yard. It should be safe there."

Robby pulled her toward him, making sure that this Victor person could see them. She wiggled away from him, and he drew her back to him.

"Robby, what's wrong with you? You should come to Victor's with me."

"No. You should come with me."

"Stop playing games," she said.

"I'm not."

"Then what's this all about?"

"Please." He reached for her hand, but she stepped back.

"Listen, Robby, as soon as daylight hits, I am leaving this place."

"To go where?"

"Dominican Republic, Montreal, Cuba, anywhere but here."

Many of her neighbors with the blankets and pillows had dispersed, some making their way back up the hill to her friend Victor's backyard, the others heading across the road to where a local priest and nuns had set up for the night.

"Please, chérie," Robby pleaded as he pulled her to him again. "Please, Caroline. I need you to be with me tonight. My place is safe, if *any* place is safe on a night like this."

He held her hand to his lips, kissed it, then placed it at his heart, which melted something inside of her. She kissed him on the cheek, embraced him, and whispered in his ear, "So it is now that you are finally inviting me to your home. This is what it takes to bring out the man in you?" Then she smiled and grabbed his hand. Cars were fewer and farther in between now, and those that went by them as they walked were packed with the dead and nearly dead.

They were both exhausted when they entered his dark bedroom. It was unbearably hot like the rest of the city, and the stagnant air grew sour. The moonlit, foul-smelling room revealed the silhouettes of the two bodies lying there, obviously dead, rendering Caroline as still as they were.

Robby gently took her arm and walked her over to each of them.

"This is Tanya," he said, then reached down and kissed her on the cheek. "And this is Minouche," he said, doing the same to her.

He motioned for Caroline's hand, but she was pulling away, stepping back, trying to make her way out of the room, out of her lover's house, and possibly out of the shaken, broken country.

But Robby would never let her go, because if the devil stirred again, beckoning the land to rattle and shift beneath them, forcing his little part of the house to collapse like a domino, encasing them all in this love, in this death, then they would truly be inseparable—he and his three lovers, bound for eternity.

ROSANNA

BY JOSAPHAT-ROBERT LARGE

Pacot

Radios were forecasting a beautiful Friday morning.
Not a cloud in the sky over Port-au-Prince. As for the
neighborhood roosters, it seemed as if they'd been
waiting for this very morning to launch their songs into the
world. A multitude of cock-a-doodle-doos echoed through
the neighborhood of Pacot.

Ahhhhh! Rosanna thought, as she slipped into her favorite
blue jeans and an airy white cotton shirt. *What a wonderful
day for a trip.*

Rosanna's aunt Solange had already put the daily work in
motion. The servants were all on their feet. The one responsible for sweeping the front yard was wielding his broom like a
soldier answering "Taps." Dusters in their hands, the cleaning
team had started the daily routine aimed at eliminating every particle of grime resting on every surface of the property.
Melanie, the cook, whose task it was to make coffee, poured
spoonfuls of grainy Rebo onto a piece of muslin cloth that
she used as a coffee filter. Soon enough, the aroma of coffee
spread throughout the house.

"Chérie," Aunt Solange called to Rosanna from somewhere on the property, "Melanie has already prepared you
some sandwiches for the road. How about a cheese omelet
before you go?"

Aunt Solange was the proud owner of two large stores in

Port-au-Prince's commercial district. The first one was a bou-tique with an assortment of expensive European ladies' dresses. It was there that the elegant demoiselles of Port-au-Prince shopped for their Pierre Cardin, Escada, or Oscar de la Renta gowns, which automatically bestowed a sign of distinction on any woman who aspired to be a part of the city's high society. In the second store, one could find a selection of luxurious home furnishings from all over the world. That was where the rich people acquired the sofas, beds, decorative lamps, mod-ern refrigerators, and other ornaments that beautified their homes. Needless to say, Aunt Solange was wealthy. Her pri-mary residence was in the old neighborhood of Pacot, an area full of splendid clustered gingerbreads and terraced villas that looked as though they had been sculpted out of the neigh-boring hills. Lovely antique furniture filled the house as in a museum. Some rare pieces from Europe and Asia made Aunt Solange's collection one of the most valuable in the country. Paintings with themes ranging from female nudes to carni-val, pieces by famous Haitian artists—including Préfète Duf-faut, Bernard Séjourné, and Edouard Duval-Carrié—added the final touches. Parked in her garage were two silver cars: a Mercedes-Benz and a BMW. One would have sworn that these vehicles had never been driven through the streets of Port-au-Prince, since they remained so shiny and clean all the time, thanks in part to Solange's young driver Da, who treated them as though they were his own.

"Ah! This omelet is so good," Rosanna declared, sitting across an elaborately carved dining room table where she and her aunt often ate breakfast overlooking a lush hibiscus and azalea garden. "Melanie is the master of omelets."

"Melanie is the mistress of everything," her aunt playfully corrected her. Melanie had been cooking for Aunt Solange for more than twenty-five years now, longer than Rosanna has been alive. Melanie had started working for Solange back when Rosanna's parents had fallen in love while pursuing their studies in engineering at the École des Sciences. They had married soon after and a year before graduation Rosanna was born. One Saturday morning, they'd decided to take a day off from studying and parenting and had left six-month-old Rosanna with Solange, who was also the baby's godmother. A fine rain was falling on the road as they returned from the beach in the dark. The surviving passengers from the camion that hit them claimed that they never had a chance. The camion driver did not see their small jeep until the last minute; as the justice of the peace report put it, the vehicle was as flat as a communion wafer.

Solange was grateful that her brother and his wife had been wise enough to leave the child with her. Having never married and with no children of her own, she saw it as a sign that she was meant to look after the girl for the rest of her life, which is why Rosanna's sudden desire to go on a trip alone to Les Cayes to research her mother's roots alarmed Solange to no end. When Rosanna's parents died, everyone had agreed that Solange was the best person to raise the girl. But now that she was a stunningly beautiful young woman—as beautiful as the corpulent nudes by Solange's famous painters—everyone would want to claim her, including her mother's family, who had barely even visited during the twenty-one years that Solange had been taking care of her.

Simply looking at Rosanna was a pleasure for Solange. The girl had her father's smooth black skin and her mother's brown-streaked curly hair, making her what in Haiti they would call a marabou, the kind of dusky beauty who poems are written about. Even when she was just a teenager, grown men would admire her as she strolled down the street, and Solange often got the impression watching her niece that an invisible orchestra was playing just for her. Solange was very proud of the job she had done raising Rosanna. The fact that Rosanna even desired to make this visit to Les Cayes to see family members who had shown little interest in her was proof of it. Very simple pleasures, not Solange's wealth, were what had always seemed to appeal to Rosanna; she preferred swimming in rivers to swimming in pools, gorging herself on mangoes and avocados to sushi and foie gras. And Solange could tell that even while inhaling her favorite omelet, Rosanna was itching to head to the Portail Léogâne bus station to catch a camion—as she had begged her aunt to let her to do—on her own.

"It's the best way for me to see the country," Rosanna had successfully pleaded her case the night before. "I want to travel like the regular people of this country do. That's what my mom would have done."

Solange did not want to smother the girl any more than she already had, but she was nonetheless worried about her. Still, she did not want to seem as though she was jealous of Rosanna's mother's family and trying to keep the girl for herself.

"Davernis can at least drive you to Portail Léogâne, right?" Solange asked.

"And my mother's brother and sister will be there to meet the bus," Rosanna completed what she thought would be her aunt's next sentence.

For lack of more elaborate stories, Rosanna had invented a whole slew of fantasies about her mother. Everything Rosanna wished she were, she imagined her mother to have been. In reality, her mother was simply a pretty girl from a poor peasant family who, because of her mother's acquaintance with some powerful henchmen in her area, had been given a scholarship to a fancy university in Port-au-Prince. This is what had put her in the path of Solange's brother. There was no point in telling that story to the girl, however. She would soon find it out for herself, and from the horse's relatives' mouths, so to speak. Besides, in death everyone is equal, and Rosanna's mother and father certainly were equal now. But Solange could not lie either, so rather than say anything she remained silent, allowing Rosanna to nurture as many illusions as she could muster about her mother.

While Solange and Rosanna wrapped up their breakfast, Davernis made his way into the dining room. He was a tall, muscular young man. He was twenty-one years old, like Rosanna, and in another type of house they might have been raised like brother and sister. Instead, she was the princess of the house, as the servants liked to refer to her, and he was the driver. That morning, he was wearing a simple watch that Rosanna had given him as a gift, hoping that he would take the hint that he no longer had an excuse to be late, as he often was when she needed him to take her to a friend's house, to a party, or shopping. Davernis also worked as a messenger in Solange's stores, which sometimes contributed to his lateness.

Before he was promoted to driver, Davernis had been a rèstavèk, an unpaid child laborer at Aunt Solange's house. Rosanna could still remember the day that Davernis's mother had brought him to the house. He was twelve years old. Davernis's mother thought he could be of use around the house, and maybe in return Solange could send him to school and, when he was a grown man, give him a job.

Aunt Solange had resisted at first.

"I am raising a young woman here," she had told Davernis's mother, a skinny toothless woman who sold mangoes at the market. "I can't have some wild young man here."

"He will be very good," the woman had insisted. And Davernis had certainly been good. He had been running chores for Solange both at the house and the store since he arrived and had been one of her drivers for two years now. He lived with the other servants on the property, in a big concrete house that Solange had a well-known architect build for her staff. He had never been in an accident, a major feat in Port-au-Prince, and treated the vehicles like they were precious jewels, often cleaning and polishing them in his spare time.

"You know that Davernis is taking you to the station," Solange repeated.

"Yes, Tatie," Rosanna answered, considering this a great concession indeed. She had expected her aunt to find some way to thwart her plans, perhaps asking Davernis to go with her to Les Cayes.

"My dear, you must be very careful," her aunt was saying now. "There are so many thieves on these buses."

"There are thieves everywhere, Tatie," she countered.

"Davernis will accompany you to the station and he will help you buy your ticket."

"Yes, Tatie." Rosanna reached under the table and, for her aunt's amusement, pulled out a massive straw hat that she had bought on the street the day before so that she might blend in better on the public transportation. She checked her purse for her camera and the micro tape recorder that she hoped to use to interview her relatives for details about her mother's life. Her suitcase, a small black roller bag, was waiting by the front door and Davernis grabbed it with one hand and started dragging it away. Rosanna and Solange followed him toward the gravel driveway where the Mercedes was waiting. By the time they reached the car, Davernis was already sitting behind the wheel. Her bag, Rosanna assumed, was in the trunk.

Rosanna kissed her aunt goodbye and Solange hugged the girl tightly, as though she had just dropped her off at college or surrendered her to some young man at the altar. When their embrace grew longer, Davernis stepped out of the car and opened the door, motioning for Rosanna to step in. He waited for her to settle in the back before starting the engine. Then, before she knew it, she found herself waving goodbye to her weeping aunt as the car slowly pulled away.

The moment they left beautiful Pacot, Rosanna and a quiet Davernis entered the real Port-au-Prince. Both sides of the streets were filled with desperate vendors proclaiming in singsong the miraculous virtues of their produce. There were beggars at every intersection, their hands outstretched, pleading, "Please, give what you can! I am dying of hunger!"

Bones barely covered by skin jutted out from holes in their torn clothes. Red eyes peered out from behind the tears streaming down their faces. One of them was holding a half-naked child in her arms, and through the glass window she bore down on Rosanna with her eyes while shouting, "For the love of God, please, help me!"

The child's reddish hair was a sure sign that he was suffering from malnutrition. The woman continued pleading with both her eyes and words as they sat stuck in bumper-to-bumper traffic leading toward downtown Port-au-Prince.

"God who is in the sky," the woman was saying, "look at such a beautiful young woman sitting in such a beautiful car. Wouldn't you ask her to help? Please, God!" The child began to cry then too, and a yellowish liquid flowed from his nostrils. "Beautiful woman, please help me, please! We have no place to stay, no food to eat, and no water to drink! Please, help!"

A great sadness emanated from the child's face. His hollowed eyes touched Rosanna to the core.

"Mademoiselle, the baby hasn't eaten for three days!" the woman shouted. "Please, help me. Throw a few pennies in my hands, I beg you, mademoiselle!"

Having spent the first twelve years of his life amidst similar poverty, Davernis was accustomed to this kind of blackmail from street beggars. Eager to drown out her voice, he yelled angrily at the woman: "Goddamn, leave us alone!"

The child was seized with fear and began to cry once more.

Rosanna intervened and said, "No, Davernis, at least have some pity for this child!" Then she took a Haitian twenty-dollar bill out of her purse, rolled down the window, and handed it to the woman. As their fingers met, Rosanna could see the layer of grime and mud on the woman's hands. No matter how often she was part of such a transaction, it never ceased to make her feel guilty for the way she grew up. If Aunt Solange hadn't taken her in, perhaps she too could have been on the street, hungry, begging.

Rosanna slowly rolled up the window as the woman cried out a loud and jubilant "Mèsi!" Thank you! The child, too, as if connected in every way to the woman, perked up.

"God will reward you," added the woman, as the car in front of them finally began to crawl forward.

"Mademoiselle Rosanna," Davernis said once they had cleared the worst of the traffic and were on their way toward Portail Léogâne, "I know you are a good person with a good heart. I've told you this many times before but you never want to listen. If you continue like this, people will always try to think of new ways to take money from you."

At the Portail Léogâne bus station, Davernis lined up the

Mercedes behind a swarm of vans, trucks, buses, taxis. A sea of people was waiting to board the buses for the countryside and horns were honking all over. Rosanna's excitement at the possibilities for the trip was growing. She waited for Davernis to step out of the car first, then took a deep breath and followed him. Thousands of people were going in all directions, buying last-minute things, corralling large animals, which would share the camion with the human cargo. Dogs were barking right and left. Goats were baying tirelessly, and if you weren't careful, the cows roaming freely in the streets could poke you with their horns. One had to squeeze and dance like a matador around bulls to avoid being gored. Women held tightly to their handbags to elude pickpockets.

"Driver!" Davernis called out to one of the safest-looking camions at the station, a colorfully painted monster that was blasting reggae music to attract passengers. The camion was called *Fate*.

"We need the front seat for this beautiful young lady," Davernis told the driver.

"The front seat is more expensive," the driver replied, leafing through his ticket book. "If she wants to pay the difference, no problem. We leave in half an hour!"

With Rosanna's cushioned leather front seat reserved, they had thirty minutes ahead of them. Davernis's order from Aunt Solange was to not leave the station until he had seen Rosanna's bus leave. But waiting in this torrid heat in the middle of the chaos at the station was tough, especially for Rosanna. In no time, she was surrounded by a horde of merchants pleading with her to buy everything from water and juice to plantain chips to cigarettes to painkillers. People were getting so close that she could barely breathe. The people's voices blended with the reverberating sounds of the horns blowing from a multitude of buses arriving and leaving. It was all getting on her nerves. More vendors approached offering kolas, patties, candy, and chewing gum. Even though she would never admit it to Davernis, Rosanna's head was spinning. Never in her life had she been so physically close to so many people all at once. As the crowd moved in on her, she searched their faces for Davernis, but could no longer see him.

"Davernis!" she called out.

"Mademoiselle!" She could see his head peering from somewhere behind the perimeter.

Turning to a roaming pharmacist in the mob around her, she asked, "Do you have aspirin?"

"Five dollars," the small man said, lowering the bullhorn he used to advertise his wares as he reached into a small black pouch for the aspirin.

To get the five dollars—an exorbitant price—Rosanna had to open her purse in front of everyone. She reached in awkwardly, and in doing so a bunch of Haitian dollar bills that Aunt Solange had secretly stuffed in her purse rose to the surface, looking like a flush in a game of poker.

"Mademoiselle!" Davernis gasped from where he was standing, the crowd now seeming to push him back to purposely keep them apart. The people around Rosanna couldn't help but notice the bills. Even Rosanna seemed shocked to see them. She was now an even bigger magnet. A group of beggars pushed in, landing on her like flies. Their hands stretched out toward her, they pleaded for help.

Now deciding to forsake the aspirin, Rosanna shoved Aunt Solange's surprise deep into her purse. There must be at least a thousand Haitian dollars there, she thought.

Then, out of nowhere, two well-built men, men who looked like they might belong to a SWAT unit, approached her. "Get out of here! Get lost!" they ordered the group of people surrounding her. "Leave this beautiful lady alone!" They shouted at the beggars as they chased the crowd away. They were responsible for security in the area, they told her.

"We'll hang around and look after you," they said, "until you board your bus."

"You are very kind," Rosanna answered, relieved that they were there, since Davernis had simply disappeared, "but I really don't need protection. I'm expecting a friend."

Hardly had she uttered the words when one of the alleged security officers grabbed her arm as the other pushed a small handgun into her spine. The one who grabbed her arm picked her up off the ground and carried her away, with the other one trailing behind. The crowd quickly scattered, and even though the first man was carrying her, he ran faster than the second one with the gun.

"Don't say a word," she heard the one carrying her say. "If you cry for help, we'll blow your head off. Do you hear?"

An intense fear invaded her, causing her to feel even dizzier. She was much too afraid to yell. Besides, everything was happening so fast that she had trouble concentrating on any one thing.

Soon she was in the back of a jeep with darkened windows. The man threw her in headfirst and quickly placed a dirty black rag over her eyes. He turned her on her belly and tugged at both her arms, forcing them behind her, ripping the sleeves of her blouse in the process. She could hear the tearing of duct tape, which he used to wrap her arms and hands together. Then he turned her on her back and placed a strip of tape over her mouth.

When the door slammed shut and the car barreled away,

she fell on the floor between the front and back seats—
cracking, she was almost sure of it, one of her ribs. Only as
the sharp pain of the fall shot through her body did she realize
fully what had happened. She was barefoot. Her shoes and her
purse were gone. Over the hum of the car engine beneath her
and the bounce of the bumpy road, she heard the loud chatter
of commerce at the port and realized that they were driving
along Bicentennial Road.

She had been kidnapped, she could now fully admit it to
herself. On Bicentennial Road, at the seashore, albatrosses
and pelicans used to glide low over the waves as large ves-
sels approached the port. This, of course, was during another
time, when she was free.

A shudder ran through Rosanna's body when they arrived at
what she imagined was the hideout. They removed the tape
on her legs so that she could walk but kept the blindfold on her
eyes and the tape on her mouth. One bandit placed her hand
on his shoulder so that she could follow him like a blind person with a guide. Underneath her feet were muddy rocks and
puddles. Then there was a stretch of dry earth. She heard the
unlocking of a padlock and felt a shove on her back: she was
being pummeled against what felt like an unfinished concrete
wall. She hobbled along a corner, offering her now severely
aching back some support. Nearby, as if in the next room, she
heard some dogs barking. They sounded like hungry dogs, she
thought, her heart racing. She wondered if eventually they
would use these hungry dogs against her. She pushed her back
deeper into the wall and tried to remain still.

A rancid smell hung in the air as the men paced back and
forth around her. One was wearing boots, she could now tell
by the way his feet hit the concrete on the ground. The other

was wearing regular shoes, fake leather loafers, it sounded like to her. There was no air passing through the room. Perhaps there was no window.

"Now," the man with the boots said, "let's get started with the important part!"

It seemed that their plans for a ransom demand had already been set in motion. The one with the boots would make the call, they decided, while the other one remained in the room guarding Rosanna.

Before he left, the one with the boots ordered Rosanna through clenched teeth, "Don't cause any trouble and you won't get hurt."

Rosanna tried to anchor herself against the wall, which was hard with both hands taped behind her back. She thought of Davernis who might be looking for her, of Aunt Solange who had not wanted her to take the camion in the first place, but had given in to make her happy. She thought of the stories of other kidnappings she'd heard in the past. The men were always beaten badly. The women were often raped. Some small children had been killed when the ransom was not paid. She thought of the shock that this could cause Aunt Solange.

Davernis drove back home as fast as he could. He was screaming like a madman when he got to the front door of Solange's compound. From the slew of words that came out of his mouth, the only ones Solange could understand were: "Rosanna has disappeared!"

"What did you say? What do you mean, Rosanna has disappeared?" demanded Solange.

"Madame Solange, I swear, I looked everywhere. She was nowhere to be found!"

Suddenly there was commotion all over the house. The

servants couldn't control their emotions. They let out loud screams and tears flowed. As for Solange, she seemed dazed as she screamed over and over, "Oh my God, please have mercy! Rosanna was kidnapped!"

The neighbors started showing up. Having somehow gotten wind of the commotion, they came over to see what was happening, then they started offering advice. Many of them had themselves been victims of the recent kidnapping wave that had struck the capital.

"You have to pay the ransom right away," they all agreed, "so that she can be released as soon as possible!"

Solange blamed Davernis. How could he let himself be separated from Rosanna?

"Why, for God's sake, would you leave my niece alone in the middle of this crowd of thieves?" Solange banged the table with her fist. Then her cell phone started to ring. The screen read, *Private number*, but given the circumstances, she replied anyway. "Hello, hello! Who is this?"

A deep voice with a menacing tone spoke at the other end of the line. "Madame, listen carefully to what I am about to tell you. I will be brief, so open your ears and open them big. First, if you inform the police of our negotiations, I can assure you that you will never even *find* this girl's body. Second, start gathering your money and make sure it is the exact amount of the ransom. Listen carefully! I will not repeat myself. Collect five hundred thousand U.S. dollars, do you hear? And then we'll tell you where and how to give it to us!"

"How is Rosanna—" Solange started to holler, but before she could finish the sentence, the man hung up.

"Who could have done such a thing?" Solange shouted out loud to herself. "Who would want to kidnap Rosanna?"

One of the neighbors, a bony pale-skinned man, whose

elderly mother had suffered a heart attack and died during a kidnapping attempt at her own house in broad daylight, had become extremely philosophical, a filozòf, in such matters. He chimed in, saying to Solange, "Ma chère, this country is a land of mystery. Mysteries enter your home quietly, and always when you least expect them. They come like a closed padlock and always without the keys to their puzzle. It's almost impossible to discover what's behind a mystery in this country. They are part of the essence of our people. They are stained into the fabric of our culture. When you hear the sound of drums coming from the depth of night, what you really hear are echoes. And never, never can you discover the true source of the drumbeats. And never mind whose hands are beating the drums. Those are the mysteries of the night. You know, madame, when the flying werewolves are in the air, one can only see the traces of their flames, but never can one guess which direction they are taking, or in whose yard they will land. Never will we know, as they fly, whose children they plan to eat during the night. But sometimes the solution to a mystery is right under our noses. In other words, what you need to know is right there next to you, though sadly, you never see it. Madame, you will never know who took Rosanna. The why, we know, is money. Money, we know, or lack of it, is the primary obsession of a poor country like ours. But as to *who* committed this crime, I am speaking from experience: your mystery will now join the rank of all the other mysteries that will never be solved in this country—"

"They want half a million American dollars," Solange finally interrupted her philosophical neighbor, lest he should go on speaking forever. "It's too much. Far too much. I have to imagine that they would take half of that, which is all I have liquid right now."

* * *

In the windowless room where Rosanna sat contemplating her fate, the heat kept rising and her body began to shake in fear. She couldn't stop thinking of all the kidnapping cases that had been in the newspapers. Of the sixteen-year-old boy who was killed and dumped on a trash heap even after his family had paid the ransom. Of the girl who had been taken all the way to the northern city of Cap Haitien and was gang raped then murdered after having both her eyes gouged out. Of the school bus full of children that had been abducted, forcing each parent to come up with a thousand dollars. Of the shoe-shine man who had been beaten on the spine with a crowbar and was paralyzed because his family could not afford the ransom. But there were also happy stories, happy endings worth clinging to. There was the girl at school who had only spent several hours in captivity because her parents had quickly negotiated and paid. Not a hair on her head was touched, she had insisted to everyone at school. They had blindfolded her, just as they had Rosanna, so she didn't know where she had been taken. All she knew was that it was extremely hot and full of mosquitoes.

There were mosquitoes flitting about Rosanna now too. By the thousands, it seemed. Flies buzzed annoyingly around her ears, occasionally landing their tiny moistened tentacles on her skin. She could also hear the man guarding her, breathing across the room, swatting the mosquitoes dead with loud slaps to his own skin.

Meanwhile, because they could not go to the police, Solange's philosophical neighbor took Davernis with him back to the Portail Léogâne bus station, hoping to find witnesses. The bus that Rosanna had intended to take to Les Cayes had already left. The street vendors who had surrounded her, and even the others who had not, but had seen everything unfold before their eyes, refused to tell them anything.

"M pa konnen," they answered to Davernis and the neighbor's repeated questions. I don't know.

"I understand." The neighbor tried to coax them with small purchases until he had an armful of wilted fruits and vegetables. "You have to come back here every day, and even talking to me right now might put you in danger, but I am a customer and customers and vendors have an intimacy."

"M pa konnen mesye," they all repeated, the fear evident in their eyes.

The guard was still looking at his beautiful captive, cowed in a corner in the unfinished house where they housed their victims. His blood was heating up in his veins, images of him and the girl whirling in his mind. He pictured her as a nightingale in a cage and himself both her potential killer and protector. The sense of power that this visual metaphor inspired vibrated through him. He had rarely felt this before—that is, sympathy for his captives. She wasn't a regular payday in his eyes. His other captives were often rich men and women, spoiled aristocrats who wanted water or even soda as soon as they got here. This one had not even groaned to have the duct tape removed from her lips and she actually seemed like a genuine innocent.

A few drops of rain could be heard tapping the tin roof above them. To him it sounded like a rhythm of Gede, the god of love and death. To her it sounded like thunderclaps, and she imagined each drop as the toll of a bell that might bring help.

"Mademoiselle, I have an offer for you," the guard said.

Rosanna could hear the mild hesitation in his voice. Even though he was the one with the gun and the power and she was blindfolded and helpless, he was addressing her the way men of his class addressed women of hers. He was addressing her the way Davernis would.

"I can let you go unharmed, mademoiselle." He tried to make his voice sound more forceful. "You are a woman, mademoiselle; you must know what I am trying to tell you. I am a man, and this desire is flowing strongly through my body. The attraction you carry around yourself creates in me the desire to make love to you. And naturally, if you allow your body to slip under mine, maybe I'll let you escape. I have the power to let you go." The captor removed the duct tape from Rosanna's mouth.

"Monsieur, zanmi mwen, I beg you," Rosanna pleaded, addressing him like someone of her own class. "You've already taken my freedom. Please don't take my . . ."

The man stood up and abruptly unzipped his pants. He pulled out his penis and pointed it toward her, taking pleasure in knowing that she would not realize what he was doing until he was already upon her.

She heard the unzipping of the pants and the thump of his footsteps when he dropped the gun on the cement. "Tanpri ede mwen!" she cried. Please help!

Her supplications had absolutely no effect on the aggressor. He had shaken off his momentary lapse of judgment in feeling sorry for her and was now saying to himself, *Another crime, why not?* Even though society had placed people like this girl above his stature, his life, his physical prowess, and his gun, would always get him what he wanted. In the end, the begging and praying meant little to him. Physical violence was the only thing those people would respect.

With this in mind, he grabbed Rosanna's arms and legs and stretched her out on the floor. He threw himself on top of her, stamping his lips roughly on her face. She squirmed out of his grasp and tried to roll away, scraping her skin against pebbles on the floor. She balled her fists and managed to squeeze her wrists free from the duct tape. Then, before he could reach her, she yanked the blindfold off her face.

The room was a gray square with unfinished cement blocks piled on top of one another; the roof was made of rippling tin. Up front was a padlocked black metal door to which this man probably had the key.

While she was contemplating a way out, the man grabbed her by the arm and threw her against a wall. He was using even more force than before. He squeezed her left arm and twisted her right one behind her back, trying to join them, perhaps to tape them together again.

She felt both her shoulders snap, the pain throbbing through her entire body. She had no more to lose. She had to keep fighting. For the first time since the guard had pulled the tape off her mouth, she began screaming. She screamed as loud as she could, and for every scream, every push, every punch she tried to throw, he countered with one of his own. She tried to bite him. He clung to her, pressing his body against her so tight that each of her movements echoed his. He picked her up and slammed her down on the ground, throwing his body's weight on top of hers, pinning her to the concrete. They started rolling together on the floor, and as she struggled to break away, he took the opportunity to snatch up her skirt with an unsettling rage. Her courage was flagging. She was exhausted. Her screams seemed completely useless. No one was coming.

Rosanna cried out one last time. At that moment he raised

her leg, chafed raw from the floor, and she felt something like a hot iron on the outside of her genitals, something like fire between her legs.

She opened her mouth to scream even louder, but this time no sound came out. There was just a feeling of suffocation as the iron attacked her flesh. The man grunted and shrieked with an animalistic joy. The pain grew so unbearable that she could no longer yell. He, however, was laughing as he hammered his hips into hers. Finally, the pain became so intense that she lost consciousness.

At Solange's house, her cell phone rang again.

"Hello. Madame, it's me. Is the money ready?" the deep voice snapped sharply.

"Sir," Solange said in a quavering voice, "I can give you two hundred and fifty thousand U.S. dollars. That's all we could put together."

"What! You're leaving the half-million behind and talking about two hundred thousand? Madame, I'll call you later." *Bang!* The same message showed up on the cell phone's screen: *Private number.*

While Solange waited, it felt to her as though the entire city was in mourning. Above the hills, a series of curling black clouds, sympathy clouds, draped the sky like a flock of bad-omen birds. Her eyes puffy from crying, Solange scolded herself between sobs. She should have never let that girl go to Portail Léogâne. She should have agreed to the half-million dollars that the kidnappers were demanding. She should have told Davernis to take Rosanna directly to Les Cayes.

Her philosophical neighbor tried to reason with her: "Madame, if the kidnappers were following your Rosanna, they would have found a way to get to her. Most of these kidnappings are well planned, you know."

The phone rang again.

"Hello, madame. A quarter-million U.S. dollars will do."

"Okay," Solange said, regaining her sang-froid, "but I need proof that she is still alive."

The afternoon drizzle started again. A smell of doom seemed to hang in the air. Rows of children were making their way home from school. Beggars sat with their hands stretched toward the sky, perhaps waiting for the love of God that had been promised by evangelists of all stripes. Solange had just left Sogebank, the philosopher neighbor at her side and a briefcase full of money on her lap. Davernis was driving. In the car, no one said anything. There was both too much and too little to say.

The booted man walked quickly down the dark alley leading to Rosanna's prison. He leapt over the piles of trash that littered the narrow alleys. The smell of decomposing flesh lingered in the air. He finally reached the front door of the cement shack.

Tok! Tok! Tok! Three quick knocks on the black metal door was the signal he had agreed on with the guard who was inside with the girl, but there was no need for this. The door was open and both the guard and the girl were gone.

The briefcase full of money under her arm, and her philosopher neighbor still at her side, Solange had Davernis drive her to the rendezvous spot, a dead-end street not far from her house, which overlooked a crowded cement shack–filled neighborhood below. At the entrance to the labyrinthine neighborhood was a trash heap that was always smoldering.

An hour went by: nothing. No Rosanna, no kidnappers!

Solange felt heartbroken and discouraged. Would everything truly end this way for Rosanna?

Her philosopher friend for once had no words of comfort or enlightenment. Finally her cell phone rang, and Davernis answered it.

"That was Melanie, madame," Davernis said a moment later from the front seat. "Someone was going by and recognized Mademoiselle Rosanna in the trash heap down there."

"What do you mean they recognized her?" Solange asked.

"She is dead, madame," Davernis explained, his eyes filling up with tears, "and her body in such bad condition that only some of her is identifiable."

"Then how do they even know? How can they even tell it's her?" Solange pounded her fist on the suitcase full of money, crying like a child. Her mind, her body it seemed, was drifting into the past, back to the Canapé Vert hospital where she'd visited her brother's wife the day Rosanna was born, back to Rosanna's baptism where she had promised to take over the parental duties should anything happen to her brother and his wife, back to the night that she'd learned of their death and had felt both agony and elation at the possibility of raising the girl herself.

And now Rosanna was gone. And suddenly the trash heap at the mouth of the slum that she had long ignored, a slum that was as much part of her neighborhood as the hilly houses of her closer neighbors, was much more visible to her. And when she rolled down the window of the Mercedes, she could clearly see in the distance this smoldering garbage heap where Rosanna had been dumped like refuse. The smell of decay in the air suddenly irritated her. Barely able to walk, Solange leaned on her neighbor's shoulder as she left the car and moved toward the trash heap. Surely there would be an investigation, some press, some sympathy. And then, just as her philosopher neighbor had said, the mystery of Rosanna's death would remain unsolved, like so many other mysteries in Port-au-Prince, whether in the slums or fancier neighborhoods. She tried to gather what was left of her courage just to keep walking through the mud and piles of trash. Then, all at once, they saw Rosanna.

"Jesus, Marie, Joseph," she gasped.

Rosanna was as naked as the day she was born. Her body was covered with scratch marks, cuts, even what seemed like burns. Her face was swollen, her eyes gouged out, leaving two fleshy gashes. There were lines of dried blood on both sides of her mouth, which remained open, as though midscream.

Solange crumpled to the ground, her knees digging into the grime that was now cradling her niece, her beautiful niece.

"She fought," Solange told those who attended Rosanna's closed-casket funeral a week later. "She fought very hard for her life and her honor. Now it is our turn to fight for our lives and our honor."

Solange had hoped that her private grief would somehow inspire a different resolution for Rosanna. She had hoped that her pleas to the authorities, to the press, would inspire someone to come forward to either deliver the killer or vow to at least try.

At the funeral, her philosopher neighbor sat discreetly in the back next to Davernis, who was waiting to follow the hearse in the Mercedes and return Solange home after the funeral. He had grown up with Rosanna, yet he could not allow himself to grieve as openly as Solange or even the throng of the girl's mother's relatives, who had heard about her death on the radio and had flocked to the funeral in Port-au-Prince to tell the stories about her mother that Rosanna had set out to Les Cayes hoping to hear.

"Ah, fate," the philosopher neighbor sighed after one such speech from Rosanna's maternal line.

"Indeed, mesye," replied Davernis, who would never forgive himself for what had happened. He would also never forgive his collaborator, who had lost him such an important payday simply by lusting over the privileged flesh of some young bourgeois girl. Now they would have no choice but to try again. This time, the aunt.

MALOULOU

BY MARIE LILY CERAT

Martissant

Stay up long enough between midnight and three a.m. any day and you will hear Maloulou. But be careful to never run into her. Everyone in Lakou 22 knew this. Noises in the night defined that yard: husbands, young men, and prostitutes who caused old doors to creak while coming in some nights; lougawou, werewolves that turned skin inside out and jumped about loudly on tin ceilings, eyeing little children for future repasts; noise there always was. But the sounds of Maloulou were unique. With precision, many could reproduce the footsteps mixed with a light clinking of chains: *clink, clap, clink, clap, clink-clap*: sometimes coming and sometimes going. It even seemed a mark of honor to wake up and recount hearing Maloulou. Older stories about Maloulou that had been abandoned would resurface some nights when the folktales of Bouki and Malis could not be stretched any further. There was the broad cassava-colored hat over an invisible head, going *clink, clap* a hundred years or so ago after the first African slaves disembarked on the island.

"Don't worry, Ghislaine, Lakou 22 came with Maloulou," Destin and Madame Destin, the very first residents to build shacks at the entrance of the yard, told my mother one morning soon after we moved there. Darkness did not worry my mother, but Maloulou would. My mother had braved the dark streets for as long as I could remember before retreating to her own cinder block–mounted bed, hidden behind the paisley-print curtain to protect me from the parade of visitors whose fees paid for our shack, my school, our food and clothing. In some ways, I was my mother's daughter; I was never afraid of the dark.

Like the Destins, other residents with nothing to do often gathered, coffee cups in hands, under bright early suns to swap Maloulou stories, as if competing for the most exciting rendition. There were those who laughed in disbelief, others appeared pensive when reports were shared about the mysterious thing that had always lived in their midst but had never been seen. Young ones like me attending to morning chores before hastily preparing for a discounted ride to school with Josaphat, the camionette driver who lived in Lakou 22, used to listen furtively, ears tuned to what was being said, eyes wide with amazement. Where the name Maloulou came from, no one really knew. One version of the story was that Maloulou came from the sea to the island with the name Nkiruka, but it was changed to Maloulou because it rolled easier on the tongue.

Nevertheless, the nomadic and infamous visitor who was said to roam our compound in the ink-blue night enthralled all. One man in particular, it was said, Roland Désir, might have come nose-to-nose with Maloulou.

Roland Désir turned mad one morning, the story went, and folks repeated verbatim the words of the person who saw it happen, his wife Marguerite, who stood in the middle of the yard sobbing, saying that maybe if she hadn't confronted Roland about the children's school fees lost in a cockfight the previous night, he might not have lost his head. Years later, Roland was still roaming the streets and corridors, speaking to himself, living under trees, sleeping under the stars, begging for food, throwing rocks at the sea or at the gagè where he used to wage cheer on cockfights.

Lakou 22 people still sought Roland to give him scraps of food. After all, it was on account of this yard that his life changed. Folks remembered how he was a proud nèg nan nò, who had moved here from up north a long time ago with his young family. He provided for all his eight children, transforming abandoned oil drums into coal stoves to sell. Sadly, what he made was insufficient to sustain his avaricious cockfighting addiction; but all agreed that he was a fine member of Lakou 22.

What made matters worse for the Désir clan were the series of unfortunate events that hit the family right on the heels of Roland taking to the streets. Folks were in agreement that it was easy to imagine Kenesou, Roland's youngest child, not living long. Less than a year had passed between him and Jean, the sibling before him, and Madame Roland's body had not fully been restored to carry a healthy baby to term. And sure enough, Kenesou was very sickly: fever, bronchitis, diarrhea, you name the parasitic disease and he had it. Many thought the Désirs lucky to have had him alive for so long, but some still believed Maloulou might have been the culprit.

Now, the death of Hermione Désir, the eldest, came as a complete surprise. She was pretty like a rainbow, they say when telling her story. By all accounts, Hermione was angelic-looking. To have seen her walking down the road and not taken special notice would be cause for concern with any man: young or old. Men begged to nestle in her hips. Wives tried to shield their mates. Prostitutes wished she'd move away. Little boys could be heard praying for the gods to send them wives like her when they grow up. Young girls were said to imitate her walks and get their hair done like hers.

The whole neighborhood trembled, they say, the afternoon Hermione Désir started convulsing. Burning cotton under her nose, rubbing alkali on her face and chest, were not enough to bring her back. She did not even wait to have the tea that had been put on the fire for her. All of Lakou 22 mourned her, even crazy Roland Désir, the father she had supposedly lost to Maloulou. He was heard the night of her burial pacing about and lamenting, "This child was too young and pretty to die," as if her death made him momentarily sane.

Mothers and wives who inherited these stories would evoke the fate of Roland to caution their men of the perils of walking dark corridors after midnight. In my head, though, I had preferred imagining Maloulou like the character Django, from the first spaghetti western film I ever saw. I envisioned Maloulou pulling a machetes-filled coffin in the dead of our nights, looking to rescue me, her own Maria, from renegades like Uncle Solon, who had mutated into a Tonton Macoute.

Mother never told me the familial relations we had with Solon. I suspected we had none. Personally, I had no recollection of his presence prior to the age of twelve or thirteen. We never went to his house; he came to us. My calling him Uncle Solon was just one of those impositions made on Haitian children, an effort at politeness by assigning a familial title to an adult stranger. Along with having to call people who curdled my blood aunties and uncles, I hated my mother for forcing me to kiss people I did not care for, but that was not the only reason I wished Uncle Solon dead. He was mother's steadiest customer. And I could tell that he was one of the best payers since we seemed to eat a bit better after his passages. He was also short, bow-legged, had a receding hairline, and eyes set too far apart, and an unfriendly face that his small, stubby legs and arms did not help. But this had nothing to do with my disliking him. One night, during an early-evening visit as my mother prepared him some plantain porridge, he came over to the table where I was slumped on my school books, put one hand on my mouth and the other under my dress, and did not stop until he heard my mother returning to the room. That's how and why my deep hatred for Uncle Solon started; and my passion for Maloulou began. Mother has had to snatch me from endless daydreams where Maloulou slays Uncle Solon and all the members of his nefarious, dungaree-clad gang.

My hatred for Uncle Solon grew deeper when he volunteered to bring me home from school to save mother the camionette fare, just so he could continue searching and playing with my bouboun under the nun's school uniform during the car rides. That nourished my plan to catch Maloulou and make an offering of Uncle Solon. Yes, I pondered the fact that I too might not survive the encounter. But not surviving was the least of the deterrents, for I was already dying in small bits. All my desires and needs to unearth the Maloulou enigma and find an ally in stopping Uncle Solon took on realness when, for the first time, at the point when night and day mixed and lying wide awake in bed wishing to hear mother turn the key, and thinking of all the bad things Uncle Solon did, I instead heard with my own ears the clinking and clapping. I listened, still as a corpse, to steps moving through the passageway toward the sea, and waited silently until the same footsteps and dangling chains ambled back.

There were a few people who told of having heard Maloulou in the night. I told no one, though I felt a tremendous pleasure for finally belonging to a special cadre of people. After a while, I did grow tired of staying up nights waiting to hear Maloulou go by. But if I wanted to come upon the one who wandered in the hours of darkness, tell on Uncle Solon and have an ally in making him disappear from our lives, I needed to know the exact times when the stroll happened, study the pace, prepare some trappings and paraphernalia, and brace for what may come.

Had mother suspected my crazed plan, she would have made me gulp down daily concoctions of hellebore until I was completely purged of my foolish idea. Curing my folly would become her personal crusade. But I kept my idea and plan in my head, sharing them with not even the wind.

In conversations with myself, however, I pulled all sorts of reasons to give me the heart to go forward. The Bible tells how little David took on the giant Goliath, I recalled. I had two giants in my life and one was going to help me slay the other. Rather than continue to endure the visits and car rides with Uncle Solon or painfully imagine the size of mother's sorrow when he kissed and hit her like what I saw him do one night behind the green paisley curtain, I was determined to risk everything. I was prepared to know Maloulou just as Roland Désir had, if only in the private confines of my head.

Amassing the items that I needed for my expedition to Maloulou was exhaustive and costly. It ate away at the tiny bit of money I was saving to buy Mother a set of gold eggplant-shaped earrings like the ones she often borrowed from her friend Fifi. I knew Mother would never muster the courage to buy them herself, feeling that she'd be wasting hard-earned money intended for rent, food, and school fees on something unneeded for our survival. I was saving those pinched coins extracted here and there to one day appear as her own magi, bearing gold earrings she would love. To protect my meager funds, I did try to get her to pay for the rope for my plan, but it didn't work. Her response to my request: "You're too old to be jumping rope! Are you getting the rope to hang the both of us?" I had no comeback. Whatever I could say would be too lame against the disarming image of our lifeless bodies hanging from some tree in the yard or from our ceiling. And a long sisal rope I absolutely needed for my mission: so I dipped in my gold earrings fund.

Collecting salt and black pepper was the easiest. Many of us in the yard put out our salt to dry if it's not raining. And whenever I came upon a calabash of salt in the sun, I would help myself. Plus, I volunteered often to be sent to market so I could purchase more salt and pepper for my mission. In less than a month, I hid away enough salt to spoil the taste of our water hole, and enough pepper to scatter about and get all of Lakou 22 fighting. Little by little, I pounded and mixed the two spices together to create a peppery powder that I'd be throwing in Maloulou's face to cause momentary blindness as I roped her arms and legs and dragged her back to our shack.

The night of my operation, I carefully arranged rags on my bed so it looked like I was tucked inside. I prayed that it would not be one of these nights when my mother would fish for me in the dark, as if fearing that I would be sucked through a hole in the ceiling. If I did not carefully plan every move, I could lose money and my quest for Maloulou would fall to the wayside. And both Mother and I would be dying sooner than our Creator intended. I chose a Friday night because that's usually when mother stayed out dancing and drinking with her clients into the wee hours of the morning. Other days in the week, some clients made quick and short stops for a taste of her on their way home, and she'd be around, going in and out through the night. But the weekends belonged to her clients.

I too had taken the habit of staying out later those nights to play with the boys and let them kiss me in the dark, disobeying Mother's directions to go home once the Pierrette twins, who were known good girls, went in to sleep. I wore Mother's faded black dress that she had worn to almost every burial procession, including that of her own mother and countless members of Lakou 22. The dress blended well with the dark. Standing in a corner of the gallery of the two-room shack recently vacated by a couple named Janine and Jean, the rope and an alfò bag containing my salt-and-pepper mixture strung across my shoulder, I was waiting in a darkness that was as thick and heavy as molasses. I replayed in my head the *clink, clap, clink, clap* of the night promeneur, and knew that I would recognize those steps in a crowd of thousands. How much time went by, I couldn't tell. Though I knew I had only blinked my heavy lids when suddenly Lakou 22 became a cane field, right under my eyes. The leaves of the cane felt like a thousand crazy red ants attacking my exposed arms, legs, and face, drawing me into a strange state of alertness.

Believing that I could be in a cane plantation wasn't hard. Léogâne, one of the remaining towns of the Haitian sugarcane empire created by France, was no more than seven or eight kilometers from Lakou 22. I could have sleepwalked to Léogâne. But what followed disturbed the expected order of things. Before I was discovered that morning at the edge of the sea by Madame André, hearing her piercing yell of "Anmwe, vin pote l sekou," Please help her, I thought myself dead and on the journey to Ginen, through this long underwater passage that Aunt Francine said all Haitians go to when they die. And the idea of dying soothed me. I would never have to speak overtly and with fear of these remembrances, never have to tell another soul of my encounters with Maloulou or be called the girl in Lakou 22 who went mad and spoke non-sense. And Uncle Solon would never touch me again.

When Madame André and Djo picked up my shivering, wet, and seaweed-entangled body from the shore, sensation in my limbs returned before my voice. But it took more than four months, plus the violent death of Uncle Solon after leaving our shack and the side of my convalescent bed one night, to confirm for Mother that I was not crazy. That got her to begin untying my arms and legs from the bed, no longer fearing that I would take off running. I was even allowed to read my old school books after I recited the daily Bible verses with her. Recording my experiences in some unused pages of some old notebook came to me only after Mother had me repeating this verse with the Bible open on my head. *But the servant who did things that deserved a beating without knowing it will receive a light beating. Much will be required from everyone to whom much has been given.*

These words started a memory flood and I could clearly see the cane field and the old woman who had appeared from nowhere in front of me; the steps and clinking of the chain made her unmistakable. There stood Maloulou, tall as a coconut tree, eyes bright like the stars above, with a metal collar connected to a chain that ran all the way to one of her feet. Without giving me time to catch my breath, take in the realization that I was nose-to-nose with her, or dig into the blindness-inducing mixture to execute the plan that I had rehearsed hundreds of times in my head, she grabbed my left arm and asked, looking down at me, in a voice as big as she was, "Why did you follow me?"

I remember stammering the words, "I need . . . help . . ." while remaining mesmerized by finally being in the presence of the one who has inhabited Lakou 22 before it was Lakou

22; the one whom the people have named, accepted as just another neighbor, feared, and blamed for undoing their lives and taking away their children.

"Children should not be out at this time of night. And those who don't listen pay for their stubbornness," she said in a hoarse, ancient voice that sounded like the scolding of a hundred worried grandmothers.

Since I had gotten a bit light-headed from the heavy and pungent smell of asafetida that enveloped the air around her, I mumbled some inaudible words.

"You can follow me, but you can't speak," she said, peering down at me, her head wrapped in a tiyon, then beginning to move away.

"Uncle Solon," I remember stuttering, determined to tell Maloulou why I had followed her. "You have to liberate Mother and me from Uncle Solon." Stunned and still immobilized by fear, I managed to add in a feeble voice, "Telling Mother how he touches my bouboun when her eyes are turned away would have caused so much . . . more pain . . ."

Maloulou stopped and turned again to look at me, her face softly lit by the half-moon overhead, revealing tender and clear eyes that seemed to see right into the profoundest corner of my soul, and let out a big sigh.

From one of the many pockets in her long dress, she drew something out and sprinkled it atop my head and on my face, saying, "He will never touch you again."

I continued crying as Maloulou patted my head with her heavy tree branch–like hands to calm me down. Her powdery potions on my face and her words must have had an impact. I could hear, but was no longer able to respond to her as she lunged into a story about a horse and life.

"Just remember, my child, you die a slave if you let this

horse guide you. You must command the horse, through the mountains of life and the valleys of death. Just be sure to always do things that will put you on the good side of life," she said. "Sa n fè se li n wè, we always reap what we sow, my child. I cannot leave you here now, can I?" She seemed to be concerned by my presence. Tightening her calloused left hand on my arm, she ploughed through the cane; the machete in her right hand pushing the blistery leaves away. At the end of the field, there was a small assembly waiting; even the mastiffs and bloodhounds were there, tranquil. Standing a short distance from the crowd, she asked twice, "Sa ki la?" What's there? And an echo of voices responded, "Bwa n ap kloure." We are nailing wood.

"Good. I am the woman of the mountain with no name who Makandal sent," Maloulou said, still holding on to me. The name Makandal reverberated in a dizzying swirl in my head. *Ma-kan-dal*, I replayed, visualizing the bench way in back of the class where I sat, and Mr. Laborde's mouth as he gave a history lesson one afternoon long ago.

"François Makandal: man, myth, but surely rebellious slave, who was burned at the stake, just like Jeanne D'Arc," he had said in quick French to show the ease with which he spoke the language. "Makandal's followers helped in killing some six thousand slave-owners in his six years of rebellion," he added in his showy style. "Makandal freed himself and rose to the heavens, perhaps still roaming the Haitian skies and forests," he laughed, "having baffled them and even us. However, myth is sacred, impermeable even. But remember, a myth is just a myth, a figment of our imagination. See you all tomorrow," he ended, dismissing the class.

In my mind that night, while repeating the short description of Makandal over and over in the same way that I repeated the Bible verse, trying to make it all stick in my head, I had imagined the tall, dark, and muscular Makandal in his ascension, the same way I effortlessly believed that Christ, Elijah, and the Virgin Mary went up to the skies, in flesh and blood. That's when I finally understood Maloulou's question, and the answer that came back was some sort of password. It became clear that she had journeyed with me into a world and time long forgotten, misunderstood, and lost within the flimsy confines of yellowed history books.

"We have been expecting you," they cried almost in unison, bringing me back to the actual moment, as they proceeded to tell Maloulou who they were.

In the order the island of Quisqueya had received them, they approached one after the other. The Taino priestess, her black hair adorned with feathers of all colors, her nagua dancing along with her copper hips in the glittering moonlight, led the procession. "I will sell them good kenèp wine that will bring on the longest sleep," she said. Then there was the Creole mulatto with eyes that pulled like a magnet, promising to place the poison in her umbilical crevasse and swearing to make the rounds of all the beds of all planters along La Ravine. And they continued to come forth: the Hausas with their bags of deadly herbs and the three Katangas who embraced Maloulou, saying, "Sister, sè an mwen, we too saw him ascending, growing those wings that took him up atop the cloud of smoke." A whole parade that perhaps I was seeing so clearly because like Roland Désir I was now considered mad, a whole parade of my history and theirs. I saw and heard them all, my tongue weighing a ton and my lips glued so that even if I had wanted to talk, I would not have been able to. What would I say? It was all clearly laid out under my eyes, the told and untold history lessons given by all the Mr. Labordes. In that very instant, if I could have spoken, perhaps I would have only told of this strange feeling of peace while holding on to Maloulou's skirt. Or I would have confessed that my fears of never seeing Lakou 22 and its memories of pain had vanished.

They had all quieted down when Maloulou finally let go of my wrist and started distributing potions and powders from deep in the many hidden pockets of her large dress: this to tie tongues; that for rendering you invisible under the eyes of the enemy; here to sweeten the last cup of water and make them sleep forever; and this to scramble memories. And a final one to remove any power that anyone has to ever hurt you again.

"My children, take no chances and be prepared to risk it all," Maloulou warned. "I must now go back to the mountain and Makandal. But I will return each night for news and supplies until victory rolls from mountain to mountain." Her words, much like her eternal journey, kept replaying in my head, blocking everything else, and momentarily making Lakou 22 and the grunting Uncle Solon and his eager hands between my legs feel like a distant drum: faint and far.

DANGEROUS CROSSROADS

BY LOUIS-PHILIPPE DALEMBERT

Pétionville

Translated by Nicole Ball

I nspector Zagribay was about to turn the computer off when his cell phone told him he had a text message. Lulled by Ibrahim Ferrer's voice, the inspector had been on the brink of losing consciousness. Only someone he knew well could text him at such a late hour. All around him the city was sleeping in complete darkness. In the last week, partial electricity rationing had turned into total blackout. In the meantime, converters were beginning to die and his own was soon to be part of the group. Owners of generators and solar panels were the last to enjoy the coveted energy. The inspector had to resort to charging his cell in his office to save a little electricity. But there was no way he was going to give up listening to his boleros once he was in bed. The boleros had the triple function of helping him untangle the threads of a current case, taking him back to his childhood, and coaxing him to sleep. And the last had become more and more of a problem. Instinctively, Zagribay turned down the music before he grabbed the phone. He might have even been waiting for that message on some level, as he hadn't even bothered to get undressed before going to bed. The sender's number, then the message, appeared on the screen. The inspector got up, picked up his service revolver, and stepped out into the heart of the night.

The car started right away and he pulled out into the street. The thick darkness reduced visibility to the immediate range of the headlights. The inspector turned right, drove a few hundred yards further, and when he reached the precinct—which was also shrouded in complete darkness—and the Baptist church, he turned left. At this hour, he could take Delmas, the long artery to Pétionville, without fear of getting caught in traffic jams. He would reach the meeting place soon after that. Though he was reluctant to inform too many people, he took the precaution of waking up a young colleague—who didn't seem particularly happy about this show of trust—and asked to meet him at Place Boyer. After he hung up, he pushed the button of the CD player. Ibrahim Ferrer's voice filled the car, leaving a melodious trail in the silent night that blended with the barking of roaming dogs and the buzz of the generators he passed.

Duermen en mi jardín
las blancas azucenas, los nardos y las rosas . . .

Inspector Zagribay's mind began racing as he drove down the bumpy road. He was getting close, he was sure of it. He had managed to gather almost all the pieces of the puzzle. Another one or two pieces—which his informer and hopefully a search warrant would soon provide—and the case would be closed. When his boss had entrusted him with the assignment, he never would have thought a story of humans transformed into cattle would take him so far. To tell the truth, neither would his boss, who knew his quixotic nature and gave him only minor jobs. But as the weeks went by, the case kept expanding. Recently, he had reached the stage of "friendly" warnings. Which proved that he was on to something big. All those warnings came from people who claimed to wish him well: his boss, colleagues at the office, his childhood friend Fanfan (who he hadn't even told anything to). Even that Maria Luz, an NGO executive he'd met at the Canadian embassy, thought she should warn him too. Far from dissuading him, all this advice had actually stimulated him. It would be such a waste to stop when things looked so good. Stopping meant being subjected to his colleagues' sarcasm and the neighborhood kids taunting him. *Hey Zagribay, how about solving the mystery of that radio journalist Jean Dominique's murder?* Also, at some point you had to show people that there was justice in this damned country. That nobody could come here and just do whatever, whenever. As if it were a jungle.

The inspector remembered exactly when the case had started to turn into something serious and go way beyond him and his boss. It was a month and half ago. He was just emerging from his sleep when his cell rang. It was close to five a.m. The ever-present crowing of roosters, the voices of early risers mixed with the sounds of a few cars backfiring, filled the air. As it did every day, the early-morning smell of coffee had jumped over the fence to tickle his nostrils. That smell was enough to justify his homecoming. The inspector stretched out his arm, groped toward the nightstand. His hand finally reached the phone. He was about to give the intruder a piece of his mind when his eyes, still foggy with sleep, recognized the number on the screen. He didn't even have time to say hello.

His boss was screaming, beside himself. Zagribay was to go straight to the entrance of Cité Soleil. A seventh corpse in a state of interrupted metamorphosis in his sector. One or two, okay. A human being's life is of little importance in this screwed-up country, but seven, that was really too much. The chief of police, a man very popular with the media, must have been afraid of losing his job and was waking him up in the middle of the night to box his ears. The problem had been brought up the day before at the cabinet meeting, yelled the chief. The president himself was upset about it. The story had already traveled around the globe, thanks to YouTube: in Haiti, "Christians" were being turned into cattle before being sacrificed during rituals honoring bloodthirsty gods from Africa. And it was easy to infer from this that Haitians were all cattle. The minister of the interior shared the president's indignation. He had promised that the mystery would be quickly solved and the murderer arrested. And there! Just this morning he had another mutant dead body on his hands. Zagribay had better move his ass instead of wasting the government's money listening to his maricón music. The boss was known as being someone who didn't mince words. He wanted results. As soon as possible.

It's easy to yell now, Zagribay was telling himself as he got up. If they'd asked for his services before, we wouldn't be where we are now. His chances of finding useful clues would have been greater, especially as the murderer always proceeded the same way. Each time, the body was crushed as if by a steamroller, then burnt to such a point that it was impossible to identify its gender. It surely came from the same brain or criminal organization. But there you are, the bosses had to wait to have three corpses on their hands to take him on board. No wonder the bastard kept doing his grisly job. What were they thinking? That he could perform miracles?

Meanwhile, the opposition was quick to claim on TV and the airwaves of dozens of radio stations that the government was incapable of ensuring the safety of its citizens. For all you know, the inspector said to himself, maybe one of the big guns of the opposition is behind this sinister show. Just to destabilize the government and indulge in the favorite game of this country's politicians: musical chairs. These people have no scruples. They'd sell their mothers to get a position in the cabinet or a seat in the national assembly. The lead was worth pursuing. But after a week of investigation, Inspector Zagribay had to face facts: there was no connection between the logorrhea of the members of the opposition and the carbonized bodies found on the streets of the capital.

His informers found nothing worth mentioning on the drug lords or kidnappers either. It didn't match the modus operandi of the drug traffickers. They were used to benefiting from efficient complicity at all levels of the state and had no need to resort to such conspicuous acts to punish people who crossed the line. As for the kidnappers, they would have ended up giving themselves away if they proceeded in this manner. This research had required two extra weeks. And in the interim, three more corpses had been added to the first three, making the front page of the local press. Same method, applied with diabolical regularity, the stiff exposed at a crossroads. He was left with the option of a serial killer, even though, as far as he knew, no case of this type had ever been reported in Haiti. In this field, no lead can be ignored, he repeated like a seasoned professor of criminology. Who knows, with all those deportees the United States have been sending back to us recently . . .

Zagribay had reached this point in his investigation when that seventh corpse fell on his hands. Seven murders in seven weeks! This was no small case. He quickly got rid of the tank top and underwear he usually slept in. He didn't have time this morning to feel bad about his visibly broadening waistline. The chief's voice was still booming in his ear. He slipped into the bathroom: a good shower, even a fast one, would wake him up for good. He turned on the faucet. The pipe produced a weird gurgling noise, the sign of an empty tank. He had forgotten to tell the cleaning lady to have it filled by the tank truck. He went over to the drum installed in the kitchen. Armed with a jug, he set out to fill the basin he had brought with him. As he was washing up, the phone rang again. Probably his boss, anxious to know if he was already on the premises. He finished washing in record time, grabbed the first pieces of clothing he could find, and rushed to his car, an old second-hand Toyota that started every other time.

The police department car stayed at the precinct: a stupid requirement from the minister of the interior to put an end to the improper use of vehicles outside office hours. Some had even been seen in bad neighborhoods when the driver wasn't supposed to be on duty. As if police cars had to be parked in front of embassies and rich homes only! Besides, those cars broke down very often, victims of the terrible state of the roads; or of the mechanics in charge of repairing them: they'd slip in used parts in place of the new ones they were selling. In any event, the inspector preferred his old unmarked Toyota to the official police car. It allowed him to go unnoticed and have no time constraints. And his car had no fear of a tough fight with the streets of Port-au-Prince.

Luckily, the old Toyota started up right away. The inspector then realized he hadn't opened the fence of the yard. He was wasting precious time. Slipping his hand into his pants pocket to extract his keys, he stepped back out of the car. After he had unlocked the padlock, he needed to remove the heavy chain which, in addition to the walls capped with glass shards, completed the security system. Then he had to open the fence to drive the car out before closing it behind him.

The fact that he was a police inspector didn't matter: he lived barricaded, like everyone else. Like those who could afford it, at least. Fortunately, Cité Soleil was not far away. Coming from Delmas 3, he had to turn left and drive along the former runway of the army airport. At that hour, the city of Port-au-Prince wasn't yet the huge bottleneck it would become until ten a.m., and then again between two and six p.m.

A small crowd told him he had reached the crime scene. A swarm of chattering people was gathered around the corpse planted in the middle of the intersection. A TV camera and three journalists from a few of the many radio stations of the capital were already there. Who had informed them? He heard a witness answer the question of a journalist with another question that was more a statement than a question. "When you see something like this, human beings turned into animals, wouldn't you say that the reign of Christ is near?" And the guy added: "It is indeed an individual who was being transformed into an ox, but the criminal's dirty work must have been interrupted by someone showing up unexpectedly." He pointed. "Look here, you can see that the feet haven't been completely transformed into hoofs. Same for the toes there . . ."

Actually, since the discovery of these strange corpses, the rumor that a bòkò had lost a bunch of zombies he had started to turn into cattle and was chasing them through the streets of the capital to dispose of them had spread very quickly. And then people started praying, reciting psalms and singing hymns even more fervently than in the Protestant churches that were proliferating in the country, almost as fast as the NGOs.

Haitians believe in all kinds of crap, Zagribay said to himself. *To me, there's only one truth. What my eyes didn't see and my hands didn't touch does not exist.*

Meanwhile, he asked the two policemen on duty to clear out the chicken coop. So far, the two cops had confined themselves to the role of amused onlookers, but they were happy to carry out the orders. The journalists grumbled that this was a democracy and they had the right to do their job.

"To hell with your democracy," said the youngest cop. "Go on, scat!"

The small crowd finally dispersed and the inspector started to examine the corpse. The body, as expected, was crushed as if a steamroller or a truck weighing several tons had rumbled over it. Impossible to identify its gender. No trace of blood: the dead person had been carbonized. The inspector made a discovery nonetheless: no gas stain on the ground. Yet the body reeked of gas. He had obviously been brought from somewhere else. No shred of carbonized flesh around either. No matches, no lighter, not even a cigarette butt left on the premises. Absolutely nothing. For what kind of audience were they putting on this kind of show? wondered Zagribay. If he could answer this question, he was certain he would get closer to the murderers or to those behind the murders.

The inspector lingered there for another hour. Just to be on the safe side, he questioned some residents of the slum in the vain hope that someone might provide information that would put him on the right track. But all he got was a jumble of contradictory statements. The blazing sun put an end to the investigation. He asked the policemen to take the necessary steps to dispose of the dead body, climbed back in his old Toyota which acted out a little before starting, and drove off, his mind tormented by a number of questions. He had hardly gone three hundred yards when he made a U-turn right in the middle of the street, enraging some other drivers. He had the distinct feeling of having seen the "witness" questioned by the journalist somewhere before. But when he was back on the scene, the man had already vanished and no one knew where he lived or where he could be reached.

Five minutes later, he remembered. He'd seen that "witness" in one of the news stories he had watched when he started working on the case. He was ready to bet a month's pay on this. From behind the steering wheel of his car—he was stuck in a huge traffic jam with a broken air conditioner and no siren to weave his way out—he made a call to a journalist friend. The journalist had several stories about the case of the corpses changed into cattle but happened to be working on an assignment just outside the city and couldn't free himself at that moment. Zagribay explained that it was extremely urgent. The journalist promised to have the stories to him on DVD by the middle of the afternoon. Which turned out to be convenient, as the inspector also had to attend a reception at the Canadian embassy for the national holiday of the neighboring country. He finally had something that looked like the beginning of a lead. He slipped the Ibrahim Ferrer CD in the stereo and turned up the volume to cover the incessant honking.

Zagribay made a detour by the precinct and ran into his boss, who seemed in a better mood than in the morning. He was greeted with a "Hi, Messiah," a nickname that emphasized his muckraking tendencies. He answered right back that it wasn't his fault if corruption made him furious.

"Me too," answered the boss. "But no matter how hard you try, you won't change this country. The art of accommodation. It's called intelligence, Dyaspora."

"Why do you do this job, then?"

"To make a living, pal. To make a living."

At least that was clear. The inspector couldn't say why

but he had an instinctive distrust of his boss. The way he lived was way over his salary. How did he pay for his villa on the capital heights? With what money did he take his family to spend weekends in Miami so often? One of his sons, who was no genius and thus couldn't possibly have won a scholarship, was a student at the University of Pennsylvania. It's a well-known fact that Yankee universities frigging cost an arm and a leg. It was easy for both of them to get rich at their jobs. All they had to do was look away, ignore certain dirty deals. Nobody here will raise questions about spontaneous fortunes. You can start in the gutter, go to bed poor as a church mouse, and wake up the next day rich as Croesus. Nobody will bat an eyelid. On the contrary: most people just dream of being able to do exactly the same thing. And those who have the biggest mouths, who rail against politicians and the corruption of the elite, are quick to swallow the word "ethical" once they're in power. Also, the chief had been in this job—for which he had no particular training—for such a long time. In a country where people in official positions are sent packing each time a new minister is appointed, this was rather suspicious. The man seemed to be part of the furniture, unmovable. Not one minister had succeeded in firing him. And for some, not for lack of trying. What did he know, and about whom?

After a lunch of fried plantains and taso on a corner of his desk, watered down with a glass of papaya milk, Zagribay set out to meet his friend at the TV station. He got permission to watch the DVDs there and to make copies of them. He had made sure to bring a blank DVD for the recording. After he'd watched the films, the inspector clenched his fist: bingo! He had guessed right. The "witness," a guy in his thirties, neatly dressed but nothing fancy, appeared in three out of the six stories; the first corpse hadn't been noticed, and a new "witness" could be seen on two others. Interesting, Zagribay thought. In both instances, the "witnesses" insisted, each in his own words, on the corpses' transformation into cattle, almost as if they wanted to make absolute sure the public embraced this scenario. Knowing how superstitious Haitians are, it was rather clever, the inspector reflected. But why? Who was behind this? He stood up and thanked the journalist, but did not share his analysis with him. He'd better leave early if he wanted to be on time for the ass-pinching party at the embassy.

Zagribay couldn't stand social functions but there was no way he could skip this one: he partly owed his job to the Canadian diplomatic services, which had financed a training program in their country. After fifteen years spent in Montreal doing police work, he had decided to come home. Fed up with the cold. Month after month of schlepping tons of clothing on his back. Whole days sometimes without a ray of sun. He had gotten out of bed one morning and just handed his boss his letter of resignation. Knowing that he was reliable, serious, and efficient, his boss had tried to talk him out of it, but Zagribay had made up his mind. One month later, he was on a plane headed to Port-au-Prince. Once there, the situation turned out to be rather complicated. The middle-class people he rubbed elbows with always managed to ask him, at some point in the conversation, when he was planning to return to Canada. Hence the nickname "Dyaspora." Even his boss used it. And yet he had made the announcement loud and clear: he was back to stay.

When he was already thinking of sneaking out of the cocktail party, a high-ranking Haitian civil servant introduced him to a woman who said she was Dominican. She was a tall, beautiful brunette named Maria Luz and was barely out of her thirties. Her auburn hair contrasted with her gray-green eyes. There was a sense of mystery about her that made her even more attractive. She was wearing a crimson dress deeply cut in the back. Very quickly, her accent made the inspector suspicious. He detected a fraud. Why did the lady want to pass herself off as a Dominican? He knew how fond Haitian men were of Dominican women. She knew it too, obviously. She assumed that identity so she could sell herself better, Zagribay thought. She was probably the mistress of some politician or rich man. But she introduced herself as an important executive of an NGO whose activities spanned all five continents. Like Doctors Without Borders, it provided primary health care for the most impoverished populations. Her story was plausible. In recent years Haiti had become a paradise for all sorts of NGOs. There were an awful lot of them. But Zagribay wasn't quite convinced. A professional reflex. It took him some time to get rid of the lady—who was rather clingy. But in exchange for getting her to leave, he had to give up his cell number.

Three days later, at the Toussaint Louverture airport where he had come to pick up a deportee expelled from Miami, he saw her sneaking out of a diplomatic lounge and rushing into the plane heading back to Florida in the company of Fanfan, his childhood buddy. Fanfan, whom he considered a close friend, had never mentioned Maria Luz, although he had been very open with him about his many other extramarital affairs. What kind of relationship could he possibly have with that scheming high-society woman?

Unlike his fellow citizens of some social standing, Fanfan had welcomed him back to Haiti with real joy. It was as if they'd only parted the day before. Fanfan, who was better connected in the capital's social circles, had been instrumental in speeding up Zagribay's hiring in the police department. Fanfan knew the chief well.

"We exchanged a few favors," Fanfan had said by way of explanation. He had never emigrated and didn't feel particularly proud about it. "Life has turned out differently for me, that's all," he'd say. "And unless you're totally down on your luck or forced to, you don't leave your country once you're past forty."

Fanfan lived in a superb villa in Belvil, a gated community modeled after those in Florida. Belvil was a small island of cleanliness and urbanization, in complete contrast to the huge, chaotic cesspool of Port-au-Prince. A city within the city, built in part, according to rumors, with drug money, as the country had become a hub for exporting narcotics to the United States.

You couldn't access the house of Zagribay's childhood friend without being seen by the two cameras—one in front, the other in back—connected to the main entrance. And one of the three guards, armed with a shotgun, showed up at the entrance before you arrived. The house was also surrounded by a wall three and a half yards high and spiked with steel nails, so that in order to get inside without permission, you'd need a grappling hook. A real bunker, that place. Zagribay had never known what his friend did to enjoy such protection. Fanfan had just reluctantly confided to him that he was in some kind of business. Import-export, he had said vaguely, like many people in this country who had a fortune with dubious origins. But that couldn't be true for Fanfan, who had introduced him to Marxism when they were teenagers. Perhaps all that security was there to protect his wife and two children.

The accidental encounter at the airport led Zagribay to take a closer look at Maria Luz. First, as she'd been relentlessly pursuing him—practically harassing him—he let her get close. Their first meeting took place in Pétionville, at a restaurant called La Cascade. He would have preferred lunch but Maria Luz had insisted they meet for dinner.

"The place is so romantic at night," she had whispered.

Zagribay had agreed, out of fear of looking like a bore. He showed up thirty minutes early. He liked to take a look at a meeting place ahead of time, a pure professional reflex. Maria Luz arrived on time. In a city where the fear of being kidnapped produced a great deal of paranoia, he was surprised to see her turn up alone, without a chauffeur or bodyguard, at the wheel of her gleaming SUV. The inspector didn't know how to interpret this. Was she reckless? Was it a calculated risk? If this was the case, to what end? Maybe she was being followed from afar by another car? While hurrying to open the door for her, he looked around, but no one else showed up.

In the course of the very pleasant dinner, Maria Luz insisted on speaking Creole, the language she knew best after Spanish, she said. "And Creole is better here if you want to communicate with everyone, don't you think?"

She was right. To the inspector's ear, her mastery of Creole was equal to that of his Spanish. Just a slight inflection here and there that revealed she had trouble not rolling the "r." Otherwise, she spoke Creole much too well for Zagribay's taste. She probably works for the CIA, he thought. And the NGO, if she really had an office there, was a cover.

At the end of the meal, under the pretext that the capital was unsafe at night, she had him accompany her to her home in the Pacot neighborhood. Once there, the inspector, inventing an urgent report he had to hand in the next day, tactfully turned down her offer of a last drink.

"Next time then," she simpered.

"Why not?" Zagribay answered, saying to himself in Creole: *Wi pa monte mòn.* Not every yes can climb a hill.

The investigation into the corpses changed into cattle was going nowhere. So the inspector decided to tail Maria Luz and asked a young colleague he trusted to cover for him. His old unmarked Toyota was a great help. He followed her for several days, enough to ascertain that the lady knew fancy people, from the chief of police to the minister of the interior and other influential individuals. He could never get over how easy it was for foreigners—especially if they were white—to have access to the highest authorities of the state. He also found out that Fanfan and Maria Luz were seeing each other pretty regularly. That said, she appeared to have no official relationship but was juggling several at once. She was living it up but not necessarily at her lovers' expense, although she didn't turn down their presents: a pearl necklace from this one or an emerald bracelet from that one. And among her regulars was his own boss.

Zagribay couldn't resist the urge to ask his boss, one morning when he seemed in a good mood, if he knew a certain Maria Luz. The man smiled and answered with a wink. The inspector wanted to know more.

"I'm serious, chief!"

"Really?"

"I'm not kidding, chief."

"Do you want a piece of friendly advice? Don't get too involved with her."

With these words, the police chief walked to his car where his chauffeur was already behind the wheel with the engine running. Zagribay bit his lower lip to contain his rage. Three days before, he had discovered that Maria Luz's NGO was in

charge of a clinic in Cité Soleil behind which stood a building with blackout windows, guarded by three armed men. He
couldn't see anyone coming in or out, as you normally would
in a public building. He introduced himself and pulled out
his badge, trying to get some information. One of the grim
doorkeepers with shades on his nose sent him to a top executive: a rich-looking Haitian, well into his fifties, speaking like
someone used to giving orders. He got on his high horse and
made it clear that, given the absence of his own superior, he
couldn't allow Zagribay to visit that part of the clinic.

"We care here for terminally ill cancer and AIDS pa-
tients," the man concluded.

A flat sentence, delivered as if he'd practiced saying it.
The inspector then asked to see Maria Luz. The man winced
before telling him that Doctor Luz was traveling. But the inspector had been trailing her the day before. It was possible,
he supposed, that she could have left that very morning.

"How long ago did she leave?" he asked.

"Two or three days, no more."

Zagribay left, smiling. He was on to something. Now he
had to find out why the man had lied. This gave him the idea
of tightening the vise around the NGO, even if there was
no apparent tie between it and the mysterious corpses. He
also got the idea of nosing around the Internet and ended up
stumbling on a blog that mentioned Maria's NGO in connection with a lab that did pharmaceutical and medical research.
Several countries had condemned it for practicing illegal experiments on humans. The blog sent him to other sources
that were blocked each time he tried to link to them. The
information was pretty thin.

That night, lying on his back, the inspector couldn't fall
asleep. Was the NGO here hiding the activities of a clan-

destine pharmaceutical research lab? Ibrahim Ferrer's voice trailed languorously in the night. Suddenly, Zagribay jumped out of bed as if a gigantic bedbug had bitten him. Why hadn't he thought of it earlier?

He grabbed his phone and called a former colleague in Montreal. His friend wasn't too happy about being awakened in the dead of night but indulged him nonetheless. They used to work together as a team in the north part of Montreal. The inspector explained the case and asked for his help in identifying the NGO and finding out what interests were concealed behind it.

Three days later, Zagribay found the information in his e-mail. The Luz NGO had been expelled from India and the Philippines for illegal activities and lab research potentially harmful to human beings. After having been subjected to various experiments and force-fed drugs of all sorts, the guinea pigs would become physically deformed. A few years before, the CEO of those labs had promised discoveries that would soon turn the world of genetics upside down. Hard to find a better place than Haiti to hide criminal activities like that, thought the inspector. They believe in all kinds of nonsense here; plus, there is intense poverty and the elite will do anything for money. All you had to do was set up a clinic, grease a few palms here and there, and that would do the trick. But if their research didn't seem to give the results they were hoping for, they might have trouble getting rid of the guinea pigs without raising suspicion. On the other hand, relying on old local beliefs to eliminate the victims was a piece of cake.

Everything seemed clear. All he had to do now was speak to his informer and then get a search warrant. For this, Zagribay had to first talk to his boss, and, provided he agreed, find the judge willing to give the order to carry out the search. No country has more respect for the law than Haiti when corrupt civil servants want to make things tough for you. The fewer people who knew about it the better, as far as he was concerned. But he had no choice, especially since he felt this was a big case.

He was close to having collected rock-solid evidence. He was going to lay it out on the desks of his boss, the chief of police, and the press at the same time. The bomb would explode in their faces. He was determined to expose what everyone else refused to do, drag the culprits to court. The profound corruption of this country's elite! With the politicians in their pocket, they were at the root of the endless misery of this island; the "most repugnant elite," as a Yankee president had called them. The proof that he was getting close to his goal was his boss's repeated advice to take it easy ("You're not the messiah, Dyaspora"), Fanfan's warnings—and he hadn't even told him anything—and the remarks of Luz, who had somehow learned of his visit to the clinic. If he waited for the whole procedure to get rolling, the birds could fly away. He had to take action.

For the first time since the beginning of the case, Zagribay felt good. He had the distinct impression of being useful, of giving back a little bit of what this country had given him in his childhood and adolescence. Fresh air was blowing into the car through the open windows. Zagribay started to sing along with Ibrahim Ferrer:

. . . *mi alma, muy triste y pesarosa*
a las flores quiere ocultar su amargo dolor.

He had just passed the cemetery when he was flanked

by motorbikes coming out of two perpendicular side streets. Floating along on the music, he didn't realize what was happening. On his left, the silver flash of the gun at the end of an outstretched arm brought him back to reality. But by the time he could draw his own weapon, the men on the bikes behind the drivers had already fired.

BLUES FOR IRÈNE

BY MARVIN VICTOR

Carrefour-Feuilles

Translated by Nicole Ball

My daughter told the police that she'd witnessed the murder of Jimmy Labissière, and that the murderer was her friend, Irène Gouin. Irène, she said, stabbed him seven times in the stomach and then went down to the hotel bar, sat on a stool, and ordered a drink that she sipped for a long time before requesting "Please Don't Talk About Me When I'm Gone" from the maestro of the quartet playing at the other end of the deck.

A week later, Inspector Joseph showed up with his questions. Inspector Joseph knew I'd had an affair with Jimmy, but Jimmy wasn't just my dead man. He was the dead man of all the people who lived on rue Tirremasse in Bel-Air and who had loved and hated him. He was a public dead man, I told Inspector Joseph right away, hissing it between my teeth. He was a dead man people never stopped talking about, trying to find with an abundance of proverbs and metaphors which part of him belonged to the devil and which part to an angel, obliterating our story as well as the ancient stories of all the other women he had been with, knowing that all we had left of him was the vague memory of crumpled sheets, moist with sweat, and the breath of old, whispered words. That's how stories are made, I concluded, telling myself that Jimmy, clutching the murderer's bottom and bawling as he was about to come, may have had a beautiful death. But nobody had talked about that. I personally had no desire to talk about Jimmy, but Inspector Joseph had forced me to cooperate. And in my reluctance to speak about Jimmy, I was hearing my voice pronounce his name. There was no logic possible when you started talking about him, no reason either when you knew that in people's mouths he wasn't dead, only an absentee. That's what they thought, since they couldn't hear him on the radio or see him on TV, leading demonstrations on the street, anymore. I didn't want doom to come out of my mouth. I wanted the idea of it to be banished. In my opinion, his life was beyond commonplace thought—any thought, actually—for it had always been a mistake, a mistake related to the immense poem of childhood, maybe. I knew it right from the first moment I saw him. Imagine a vast, dark room; no glimmer of light ever slips into it. He told me I was that glimmer, and I'd forgotten to hear his words sliding over my skin, like his fingers when we made love. I let it happen. When the young president had started to build his underground army, Jimmy was at the heart of the movement, with the enthusiasm of a mad child. He'd spent six months, a year, maybe more, in a training camp. He himself couldn't remember when he told me about that part of his previous life. A whole eternity spent waiting for a sign from the president. Many were waiting like that. Meanwhile, the president was making speeches, stirring up the people. Jimmy was inside that crowd too.

One morning he got the call. He was shaking on the other end of the line, as if he hadn't been floundering in the smelly mud around the Saline. A load of weapons to transport to Camp-Perrin, along with money, lots of money. No. He did not understand, could not understand. He'd hit the road in a van, in the company of a comrade. In the middle of nowhere, the van started to smoke and backfire before stopping smack in the middle of the highway. There was sand and cane syrup in the gas tank. At some point, a man with his face eaten by a salt-and-pepper beard popped up; he offered to help, then pointed his gun at Jimmy's temple and took the money and ammunition. A setup?

When he called to report that the mission had failed, the phone rang in vain. There was no answer, as there had never been any such number. That was the day he was murdered. Not on the day before my birthday, in that small hotel room where he went to look under the skirt of that snotty girl, his mother had said when I came to offer my condolences. Ah, that snotty girl everybody in town described as a rich girl at odds with her family, twenty years old, not black-black but a burnt-earth color. Yes, he was dead before our encounter. I imagined him faking sleep, gone on another road, toward absolution, love, or another girl's breast.

Yes, pain and sadness had arrived the day people started to turn around on the street to look at him, naked under his mask of a public character wanted by the police. I had met him, had reached out to him, not knowing that everything had become, literally and figuratively, cold around him, and that he was in a way pouring boiling water over his own head. We made love inside that madness. Voices, carried by the winds, were speaking inside of him. I had met him during that period. In front of a movie theater, on Lamarre Street. He'd come to see *Bird*, the seven p.m. show. He'd come out of the theater and was tying his shoes on the sidewalk when I spotted him. I'd been selling junk jewelry to make a living for me and my daughter; so I showed him a wristwatch and asked if he'd like to buy it for his wife or girlfriend. Not knowing that I would become his girlfriend a few moments later. That same evening, we slept together in a crummy hotel on Grand-rue. No fuss. We had a long talk about Charlie Parker, who, as a teenager in Kansas City, played the recorder while he rode his mule and entertained big dreams listening to Count Basie's orchestra. He told me he was my Bird, and me his Chan, the dancer Bird admired. I told him no, let's switch roles and get it right, I am the Bird and he's the Chan, but he wouldn't hear of it. And sleep fell upon us, all of a sudden.

After that, we'd meet at his place, not far from the cathedral, on rue Borgelat. A very dark two-room apartment that smelled of mold and cold tobacco, because ever since my husband had left, aside from occasional one-night stands, I had no steady man in my life, which was all right by me— the body has its needs—as long as my lovers didn't promise me the sky and the earth or rain from countries where it no longer rains. I've got my home, you've got yours. As the police were after him—he rarely went out, and only at night, in disguise, taking dark roads with their streetlights out—we agreed I would be the one to go visit him. Aside from the films he'd go see secretly, I had become his only contact with the outside world. I'd show up at his place three times a week: on Tuesdays, Thursdays, and Saturdays. Like a rebellious girl, I was attracted to the danger he represented. I didn't know why. I suppose it gave me the exhilarating feeling of betraying somebody, something I wasn't completely conscious about, but it really turned me on. To the point where I wouldn't remember if I truly loved him. We'd spend our evenings talking travel, although neither of us had ever left the island. The only sea he knew was the one polluted by the barrels of toxic waste foreign cargo ships dumped into the harbor of Port-au-Prince. Once, on a whim, I brought him back a shell from the sea-fest in Pestel where I'd taken my daughter. I made him listen to the sound of the waves inside it. Yes, everything was fine, until that time when he forced me to spend the night. He heard me moan in my sleep as I was touching myself. At first, he didn't seem to mind; then, a week later, he started to think—wrongly—that I was seeing another man. From that point on, he'd made surprise visits to my home. Most times he'd run into my daughter, sitting on the stoop in front of the house, smoking a cigarette. She was rather nuts—had always been so—but was very beautiful, with big black, sunken eyes, a subtle smile. She knew what he was coming for, so she'd look him up and down and stick her tongue out at him.

Jimmy was buried at the national cemetery on a Saturday morning. Dirty, ragged children wept and put flowers on his grave. That day, there were also women, many women, most of them very beautiful, wearing long dark dresses under the shade of their black silk mantillas. I was there too, with my daughter, in the background, dry-eyed. I had the impression that we weren't there for his funeral but for an ultimate erotic parade, a way for each of us to prove to him that we loved him more than anything, more than that tall, big-boned woman who was looking disdainfully at me from behind the gray designs of her fan, sweating in the heat of the last days of summer.

One afternoon, in the middle of our endless interviews with Inspector Joseph, my daughter came out of her room almost naked. She leaned over the inspector's ear and told him that if he went looking into the crumpled sheets of the hotel room, he could find, in the play of the shadows created by the subdued light of the lamp on the bedside table, the meanderings of the murder, how the scene had unfolded. The inspector knew she'd been born nutty and he laughed, but that same afternoon he took us to the crime scene, to that hotel high up in the Carrefour-Feuilles neighborhood, to that room with a view over the harbor and the rusty roofs that hemmed in the sea. He took pictures of the hotel which had been deserted since the night of the crime, of its entrance lined with bougainvilleas and oleanders, of the walls of the room decorated with cheap paintings, of the bedspreads, of the private cop with his hunting rifle who had seen the young woman arrive on Jimmy's arm, her steps heavy with alcohol, both laughing madly.

After the visit, we walked part of the way home, and my daughter kept repeating that in the room she had felt the presence of Irène Gouin, who had bent over Jimmy's blood-soaked body and felt sublime. She was talking nonstop, deciding even as she was detailing them how the facts were to be arranged. And me, to cool off the situation, I reminded Inspector Joseph that she has never been in her right mind. She pretended not to hear me, and kept on talking as if she wanted to take control of the situation, deconstruct the hypothesis of unpredictability and randomness of Jimmy's murder: Irène's act and her state of mind at the time, the strong smell that night of salt and seaweed, of the sea rising from the harbor, filling the city streets with their brackish fragrance, Jimmy's ugly skin and bones, the golden reflection of his Barbancourt rum on the rocks, and the bubbles in Irène's Coke at the hotel bar, before they went up to the room.

She encouraged the inspector to get rid of his pretentious desire to understand everything about a life that took pleasure in secrecy, the way a virgin might get pleasure from her little perfumed firebrand, she said, explaining to us that sometimes, when she had nothing else to do, she imagined she was the murderess Irène Gouin, and that they resembled each other down to every detail of her face, like two drops of water at the bottom of the ocean.

On the Chemin des Dalles, near the Saint-Géraud bridge, we stopped a cab and settled into the backseat. The cab was really a pile of scrap metal, a small apple-green Datsun that you could immediately tell dated back to the '70s. A little old guy with a straw hat on his head was at the wheel, driving slowly. He threw himself into rue Pavée, and taking advantage of the traffic jam, started to talk, mumbling through his teeth. Seeing we didn't pay any attention to him, he put on some konpa music by Shleu-Shleu. We got off at the entrance to my neighborhood, at the top of the Bel-Air hill. My daughter headed straight to the stand of the spirits seller, Brigitte. She was thirsty, she said, although our house was nearby. Scratching the back of her head, she ordered a rum taffy. Inspector Joseph and I caught up with her right away. She was swaying her body more and more wildly. I sometimes thought I'd brought her into the world so she would become my master and I her slave, I told the inspector, as if she was the one who had tinkered with me, knowing she was the prolongation of my dreams, my shipwrecks. I had projected myself on her, wondering on which of her shoulders she would have to bear my cross. But she was more clever than I was and had escaped in time.

Then the inspector left me and walked up to my daughter as if to give her a kiss. He held up his hands too, like he was framing her in his camera, before moving closer.

"Oh!" she exclaimed, as if she'd never seen the man before. She swallowed her rum in one gulp and a few drops escaped from the corners of her lips. She handed the empty cup to

Brigitte, coughing in the loose end of her blouse, wiped her mouth with the back of her hand, and thanked her. She then lit a cigarette, grabbed the inspector's arm, and led him to our place, except that all the inspector wanted was to talk about Jimmy.

Before our conversations, I usually offered him coffee and cookies, but this time I didn't find any in the kitchen. So I joined them in the living room. It was very hot. The inspector was helping my daughter open the two sides of the high window that looked out onto the façade of a big white house on the other side of the street. I walked up to them.

My daughter said, "Come on, Manman!"

The inspector didn't see my knife entering the back of his head, and blood, not thick but clear and sweet-smelling, spurted onto my face.

"That big white house is where Irène Gouin lives," my daughter said as he was dying.

Irène Gouin's house, she explained, was a mix of high tech and refinement, a hotel with a gym and a large room for brunches, a white marble porch at the entrance, a living room with a glass ceiling, a white Chesterfield couch, a vodka bar, a sun deck, and spacious, luminous bedrooms. An electrical system allowed you to create a mood with all shades of blue, tile-and-chrome bathrooms, deep oval bathtubs, thick white wall-to-wall carpeting, pop art–colored objects.

Yes, Irène Gouin's house, my daughter went on, had two duplex suites with their own swimming pools. The top floor was for B.H., a famous singer. It included an immaculate bedroom and, at the head of the stairs, a small living room opening up onto a deck with a view of the city's rooftops and a tiled swimming pool all lit up at night. The bedroom led to a second deck—summer breeze and diving under the sky.

Irène Gouin, my daughter said, wanted nothing to do with the neighborhood people and even less with the good old city of Port-au-Prince, which sometimes takes itself for London or Paris.

Everybody was dirt on her shoes, she said. When she arrived in the neighborhood, Irène Gouin didn't introduce herself to anybody, and they all understood her need for solitude, and Irène Gouin had always been very composed. Irène Gouin never wanted to have company, couldn't stand heroes, Saturday-night drunks, and Sunday Christians. At first everybody had doubts about her, but after a month they thought they were lucky because she didn't behave like those young Dominican girls with hennaed hair who partied all night long.

From her window, my daughter concluded, she could sometimes see smoke billowing out from that Irène Gouin's cigarette or hear the notes of "Please Don't Talk About Me When I'm Gone" looping, over and over again. My daughter was Irène Gouin.

PART III

WHO IS THAT NOIR?

THE LAST DEPARTMENT
BY KATIA D. ULYSSE
Puits Blain

The languorous drone in Foufoune's ear meant that her international call had gone through. She'd been on the phone with relatives for hours, explaining through scalding tears how she came home after work and found her elderly mother dead. Her message was met with perfunctory sympathy. Foufoune and her mother had lived together for years. She would miss her more than most. Wedged between everyone's words of condolence, however, was relief. And blame. Dona "Gwo Manman" Malbranche had been as happy as a prisoner in solitary confinement.

Every morning after Foufoune left for work, Gwo Manman would take her place before the television to chat with the strangers who lived inside.

"I wish I could sprout wings and fly back home," she often confided to Bob Barker, host of *The Price Is Right*. When the Showcase Showdown ended and the last prizes were distributed, Gwo Manman would turn off the television and sit for hours in silence. Until four o'clock. Her most trusted friend and confidante, Oprah, would nod knowingly each time Gwo Manman explained how Foufoune had kidnapped her from her home and was forcing her to live in the worst kind of exile.

When all her television friends were gone for the day, Gwo Manman would sit and stare at the wallpaper, imagining the distant place that used to be home and the freedom that was hers to do whatever and go wherever she pleased. A map of Puits Blain's nameless alleyways was imprinted in her memory as clearly as the lines in the palms of her hands. Sitting in a chair thousands of miles from home, she went for long walks along Route des Frères, visiting with friends for hours. Being trapped inside an apartment day after day, week after week, month after month, and year after year was torture. She missed the roosters announcing the dawn, the ominous lights flickering from Boutilier and Morne Calvaire.

"You're hardly a prisoner in exile," Foufoune would tell her mother when she complained. Sure, Gwo Manman got to dress up once in a while for a wedding or a funeral, but being taken out of the apartment only for special occasions made her feel like a clown, a madigra mal maske.

When Foufoune came home from work at night, she was always too tired to do anything but sleep. Too tired to ask Gwo Manman how she had spent the day. Gwo Manman would want to talk about her garden back home, her house, her friends who sold lwil maskreti behind the cemetery and fried food to the taxi drivers waiting to ferry passengers to the end of the road just beyond Hotel Flamboyant. In the States she had rain, sleet, illnesses she'd never even heard of—she didn't want to talk about those. She had changed, and hated the person into whom America had turned her. Once, while Foufoune was at work, Gwo Manman unlocked the door and escaped. She wandered into the unfamiliar streets, improperly dressed for the snow that reached her ankles. She turned a corner, then another, then another; soon she could not find her way back. Hours later, a good Samaritan found her shivering and dazed.

"What's your name?" and "Where do you live?" the good Samaritan had asked. But all that was more English than Gwo

Manman understood. He took her to a nearby hospital. Foufoune spent an entire day trying to locate her mother that time. She prevented a reoccurrence by having a sturdier lock installed. Gwo Manman tried but could not get out of the apartment without a key, forcing her to retreat further into the wallpaper and the television world. But even that had changed. Bob Barker was no longer a resident. Just when she had gotten used to him, a stranger came and took his place. Even Oprah was not the same. She spoke only in tongues now. She'd become distant and unfriendly, prompting Gwo Manman to try and smash the screen with a mop, spraining her frail wrists. When Foufoune came home and found her mother hitting the television screen, she covered it like a corpse, saying, "The TV people won't be able to bother you anymore."

Dona Malbranche died the day after she turned seventy—a gift from God, as far as the old woman was concerned. The frown on her face was a perfectly inverted grin. "Ki te mele m." She had drawn her lips tight on the "m" to intercept her final breath. "Ki te mele m," she used to tell Bob Barker and Oprah—her companions and life's witnesses. She no longer cared.

When Foufoune returned from another double shift and found Gwo Manman slumped over the chair, her instincts as a nurse rose up like a tsunami. She lunged toward her mother, determined to pry her loose from Death's stubborn grip, but her limbs had as much life left in them as dried gourds. Foufoune dialed emergency, saying, "Hurry, please hurry." The bottle of lwil maskreti clutched in her mother's hand had spilled on her good rug. "Please, please hurry!" Within minutes the apartment was flooded with strangers in uniforms. Everyone shook their heads sympathetically. Foufoune sniffled and sobbed as she unclasped the gold necklace which Gwo Manman never would have parted with while she was alive. It had been a Mother's Day present from her other daughter, Miriam, who still lived in Puits Blain. Foufoune continued to sob as her mother's lifeless body was carted away; suddenly stung was she by the realization that if Gwo Manman had had a choice, she would have been savoring breadfruit grown on her own little patch of land in Puits Blain, instead of dying alone abroad.

Foufoune put off calling her sister for last, hoping someone would do her the favor of forwarding the news. No one did, of course; the call was hers to make. She adjusted her earpiece with trembling fingers. Her sister would answer momentarily, and sever the sliver that was her last nerve. Miriam had always sided with Gwo Manman: *The woman is old enough to know where she should live. She's not a child. If she doesn't want to live in the States, you must respect that.*

Foufoune had considered sending her mother back, but after just a few weeks in the States it was already too late. America did not agree with Gwo Manman. She had an allergic reaction to the very air. She changed as soon as she left the island. At first Foufoune thought her mother was just homesick and would overcome it soon, but Gwo Manman's condition steadily worsened. When after several months Gwo Manman grew even more despondent and sickly, Foufoune had her seen by the best physicians she knew. And out came the diagnosis she dreaded: onset dementia, Alzheimer's. She knew all too well how those diseases ravaged the mind.

"I never got sick back home," Gwo Manman argued, even after Foufoune was careful enough to make up the best lie rather than translate what the doctors had said. "I wasn't sick until I started to live à l'étranger," Gwo Manman maintained. "You have the flu," Foufoune explained. "A very bad strain. You'll get better soon."

Miriam was singing along to an old Coupe Cloue tune while stirring a bubbling pot of cornmeal when the phone in her apron pocket rang. She set down the long-handled wooden spoon and turned off the radio. A light rain was falling, rinsing the dust off the flamboyant branches over her porch as well as the splotches of blood where she had cleaned goat meat the night before.

"Alo." Miriam had decided she would send the caller away, or else risk having too many lumps in her signature dish which today she would serve with black beans and salted herring. Customers would start arriving soon for their noonday fix. She would not disappoint them. The goat meat she painstakingly cleaned was now marinating in a special concoction. By nightfall, every bit would be gone. People would come from far away for a taste. Kenold and most of the other guys who sold those brightly painted canvases up the street from the lycée and Anne-Marie Javouhey elementary stopped by Miriam's for food on their way home. In all the years since she quit a back-breaking factory job to open the eatery, she had never let her customers down.

"Alo?" Miriam repeated, annoyed. Jean-Jean, the man she hired to clean the latrine behind her house, walked by with his shovel in one hand and a cell phone in the other. Miriam's house was equipped with indoor plumbing, but she kept the old relic behind the house for customers. Miriam's thoughts shifted to the days when hers was the only household in all of Puits Blain with a telephone. Nowadays, everyone had phones: maids, stall keepers at the marketplace, farmers, tap

tap drivers, even Jean-Jean—a man whose profession required him to work under the cover of night when no one would see or judge him.

"M-m-i-s-s Mi-ria-m," he stuttered, his head bent low due to chronic humiliation, "I'm c-coming tonight to start that j-job for you."

"Kapitèn Poupou!" a group of giggling children saluted Jean-Jean. Ashamed, he pretended not to hear.

Miriam nodded. Now was not the time to explain why the job would have to be postponed. She would speak to Jean-Jean later. Perhaps she should have him seal that hole and make the old latrine disappear like the thatched huts and tin-covered shacks that used to populate the area. Puits Blain was no longer an idyllic haven. The kenèp groves were gone. The cornfields had been replaced by top-heavy palaces with high walls surrounding them. Tightly clustered wannabe mansions and the ever-expanding bidonvilles did not spare a single sapling. On the upside, there was now a Culligan water depot just steps from her porch, making it much easier to run her business. The cyber café halfway down to Kay Peshòt—right in that spot where Papa Malbranche used to tether his blind horse—stayed packed with those seeking escape via the Internet. Hotel Flamboyant's sparkling point of light stood on land where, it was said, a girl once turned herself into a mabouya to escape a beating. Miriam's umbilical stump was buried under the flamboyant tree in her front yard. So was Foufoune's, but that meant precious little to her sister. The dirt path where Gwo Manman used to ride her mule was now a bustling artery that accommodated the United Nations' fleet of tanks hell-bent on keeping Haiti safe. Minustah soldiers manned every few feet, catching gang members before they could disappear into the convoluted alleyways. Gone were the days when

Puits Blain did not need guarding. Yes, Miriam resolved, it would be best to have Jean-Jean seal the latrine and demolish the decrepit wooden shack surrounding it once and for all. Anyone could hide in there. Why hadn't she thought of this before? Her customers would have to manage without it. Miriam shook her head. Her old Puits Blain no longer existed, but unlike her sister, she would never abandon her ancestral land to live elsewhere.

"Alo," Miriam said a third time, keeping one eye on her steaming pot of cornmeal. She realized by the loaded silence on the other end that it was Foufoune. Gwo Manman's children knew each other so well that they needed to maintain at least one ocean between their respective homes. Same mother, same father, same ancestral blood in their veins, but those two had even less love for each other than a goat and a butcher. Foufoune liked to think she was accidentally switched at birth. Nothing else could explain why her blood turned to ice whenever she even thought about her sister. Hatred raged inside of them like a parasitic cancer. The disease spread over the years, taking control of their lives, until one could no longer bear the sight of the other.

"It breaks my heart that my only two children cannot get along," Gwo Manman often lamented.

"I have no problem with my sister," Foufoune would lie to appease her mother. But to her friends, Foufounce would say: "Miriam is jealous of me because I made it and she's nothing."

"Hello, Miriam?" Foufoune said timidly.

Miriam knew what her sister had called to say: their mother had died; no one needed to tell her that. Just as she was cleaning the goat the previous night, Gwo Manman had stood under the flamboyant tree and announced that she had had it with the snow, the sleet, the wind, and the crazy language that always left her mind in a jumble. Foufoune's apartment was a jail cell she would escape, and soon.

Yes, Gwo Manman had whispered in the darkness, *I'm on my way home.*

"Who is this?" Miriam asked sharply. A doctor might have just signed her mother's death certificate, but Gwo Manman had been dead for years, as far as she was concerned. The day Foufoune put her on that plane and made her say goodbye to Puits Blain was the day Gwo Manman had passed away. Taking a fish out of water suffocates it; putting a bird in the most beautiful aquarium drowns it. Every time Gwo Manman looked out of the apartment window, all she saw was sky and shapeless air—sheer torture to a woman who preferred her bare feet on a packed-dirt floor to fancy tiles, or even Foufoune's pretty rug. As far as Miriam was concerned, Foufoune might as well have put a bullet in the old woman's heart.

"Miriam, is that you?"

Who else could it be?

"Gwo Manman ki te nou." Foufoune's throat tightened around the words. *Our mother has left us.*

"I've heard," Miriam lied. "I was about to call you when the phone rang." With her free hand she picked up the wooden spoon and resumed stirring her cornmeal. Elderly people like Dona Malbranche died every day in the diaspora, leaving relatives to bury the truth in distant graves. Some who did not believe in cremation became sudden converts; get rid of the evidence!

"Manman nou mouri," Foufoune's voice broke. *Our mother is dead.*

"When are you bringing her body?" Miriam asked, her eyes narrowing.

Foufoune scratched her head. She saw no reason to bring

the body back to the island. She could not be expected to travel all that distance every time she wanted to place a wreath on her mother's grave. She was a naturalized citizen, an expat; the tenth department was her new patrie. Why did her sister always go out of her way to be so damn difficult?

"Bring my mother back," Miriam snapped. She was addressing a brazen kidnapper, not her sister: "You can't keep her a prisoner anymore." Hadn't the ransom been paid in full? Hadn't Gwo Manman paid the ultimate price for her freedom? "You need to bring her back where she belongs."

Foufoune sniffled, hearing accusation after accusation between every two words. "If wanting to give my mother a better life was my crime, then I'll take the blame."

"But you didn't give her a better life," Miriam hissed. "You cheated her out of her life. You stole years from her. Years! She was living in exile. She was confined to the life you thought she should live. Gwo Manman did not want to be in the States." There! She had said what she'd meant to say for years. No more civility. No more pretenses. "Gwo Manman never stopped crying," she added. "She wanted to come home. Her life was here in Puits Blain. She was happy with me. Everything she was familiar with was right here. You locked her up in an apartment morning, noon, and night. She was free here, not trapped like a tortured detainee."

"Gwo Manman had a good, happy, comfortable life with me," Foufoune argued back. Only Miriam would be so callous as to talk to her that way at this horrible time. Puits Blain had become unsafe, hadn't Miriam heard? It was just like her to pretend things were not what they really were. Wasn't it only a matter of time before their mother would have been robbed, or worse? Any number of things could have happened to her. What did Miriam have to offer Gwo Manman anyhow? Selling rice and beans to a bunch of sweaty passersby was hardly a life of luxury.

"I talked to Gwo Manman often," Miriam said. "I called her after I knew you'd left for work. She hated the life you forced her to live. If you had sent her back to me, she'd be alive today."

"How you talk!" Foufoune snapped. "Why didn't you come get your dear mother if you were so concerned about her well-being?"

"And have you send the police after me at the airport? You had yourself declared her legal guardian. You just bring Gwo Manman's body back to me or I swear you will pay." Miriam slapped the phone shut.

Sympathy clouds hovered over Brooklyn, D.C., and Miami: places where relatives of the deceased lived. More rain fell over Puits Blain, but the heat spell would not be broken. Miriam put the phone back in her apron and focused her attention on the massive pots bubbling with aromatic food. Her house and place of business—a respectable concrete-block two-story—would soon fill with mourners. But first she would finish cooking. Death and mourning always made people famished.

Word scurried via scared rèstavèk children all the way to the stalls lining the cemetery's wall, where Gwo Manman's friends sold bottles of a cure-all the old woman swore by. The oil might not have extended her life by a minute, but just before she died Gwo Manman had looked for the last bottle of lwil maskreti she owned and clutched it as if it would go with her to the next place: the Last Department. The thick brown oil did nothing but spill on Foufoune's pretty rug. Ki te mele m. She didn't care.

* * *

Grudgingly, Miriam shut down her business and opened the house to visitors who came to shake their heads and grunt. Je wè, bouch pe. What was there to say? Gwo Manman was made to leave her home and die in a place whose name was like rock salt inside her mouth. The Gwo Manman everyone knew never would have allowed herself to live or die anywhere but in Puits Blain.

Miriam dutifully wore a black dress and positioned herself near the doorway to welcome visitors/spectators and set the tone for the gathering—a dark theater in which she would be a reluctant star. All eyes would be on her tonight. Po dyab, pitit. Take heart, my dear! The uncooked goat meat she had prepared went to Jean-Jean, a tip for the job she hired him to do.

"Mèsi, mèsi, Miss Miriam," he had said, quivering at his good fortune. Miriam had also thrown in the change he returned from the sacks of cement she sent him to buy. She would have him seal the latrine after the funeral. "Mèsi! Mèsi!" Jean-Jean sometimes lost his stutter when he saw money.

There were a few faces in the house Miriam did not recognize. Death dragged impunity in its wake, so no one was turned away. Gwo Manman would have been pleased. The more mourners the merrier!

Faces brightened when the subject inevitably turned to Rhum Barbancourt. Miriam had always suspected that their mother's delectation for rum was another reason why Foufoune had flown down to Puits Blain years prior, packed up a few of Gwo Manman's clothes, and taken her away.

"I don't want to live in America," Gwo Manman had protested. "I am too old for that. What will I do there? I'm afraid of the cold. I don't want the snow. I want to live in my country."

"Gwo Manman, please." Foufoune had swatted the air around her with dismissive hands. "Look around you! Puits Blain is all dust, don't you see? You'll be happier with me in America." Besides—this she had thought but dared not say— I work too hard to have my mother live like this. Foufoune sent enough money monthly to keep her mother living very well, but Gwo Manman insisted on sitting with the stall keepers behind the cemetery. She liked the taste of Barbancourt in her mouth. She liked that wild drum music. Rumor was that she had a boyfriend. No, boyfriends—at her age! She liked to be shirtless under the noonday sun; said it had healing powers: *That's why I never get sick!* she'd say.

Gwo Manman cursed the day she'd allowed Foufoune to take her away. But admitted she had been curious about the foreign place too. She had dreamed of being able to say that she went there once. Only once. And came back. But Foufoune had tricked her. There was never a return ticket.

Foufoune arrived several days later with Dona Malbranche's body in a gorgeous coffin.

"You look well," Miriam remarked upon seeing her sister for the first time since she came and took Gwo Manman away years ago. Not a single crease in Foufoune's flawless features. Hair, as usual, in a classic chignon. Foufoune had always been the beautiful sister, "the one who's going to amount to something," everyone, even Gwo Manman, would say.

"And you haven't changed," Foufoune said, eying the tufts of unruly gray around Miriam's temples, the head tie she must have borrowed from a charcoal vendor, the rust of subpar living in her sunken eyes. Koshon Mawon! The words tickled Foufoune's lips, but she did not speak them. There were stains on Miriam's skirt: blood, no doubt—probably from cutting off fish heads to make soup. Koshon Mawon! Long ago when they attended Anne Marie Javouhey elementary school, Foufoune and her girlfriends had made up a song which they liked to sing whenever they saw Miriam approaching:

Miriam Malbranche is dumber than a twig
Her mother, her sister:
No one wants her
Not even a wild pig . . .

Miriam threw her arms around her sister, saying: "We have only each other now."

Foufoune, in turn, kissed her on both cheeks.

That night while Foufoune rested, Miriam paced under the flamboyant tree. Gwo Manman did not die peacefully—that much she knew. She suffered. Li soufri. Miriam held her belly. She wanted to scream, but swallowed the pain.

A few other relatives flew to the island to say their good-byes. They booked rooms at Hotel Flamboyant, where the pool sparkled and massive generators guaranteed the power would stay on. They brought laptops in order to meet deadlines; they still had to make a living. Nouyòk pa lan jwèt a moun, surely Miriam understood. Business reports and dissertations did not stop for death.

No one planned to stay Down There too long after the services. They all led busy lives. They would spare a day or two, and then mount their winged friend to return to their respective chapters in their respective storybooks. During the services, however, they would be most dedicated, most single-minded, most unwavering in their show of grief. They would not be reproached. By the time they were through, all of Puits Blain would know just how much they loved the old woman they hardly knew.

* * *

The stained glass inside Église Saint Pierre rattled with their screams. Eyes darted between the pews to see who was crying and how many teardrops were actually shed. Some of the practiced mourners would have outdone themselves had the body been displayed. They felt cheated.

The procession to the cemetery boasted an impressive number of those who had succumbed to sezisman. Long-lost cousins swooned, dropping down in front of moving cars. There were wreaths galore (more flowers than Gwo Manman had seen in life). The affair cost many, many thousands; everyone was duly impressed. The casket, copper of course, came with a sixty-year moisture and water seal warranty—just in case. (*You know Haiti and hurricanes*, the dealer had said). Gwo Manman's burial clothes—an elegant mother-of-the-bride two-piece—were precious. Pity no one got to see how prettily she was dressed. And who among them would have discerned how much she loathed the outfit?

These clothes make me look like a clown, Dona would have said, if she could have seen herself. *I look like a madigra mal maske.*

At Miriam's house after the interment, there was no place to punch a pin. Everyone ate their fill. Barbancourt 5 Star flowed like Saut d'Eau's waterfall. A young man complained there was not enough ice. His drink was not cold enough. "In this heat, the mourners need ice. Where is the ice?" he wanted to know.

"Why are you here?" Miriam asked the disgruntled mourner. "Did you know that the woman whose funeral you attended never once owned a refrigerator? But does that matter? You want ice. We're out of ice. Don't move. I'll see to it that you get your ice."

Foufoune asked Miriam what was wrong.

"We're out of ice," Miriam said, shaking with disgust. "This boy is crying for ice. We're out of ice."

"Where is the ice?" Foufoune asked, desperate to do something—anything—right. The parched earth under her feet had shifted when she watched her mother's coffin being worked like an oversized pacifier into the tomb's mouth. Tears had spurted out of her eyes when she heard Miriam scream: "Not again, Manman! Don't leave me again, Manman!" Foufoune's heart had softened. She realized then that she did, in fact, love her sister. And Miriam loved her.

Burning tears stood in Foufoune's eyes. It took burying their mother to see that she could never have despised her own flesh and blood. And Miriam had been so generous. So selfless. Miriam had been the one who handled every detail of the funeral. Trying to plan it from thousands of miles away was a logistical nightmare. Perhaps Miriam was right about everything else. Perhaps she should have sent their mother back to Haiti to live. Perhaps Gwo Manman would still be alive today.

"I'll take care of getting more ice," Foufoune said. She would crawl on her knees all the way up to Caribbean Market and carry bags of ice on her head, if that was what Miriam wanted. One day she would tell Miriam that she regretted taking Gwo Manman to the live with her in the States. One day she might even ask for forgiveness. Her sister had been right all along: Gwo Manman belonged in Puits Blain. She knew that now. How could she have been so selfish? So blind? Her mind raced with regret, but what came out of her mouth was: "Where can I go to get more ice?"

"I'll take care of it," Miriam said. She summoned Jean-Jean, who barely looked like himself in his fine funeral clothes. His work clothes were in a satchel by the outhouse, which he would start sealing "after the last mourner leaves," as Miriam had instructed him when he arrived much earlier than he was told. Pending jobs made him uneasy. The sooner he sealed the hole, the less of a chance Miriam would have to change her mind; and the sooner he would get the rest of his money.

"Leave your shovel behind the house," Miriam had instructed him before the funeral. That thing was like an extension of his hand. He carried it everywhere, always hoping someone would hire him. "You can start tonight," Miriam had added, to his delight. She had read the impatience in his eyes, though she was the one who could no longer wait once word had reached her ear about some sneaky schoolgirl who had dropped her newborn into a nearby latrine. A suspicious houseboy had followed the trail of blood from the outhouse to the girl's thighs, and she'd confessed. Jean-Jean almost slipped into the hole and died himself, when frantic neighbors sent him down there with a bucket on a rope to try and scoop out the remains.

"I remember your mother well," Jean-Jean said. The thought of getting paid in just a few hours had cured his stutter for now. "She was a good person." Gwo Manman always had a kind word for him. He would do anything, anything at all, for the Malbranche family.

"We need ice," Miriam told him.

"I'll get it," replied Jean-Jean. For once, no one seemed to care where his hands had been.

Miriam embraced her sister, saying, "Pran kouraj. You did what you thought was best." She lifted up her hand and her voice: "A toast to Gwo Manman!"

Someone gave Miriam a fresh bottle of rum. She put it to her mouth and drank. She passed the bottle to Foufoune. *Do this in remembrance of me.*

"To Gwo Manman," Foufoune said. The liquid burned her throat on its way down. She was not a drinker. Her petite frame had never been able to meet rum on its own terms. A single sip would send her head spinning. But for Gwo Manman . . . just this once . . .

When Jean-Jean returned with the ice, the disgruntled mourner thanked him and drank and toasted for several hours before he stumbled out of the house. Foufoune, too, continued to toast her departed mother until her stomach churned and her thoughts began to swirl. Everyone was now stumbling with five-star grief. Foufoune teetered toward the bathroom. It was occupied, but she could not wait.

"Of course," Miriam said when Foufoune, trembling like a little girl, asked her sister to escort her to that wooden stall behind her house. It had been years since she last used it, but if memory served her correctly, it would be pitch-black inside and densely populated with flying roaches. She would have waited, if she could have, but the rum had instigated a riot inside her stomach and everything she'd ever eaten in her life was seconds away from a violent uprising.

Miriam listened as Foufoune retched into the thirty-foot drop.

"Water." Foufoune could barely say the word. She would splash her face with water; surely that would make her feel better.

"Yes," Miriam responded. "I'll get you some."

Miriam returned to the house for a pitcher. Jean-Jean was leaning against the wall, an anxious look in his eyes. The last of the stumbling mourners kissed her goodbye and said, "Be strong."

Miriam filled the pitcher and headed back to the outhouse. Foufoune slurred something Miriam did not understand as she bent over the latrine, vomiting—too intoxicated to care about the stench or the roaches. Her chignon was still intact, Miriam noted.

The back of Foufoune's neck was bare, except for the heart-shaped links of a gold chain which Miriam had given to Gwo Manman one Mother's Day—purchased with money she should have used to extract a molar that was so infected it ended up costing her half of her bottom teeth. Miriam wondered if Foufoune had taken the necklace off their mother's neck after she died, or if Gwo Manman had willingly given it away.

Without taking her eyes off the gold hearts, Miriam gripped the pitcher in a tight fist and drenched Foufoune in a vengeful baptism.

Stunned, Foufoune turned to ask why. In that second, Miriam reached outside the door and wrapped her fingers around the wooden handle of Jean-Jean's shovel. She shifted her weight and steadied herself on her callused heels, leaning back just so. As deftly as stirring lumps out of her cornmeal, Miriam delivered a blow so precise that Foufoune's chignon came undone. She fell sideways over the latrine's mouth. Miriam hit her again and again.

"This is for Gwo Manman."

Blood streamed out of Foufoune's mouth. Her eyelids pulled back in blinding shock. Miriam snatched off the heart-shaped necklace, and with a strength she didn't know she possessed, worked Foufoune's ever-so-svelte little frame into the hole. Foufoune's body went through with minimal force, landing with a sound as faint as a serving of rice and beans onto a Styrofoam takeout container.

Miriam held the necklace in a clenched fist, peering into the darkness. She tried but could not see her sister below.

Thick mud clogged Foufoune's mouth, her nostrils, her ears. Her head was heavy with mud—was it mud? She could not move her legs. *Dear God, help me*, she tried to say, but the words could not make it past the gunk in her throat. She attempted to lift her hands toward the strange dappled light filtering out of the darkness, but the movement caused her to sink even deeper.

Miriam covered the hole with a sheet of plywood. Soon Jean-Jean would pour concrete, turning the latrine into a memory. She sighed heavily as she returned to the house. Jean-Jean was standing like a shadow on the porch, waiting for her to give him the word. The sooner he started, the sooner he would be done. The sooner he would be paid.

"Everyone is gone," he said.

"Then get to work," Miriam told him. It had been a long day. She was tired, but took comfort in knowing that her mother and sister had both returned home to her in Puits Blain. This time to stay.

DEPARTURE LOUNGE

BY NADINE PINEDE

Cap Haitien

D renched in sweat. A bad idea to wear black cotton, even if it hides stains. A worse idea to lie to my boss at The Well-Seasoned Traveler and tell him I'm fluent in Creole. So he booked me as a private tour guide for Miranda Wolcott, who has her own show on the Food Network. The best thing about her show is that huge house in Westport. Now she's writing a cookbook on "Caribbean fusion," and she wants to include Haiti.

I've been waiting at Toussaint Louverture International Airport an hour to meet her flight coming in from Kennedy before we fly north together to Cap Haitien. We have only three days, which is way too short, but Miranda has to be back in time to tape her Easter special. We're traveling with two Haitians from Plant for Peace, some nonprofit group. Not that anyone can seriously believe planting trees can change the world. Anyway, they're taking care of security, plus the van and driver.

There was no way I would tell anyone my real reason for coming. What could I say? My dead grandmother told me to do it? It started like this: A few months ago, my phone rang in the middle of the night. I picked it up and heard those bleeps you get when someone's trying to send you a fax. So I lurched to the fax machine, thinking it must be a last-minute itinerary. All I got was a blank sheet.

First thing in the morning, I called New York and asked them what was so important that they tried to fax me in the middle of the night. Josette, the new executive assistant from Paris, was as charming as usual, but she insisted no one from the office had sent me anything yesterday. She liked to speak French to me so she could correct my pronunciation. A nice way of feeling instantly superior.

Then my mother called. She'd just been to church to light a candle for Grandmère Lucille who died two years ago on that day. We talked about her for a while. I was just about to hang up when out of curiosity I asked her what time of day Grandmère Lucille died.

"Three-thirty. Why?"

"In the morning, right?"

"Of course. You don't remember how we tried your cell?" I'd turned it off after a fourteen-hour day dealing with one client's stolen luggage and another's food poisoning, and then that valerian tea had knocked me out. One of my biggest regrets.

"No reason. I have to go now. Love you. Bye." I looked at the fax. The time stamp was three-thirty a.m.

The next night I dreamed Grandmère Lucille was angry with me, but she wouldn't tell me why. Then I dreamed she was crossing the street, only it was a street in Haiti, and she was waving over at me to join her, but my street was in New York and there was too much traffic. When it was finally safe for me to cross over, she was gone.

After a month of this, I couldn't take it anymore.

Which is why I lied to get this job. That, and the fact that bankruptcy is staring me in the face. And I have no idea how I'll make it through this week.

The news is bad. Haiti is suffering the worst drought in years. The rainy season is months away, yet people still pray for a miracle. Haiti's floods are as violent as its politics, sweeping away entire villages. What used to be forest is now something more like a desert. There's a Haitian proverb for hard, brutal rain during bright sunshine. *The devil is beating his mother.* Grandmère Lucille explained that one for me. The sunshine is the devil laughing, and the raindrops are his mother's tears. You'd think with all this humidity there would be rain. I seem to be sweating more than I ever have in my life. I scan the airport departure lounge for a ceiling fan because the air-conditioning, if it ever existed, is kaput. Where the hell is Miranda Wolcott? Her flight landed an hour go. I've left three messages on her cell. Customs wouldn't hold her up that long. The way things are going, we'll miss the last flight today. Driving to Cap Haitien is out, thanks to illegal roadblocks and gangs that specialize in trailing cars from the airport to rob them at gunpoint. Or kidnap the people and hold them for ransom. I'm glad we have security.

I ask Manuel if we'll really manage to do everything on the itinerary. He's an agronomist and the program manager at Plant for Peace. Nice guy from what I can tell so far. The three of us will fly north, via Aérogare Guy Malary, to meet Alexis Auguste, the director, and visit some co-ops. Then we'll drive to the border to meet a few farmers before we head to the Central Plateau to the training center in Papay. Manuel tells me not to worry. His eyes seem genuinely calm as he pats my hand. I've seen that kind of look before, mainly on blissed-out Buddhists and born-again Christians. Actually, he looks a bit like my older brother Philippe, the one my mother worships. The Saint of Our Family. Youngest partner in his law firm who works pro bono for Haitian detainees. The only thing he can't do is walk on water. Too bad I can't stand his Polish wife.

"On the last day, we leave at dawn," Manuel says.

"Why are we missing the big march?" It doesn't make any sense to me, until Manuel gives me a tight smile and changes the subject. My guess is someone doesn't want the march to happen, and Manuel is expecting trouble. I don't really want to know more. Politics has never been my thing.

I'm sitting right under a ceiling fan to cool off and look halfway presentable when Miranda finally shows up. Maybe I should use this time to rehearse my script. Did she read any of the books I suggested? Did she watch *The Comedians?* Okay, so it was filmed in Africa, but Graham Greene got a lot of details right. Nearly fifty years later, the airport's murals and the earnest slogans could be the same, except for the face of the president. The tarmac is still pockmarked asphalt that shimmers in the heat. The mountains are dusty from erosion. Men dressed in starched white shirts wait outside the airport terminal, dreaming of departure.

Miranda first told my boss that she wanted to "see some real voodoo." *Vodou*, I corrected her by e-mail. What did I really know about it? The last time I was here, I was just a girl. "Baby Doc" had recently been exiled, and people were hopeful about the future. My family decided it was safe again to visit.

Despite Haiti's tragic history, or perhaps because of it, we were always proud of where we came from. The world's first black republic. The second republic in the New World, after the U.S. The first country created from a successful slave revolution in 1804, boycotted for decades should any other slaves get the same idea.

Back then, when we arrived at the airport, a smiling crowd of black and brown faces lined the balcony overlooking the tarmac, waving as we disembarked and made the long hot walk to the terminal. I thought the crowd was there just for us, filled with our relatives who wanted to welcome us back. This must be what it feels like to be home.

Politics and Vodou were all most people knew about Haiti in those days, and they were both steeped in blood. The politics were the reason my parents had left and couldn't go back. One uncle was assassinated, another thrown in jail for a year. More than that they wouldn't say.

They didn't talk much about Vodou either, since we were raised as Catholics (although my father only went to church on Christmas Eve and Easter). My mother did tell me some stories, but just as I'd get all caught up in it and suspend my disbelief, she'd let me down with: "Of course, it's all non-sense." For months before our family trip to Haiti, I'd been begging my parents to let us attend a Vodou ceremony because I thought it would be a cool thing to tell my friends. So they finally relented. I'd been looking forward to that night for a long time. We all went together, with Philippe on one side of me and my mother on the other.

The Vodou priest, Monsieur Duval, began by explaining that this was a real ceremony, and that we should forget most of what we'd heard or seen in the movies.

"I will not stick any pins into any dolls," he said smiling, "and if you behave, I won't turn anyone into a zombie."

I rolled my eyes when the crowd laughed. The drummers began slowly. From the left of the amphitheater came a single file of men and women dressed in white, doing a two-step meringue shuffle to the beat of the drum. Duval picked up a bottle from his altar. He took a swig and sprayed it out into the air.

"Do you think it's rum?" Philippe's eyes were bright with excitement.

"I think it's gross."

Monsieur Duval was tall, with the broad-muscled shoulders of an athlete and smooth caramel skin. He would have looked just as good in a designer suit as in the white robe of the ougan. He probably still had some business suits from his days as a chemical engineer, before his father summoned him back to Haiti to assume the mantle. My parents knew him as a student in Paris, where he was a real bon vivant, popular with the French girls he took dancing to all the best jazz clubs.

The believers were now in the middle of the room, chanting and clapping between the drumbeats. Their luminous faces seemed even darker in the candlelight. Duval pointed to one of the complicated line drawings on the dirt floor. To me it looked like a cross standing on a coffin. "These are vèvès, which we draw with cornmeal and wood ash. Each lwa has his or her own."

A murmur rippled through the crowd. Duval set fire to a small pile of twigs near the vèvès. The smoke snaked along the poto mitan, the middle post holding up the temple. Grandmère Lucille would always say women were the poto mitan of the world. Then one day I asked her why all the priests at our church were men. Her face lit up and she hugged me tight, like she was proud of me.

Duval closed his eyes and muttered a few words while the believers circled him, still doing that two-step. The hypnotic chanting became a call-and-response, lulling me to the edge of sleep. I rubbed my eyes and opened them wide.

"Look at that!" I cried out, and my mother hushed me.

A woman had stopped right in front of us. She had the darkest skin I'd ever seen, a kind of midnight-blue, and her arms and legs were trembling in spasms. She threw back her head and screamed. I grabbed my brother's arm. No way would I let my mother see me get scared.

"What's happening?" I whispered to Philippe.

"She's possessed, in a trance."

I glanced at my mother and her expression of calm be-musement.

Now the woman was bent over, still shaking, lunging to-ward Duval. She grabbed his bottle from the floor and drank from it. We all gasped when we heard the sound of glass break-ing and saw her chewing.

"No way," said Philippe. My mouth hung open in disbelief. The candles glowed brighter, as if fueled with gasoline. The possessed woman picked up a piece of wood from the fire and put it in her mouth. I flinched but didn't turn away. A stream of black and red trickled from her lips, inching its way to the white of her collar.

Please don't let her come over here. I should never have insisted on sitting in the front. Now she was bent over again near the fire. Only when she turned to face us did we see the white rooster she held by its feet, which she began to swing in circles above her head.

Oh no. Not that.

It was all over in less than a second. Blood gushed from its severed head, and the rooster's feet seemed to tremble and kick in her hands. The crowd let out a collective groan with hands over mouths. The gods ride the possessed like horses, Monsieur Duval had explained, and of course they demand sacrifices. The rooster's lifeless corpse was laid to rest on the vèvè by the fire.

I had always been the squeamish one, letting Philippe hack the family of snakes in our rose garden with a hoe, or drown my mouse Ivory, white like that rooster, in a jar of alco-hol when it grew a huge tumor in its neck. Later I would laugh and pretend I'd never been scared. I stared at the ground to the stop the awful rollercoaster in my stomach. If only I could manage not to throw up. By the time I realized Philippe was nudging me, it was too late. Here she was. The possessed woman's mouth was splattered with blood and soot. She was looking right at me, still holding a charred piece of wood from the fire.

The audience was quiet, the drums muted. She stood in silence in front of me, as if she could hear my heart pounding. She took my right hand. Her eyes were strange, like a tunnel of darkness, but suddenly I wasn't afraid anymore because it felt like I had stepped out of my skin and was floating to the ceiling, watching all of this from above. She turned my hand over and using a sooty twig, she marked my palm with an X.

I looked down at the mark, then back at her, thinking she would say something to me, but she dropped my hand and spun away, joining the believers in their hypnotic shuffle around the fire. A few minutes later, she fainted and was carried off. The drumming died out and the candles were extinguished. The house lights came on to reveal the bare earth spattered red.

"Whoa! What a show," Philippe said in what sounded like awe.

"It wasn't a show." My voice was smaller than usual. My mother and father took turns reassuring me. Of course it was all just a show, there's nothing to be scared of. Their words were like water trickling over stone. Later, when I told her about it, Grandmère Lucille said I was right, it was a good sign. But she never did explain what she meant. That's the way she was, always an enigma.

If only Grandmère Lucille could see me now. I have her spiral notebook, where she wrote her unsent letters and jotted down the names of herbs and what they do. There is a family legend that when Grandmère Lucille worked as a maid in Haiti, she had used her leaf medicine to save a black American woman's life. Who knows? I might have to save someone's life too. When I once asked her about it, Grandmère Lucille replied with a typical Haitian proverb: "Only the knife should know the heart of the yam." Another secret she would never tell, and now it's too late. It was frustrating always being told to mind my own business, when all I wanted was to make sense of things. Still, I loved her more than I've ever loved anyone, and this little notebook is all I have.

A woman calls my name, and my heart sinks. Her hair is cut in a smooth white bob. She's slender and prettier than the photos I saw online.

"Fabienne, is it? Fabienne, I'm terribly sorry for the wait," she says with that Boston Brahmin accent that immediately makes me think of the Kennedys. No surprise there. Miss Porter's, Radcliffe, English, magna cum laude.

We shake hands. Her sunglasses are propped jauntily on her head, showing off gray-green eyes, those high cheekbones that age gracefully, and lightly freckled skin without makeup or a trace of sheen. Even more annoying is that she's actually smaller than she appears on television. I suck in my stomach and straighten my back.

Her sleeveless white linen shift is completely unwrinkled. The dress I instantly recognize as Eileen Fisher, that New York designer whose cheapest organic cotton tanks are still fifty bucks. The kind of clothes Philippe's wife buys all the time. Way out of my league.

"Anmwe!" a woman near the front door screams. Nobody moves to help her. "Anmwe!" she screams again, before slumping down in a chair to cry. She probably turned away for less than a second. Now her suitcase is gone.

When I glance over at Miranda, she is yawning. Then she turns her back to the front door. She looks like she's studying the rusty single-propeller plane idling on the runway, ready for boarding.

"I'm so pleased to meet you," I hear myself say in a forced bright voice as I pick up my scuffed backpack to line up behind her for another passport check. We are last in line and will probably have to sit together on the plane.

"So where are you from?" she asks me.

"I'm Haitian."

"Of course you are."

What does she mean by that? Something like rage rises in me. There are some clients I know will push my buttons. She probably hasn't read a thing I sent to her personal assistant. An hour late and she just waltzes in completely unruffled and expects it all to fall into place because she has someone like me sweating the details. Naturally, she's one of those lucky people who can't imagine what it means to worry about mundane details like money. Which is never far from my mind these days.

"Our neighbor's nanny is from Haiti. Solange."

Please don't ask me if I know her.

Miranda continues in her blithe staccato: "How long did you live here in Haiti?"

The short answer is "not long," but I never say this right away. I first explain that my parents were born and raised in Haiti, where I was born. Grandmère Lucille took care of me until I was two, while my parents finished college and looked for jobs. Then we moved to the U.S., where my classmates asked me if I stuck pins into Vodou dolls. Oh, and if we were responsible for AIDS.

Yet wherever we lived, our house was filled with Haitian music, proverbs, legends, paintings, sculptures, and the earthy scent of rice with wild black mushrooms. Living in Haiti was a state of mind, and my parents were ambivalent immigrants who passionately nurtured their memories. Even so, no matter how hard they tried, each passing year felt like the tide ebbing, making them strangers to their own homeland. Philippe and I ended up speaking English at school and at home, and hearing Creole only when my parents spoke to each other. We always understood what they were saying, even though we couldn't speak the language ourselves. The technical term is *auditory comprehension*, not the same thing as fluency.

It's only three days. I can fake anything for that long.

"Only a few years, but don't worry, I'm fluent in Creole." Could she see right through me, or was I just being paranoid? With some people, you know exactly where you stand. A conservative political commentator once wrote an editorial in the *International Herald Tribune* about the "Tahitians" on their boats to Florida. I wrote a letter to the editor, pointing out that those poor "Tahitians" would have had quite a long way to row if they ever wanted to reach Florida.

But Miranda isn't like that. Maybe the sad state of my birthplace is embarrassing me, though I will never admit that to her. It's complicated to try and explain how I can be proud of a place most people see as a hopeless basket case. So I have to be a ruthless editor, slashing away at paradox to clear a path of understanding.

"My parents left Haiti because of Papa Doc Duvalier. They both received scholarships from the French government to study in Paris, where they met." I try to sound nonchalant and not intent on pleasing her one way or the other. Try to make her like you without being obvious. Desperation is a turnoff.

Never let them see you sweat. It makes those people anxious. I want some positive response from Miranda, but she remains uncommitted as we climb the rickety steel steps into the plane. "Would you prefer the window or the aisle?" She shrugs off my question and takes the window. Thank goodness, because I get vertigo. The plane rattles down the runway, bouncing us up and down like a trampoline.

Miranda pulls out a paperback from her raffia tote bag and puts it on her lap. Zora Neale Hurston's *Tell My Horse.* Oh God. That would be just like Miranda to think she can learn something real about Haiti from that book. Zora actually wrote that Haitians are all liars. When I saw that, I couldn't read anymore. On the other hand, she did say she loved her Haitian maid Lucille, which is a neat coincidence. Then again, I guess Lucille isn't such an unusual name.

"At last," Miranda says, peering out of the dust-caked window, "the ride of our lives."

The plane clears its throat as it prepares to take off. There are no announcements about exit doors, oxygen masks, emergency landings, seat cushions, flotation devices, or seat belts. I fumble in the gap between our seats for a buckle. There are no seat belts.

When we finally land at the small airport in Cap Haitien, Miranda's face is still a serene mask. If she feels any of the nausea I do, she hides it well.

We elbow our way through yet another crowd to reach our white SUV, parked in front of the airport. Alexis Auguste is standing by the front passenger door. He's a good-looking guy, tall and slender, with small round glasses. Around fifty or so, with a dark smooth face and just a sprinkle of gray at his temples.

I know it's him from the photo on the Planters for Peace itinerary. Alexis shakes hands with all of us. Miranda can't stop smiling when he opens the door for her so she can sit in the back with him. Great.

Manuel is driving us to our hotel and telling us a bit about the city. On either side of us are canals filled with what looks like raw sewage.

"Cap Haitien was once known as the Venice of the Caribbean," Manuel says with pride, as if he's oblivious to the crumbling boulevards and fetid air.

There are people everywhere. Women in bright dresses carrying baskets and bundles on their heads, men sauntering by in crisp shirts and jackets despite the muggy hundred-degree heat. The paint peeling from the wooden shutters of our hotel makes it look shabby from the outside, even with those graceful wrought-iron balconies. This once grand establishment is now nearly empty. Manuel complains that the tourists on the cruise ships who disembark on the paradise beaches at Labadie never make it into town, and they're never even told they are in Haiti.

Inside, the hotel has good bones, graceful archways. It's a peaceful oasis in the middle of so much heat and noise. There's a well-stocked bar I can't help but notice. Good for a nightcap. On the other side of the lobby are some men in crisp shirts grouped around a whiteboard. They are all dark-skinned, except for a few dressed in business suits pointing to charts on the board, who are light-skinned with wavy brown hair.

I can't stop staring at that painting on the wall. A woman half underwater, floating on her back, with a tiger standing by the shore, watching her. Are there tigers in Haiti? I almost ask Manuel. Of course not, he would say, except in a painter's mind. The woman isn't afraid of drowning either. For a moment I'm floating like she is, until I hear Miranda's voice. "No signal," she says, holding up her iPhone. "Can I try yours?" I hand her my cell and watch as her face lights up. It turns out there are no more single rooms, so Miranda and I will be sharing. Just my luck. All I want is so simple: a shower with real water pressure and an insect-free room to sleep in. But it's hard to sleep when I can tell I have failed to impress Miranda Wolcott. I end up not sleeping and imagining all of my worst fears: flying cockroaches and rats crawling over my body and bats entangled in my hair. Did I mention how scared I am of insects and rodents?

The next morning we travel to the border, then down to Hinche. We visit Alexis's cooperatives and hear long talks about the hairy Creole pigs and their importance to small farmers, the dangers of deforestation, the need for sustainable agriculture and food security. Manuel and I quickly become buddies. I sit in the front seat and chat with him as he drives us to our next destination, two pros in the travel business, trading horror stories and talking shop. Now Miranda, on the other hand, is getting the star treatment from Alexis. I wonder if they know each other from somewhere else, the way they're so chummy. Maybe he's softening her up for the Big Ask. Sure. That's what I tell myself when I get annoyed at how he fawns over her.

As we're standing on the banks of a river that is shallow from the drought, Alexis looks more serious than I've seen him. "This is the Massacre River, where in 1937, the Dominican dictator Rafael Trujillo ordered the slaughter of at least twenty thousand Haitians." No one says a word. We stare at the river. "It was a genocide, an act of ethnic cleansing. This river ran red with Haitian blood."

I feel a sick heaviness in my chest and try not to picture bloated corpses floating past us. No one moves—as if in silent agreement, we want to honor the dead. Then Alexis turns around and leads us across the river, hopping from stone to stone. On the other side, we push through tall stalks of sugarcane and stop in silence at a scarred tree.

"Here was a Dominican prison," Alexis says. "Only this tree survived, a silent witness to history."

We finally reach an unassuming wire fence. A factory billows smoke in the distance.

"This is the real border," explains Alexis, "but most people don't realize that."

There's a group of farmers up ahead, waiting for us. I feel lightheaded from the sun and my exhaustion, and now I'm supposed to say something to introduce myself. The phrases I copied from the Creole grammar book are right here in my tiny reporter's notebook. When my turn comes, I stand up.

Sweat tickles the hairs on my upper lip. I clear my throat. "Mwen rele Fabienne," I start to read aloud, but my hands are trembling and the words are swimming off the paper and sliding into the earth. I clear my throat and squint at my notebook. I try to hear my mother's voice speaking Creole, to imitate what she would have said. It's no use. My voice trembles while I sniff back tears.

"You're crying," says one of the farmers. I look up and recognize his face. Earlier, when we were walking through his land, he had spotted me and called out in Creole, "You're Haitian, aren't you? I can tell by your beautiful skin." But now his voice is sharp: "You're crying, but we're the ones with a reason to cry."

I have a reason too. I can understand my parents' language but can't use it here, now, for a simple greeting. I can translate long speeches from Creole to English for Miranda, yet can't string together one simple sentence when I need to. I am functionally illiterate in what should be my mother tongue, a fumbling tourist in what should be my homeland. The farmers stare at me in silence, and I look down at the ground, wishing it would swallow me up.

The farmers begin to tell stories of being threatened and forced to sell their land so a free-trade zone can be built. "We will fight for this land until we die!" they yell, waving their machetes. But some say they're afraid of what may happen if they don't sell. Alexis listens to all of it along with us, then he asks if there's a way they can put their heads together.

"What people learn with their eyes, they don't forget," he says. He holds up a small poster of a big fish ready to eat a little fish, with other small fish swimming away in fear. His next poster shows all the little fish biting the tail of the big one. "Are fish more intelligent than people?" he asks.

The farmers murmur, shaking their heads.

"You need to unite in your battle," he adds, "then we can accompany you."

The farmers applaud Alexis and gather around him, all talking at once. Miranda is beaming, like a woman in love.

The next day we survive the bruising ride over bumpy dirt roads to Hinche, where I volunteer to help out with interpretation for a radio interview in French.

"Are you Haitian?" the interviewer asks me.

I pause before replying. I mention that my grandmother Lucille was from a village near here.

Miranda abruptly says that she and Alexis are going somewhere together, and she doesn't need me for a couple of hours, so I go off to find some of the plants in my notebook. I even find the serpent's herb, and it looks exactly like Grandmère Lucille drew it.

That night in Papay, we sit with Alexis under the gazebo of his modest house, nestled in a heavily guarded compound. For a man about to lead a march, Alexis looks enviably serene. He's showing us the posters, like the ones with the fish, that he uses with people who can't read. Small bats flutter in the distance as night approaches. When Alexis's wife appears to announce that dinner is ready, Miranda seems a bit annoyed, and for a moment I wonder if Alexis is the real reason she came here.

Alexis speaks eloquently the following morning about fighting the Plan of Death, his name for what the World Bank, the IMF, and the U.S. want. He tells the audience gathered there that alternatives exist, and that just as two hundred years ago Haiti inspired the world with its revolution, it can again be an inspiration in the fight against globalization. For the first time, I really listen and let his words sink in. His call to arms lingers in the air. And then it rains. The steady drumming on zinc roofs is greeted by chanting and singing that lasts for hours.

Miranda stands up to present a painting she had secretly bought in Cap Haitien on our behalf, and which she is now offering to Alexis so that it can hang in the new dormitory. She thanks the crowd with the only two Creole words she knows, "Mèsi anpil," and then sits down to thunderous applause. As I'm about to head back to my room, Manuel grabs my arm.

"This morning, an old woman came by the center and left this for you." He hands me a stained envelope, with nothing written on it. "She said she heard you yesterday on the radio, and she knew your grandmother. She didn't tell me her name."

I wait until I'm in my room to open the envelope and pull out the folded yellowed pages, torn from a notebook. It's Grandmère Lucille's handwriting all right, and the torn pages are from the very same notebook I brought with me.

I can't wait to tell Miranda the whole story, to see the look on her face when I say, *Guess what? My grandmother knew Zora Neale Hurston. She helped her when Zora came to Haiti and wrote* Their Eyes Were Watching God. *She's that Lucille, the one in* Tell My Horse. *My grandmother.* This must be the reason she visited me in my dreams. To show me this.

It's three in the morning by the time I drift off, lulled half-asleep by the farmers' vigil. First the murmured Latin phrases, the Gregorian chants from nuns in sky-blue habits who came by bus for the march. Then the soft acoustic guitars of troubadours in straw hats, their lyrics as sweet as the wild honey from the bees of Papay. Dawn approaches, and for the first time in my life, I hear gospel music in Creole.

"*We need to love one another other,*" a woman's voice sings, soaring and fading, trying to sow love in the dusty path of death.

We have two SUVs for the long ride back to Port-au-Prince, because some people from this center are coming with us. And, of course, Miranda is in the other van, so my story will have to wait. Despite the warnings not to march, the people voted to go ahead. Alexis's eyes are calm but red-rimmed when he shakes our hands and thanks us for coming. He kisses Miranda on both cheeks and they look right into each other's eyes. Am I out of it or did something happen between them? It's true I didn't see her much last night. Who cares?

I feel triumphant this morning. Nothing can bother me now. Alexis tells Manuel and the other driver to be careful. I take my seat of honor in the front, next to Manuel. Our two SUVs are whisked through the gates that quickly close behind us.

We're stopped by uniformed men who, after peering into the cars, brusquely wave us on with their guns. I've never seen so many people with guns. We pass a village perched on the edge of a steep cliff. Below is the Lac de Péligre, the Lake of Danger.

Manuel is telling us how Americans created the lake in the 1950s to stop up Haiti's largest river, the Artibonite, the lifeline for this region, known as Haiti's breadbasket. The U.S. Army Corps of Engineers planned the dam. It was supposed to be a development project that would bring electricity to millions. In Port-au-Prince, assembly plants and agribusinesses, along with some lucky families, did receive electricity. But upstream, peasants from the valley who used to live alongside the river ended up fleeing with whatever they could carry. These were the "water refugees," whose pastel dwellings cling hopefully to these cliffs. I peer down at the charred skeleton of a truck at the bottom of the ravine. A tiny swerve in the wrong direction. That is all it took.

In the departure lounge at the airport, I hug Manuel goodbye.

"Don't forget to plant a tree," he says smiling, holding me a fraction longer than I expect. He seems kind of sad to see me go, or am I just imagining things? I watch him walk away. He does not turn around or look back. I line up to take my seat next to Miranda.

Good morning, friends, says the e-mail from Alexis the day after the march. *It is with a sense of great urgency that I write to you today to denounce the vicious attacks that took place yesterday in Hinche against peasants leaving the Congress.*

Alexis describes how, after dropping us off at the airport, Manuel turned right around to return to Papay. He was driving alone, hoping to make it back in time for at least part of the march. Near that turnoff by the Lac de Péligre, he was flagged down on the road. Perhaps he thought he could help, or maybe he recognized someone. In any case, a few witnesses said Manuel got out of the SUV and was quickly surrounded by a group of young men with guns. They forced him into the backseat. The white SUV sped off. Manuel hasn't been seen since.

WHO IS THAT MAN?

BY YANICK LAHENS

Saint-Marc

Translated by David Ball

W ho is that man? Orélus thought about it every day. Several times a day. Every night. For almost ten days now. He'd tried an infusion of soursop leaves, as he had every other night to calm himself down. Nothing helped. It was close to half past midnight and he couldn't manage to fall asleep. To make things worse, it was particularly hot that night. Stifling. In this town of Saint-Marc, flat as a cassava. Flat as the palm of your hand. Who was that man sitting next to him in that SUV barreling toward Port-au-Prince? A trip that had turned his life upside down. Who was that man? He probably had a wife and kids, a mother.

Orélus flapped an old school bag in the air, first near his face, then around his left shoulder, and finally over his right shoulder. Despite the repellent coils to drive off the mosquitoes, they still made their usual rounds and were whining away relentlessly at his ear. So Orélus kept trying to chase them off by shaking that old satchel. It didn't work. And it was hot enough to fry an egg—or your skin. Orélus had to get out of bed and sit right next to the window with the hope of getting some relief, and maybe, in the silence of the night, finding an answer to question that haunted him: who is that man?

His wife Yva was fast asleep, exhausted. She'd just gotten up to give her daughter a bottle, then went right back to sleep without even realizing how uncomfortable it was, what with the heat and the mosquitoes. Yva didn't complain. Yva rarely complained. And luckily didn't ask too many questions. Which was quite convenient as far as that incident was concerned—the incident that still made him shiver sometimes, just thinking about it. Orélus looked at his daughter Natasha for a moment. She had come into his life a year ago and he'd promised himself he would give her a better life than his own. That incident had made him even more determined. And he could see the scene of her birth at the hospital once again. Since from now on everything was connected.

In his mind, Orélus went over that day, the third of July, for the nth time.

Just like every month, he was getting ready to leave for Port-au-Prince and go to the main office of the health organization he worked for, to turn in his report on the assignment he'd completed over the past month. He had visited every corner of the main towns of Bas Artibonite and meticulously filled out the questionnaires: *Age, sex, number of children, marital status, date of last visit to doctor, declaration of illnesses,* etc. He had slept very late the night before, in order to file the papers according to the organization's guidelines. His employers liked him, and Orélus was very much attached to his job, which not only allowed him to feed his family (the beginning of dignity), but to pay for his younger sister's computer studies and be generous to strangers who'd been pummeled by misfortune. His compassion had saved him on that third of July. It made him all the more aware of his own good fortune and he had no desire to lose it.

He'd had a hard time waking up that day and had almost run to the station where the trucks left for Port-au-Prince.

They were all full already, and time was passing. He looked desperately at his watch several times. Then a friend he hadn't seen for a few years walked over and jumped for joy when he spotted Orélus. Pierre had left Saint-Marc for the United States when he was a teenager. His school friends heard from him once or twice, then silence. Orélus was sociable and liked companionship. They embraced each other with mutual warmth. They exchanged the usual questions friends ask after a long absence, but Orélus couldn't help looking intently at the trucks to see if luck was smiling on him at last. Pierre asked him what was making him so impatient. When Orélus explained that he needed to get to Port-au-Prince for his work, Pierre told him not to worry. A friend was going to drive to Port-au-Prince that morning and he was alone. Pierre called that friend on his cell and the man agreed to take Orélus with him. Orélus thanked Pierre warmly for putting an end to his anxiety.

Ten minutes later, Orélus was comfortably seated in a brand-new SUV with four-wheel drive. He immediately stopped worrying. He exchanged a few words with the driver, whose name was Dudley and spoke Creole with a strong English accent. Although the guy was driving extremely fast, Orélus was so relieved that with the help of the air conditioner, he dozed off after the first few minutes. He remembered being suddenly awakened by the squealing of the brakes on the asphalt and realizing that the driver had just dodged a truck speeding in the opposite direction. Orélus promised himself not to fall asleep anymore. He tensed up a bit. All the more so as he noticed Dudley glancing constantly at his rearview mirror, trying to keep the car behind them from passing. Orélus knew those drivers—all too many of them—who staked their honor on the wrong things. And risked their lives for totally childish reasons. He said to himself he'd rather get there fifteen minutes late, but alive. Orélus told Dudley in a tone neutral enough not to offend him that he wasn't in that much of a rush and it would be a good idea to let the impatient madman on their heels pass them. Taking advantage of that moment, when Dudley wasn't paying attention, the vehicle went ahead and passed them and, to Orélus's great surprise, swung a quick right and blocked their car.

Three men got out, each with a gun in his hand. The first came over to the driver's door and aimed his 9mm at Dudley's head. He made him get out and sit in the backseat. He then sat down next to him, against the left door. Orélus thought it was a classic attack by an armed gang, as happens sometimes on these roads—until the moment when Dudley said, "Elien, what's happening?" And Elien answered, "You'll find out what's happening soon enough." So Dudley knew them. This left Orélus completely at a loss.

The second armed man had already walked around the other side of the vehicle. He asked Orélus to move to the back of the car, pushed him in right next to Dudley, and sat down against the right-hand door. The third man got behind the wheel and took off fast. Orélus had the feeling he had landed at the wrong place at the wrong time, and with the wrong person. He also knew that people sometimes lost their lives because of such unfortunate coincidences. They weren't far from Titanyen canyon: all the ghastly stories about the place came back to him. Titanyen, an isolated garbage dump where organized gangs and politicians got rid of their unwanted corpses. Orélus thought of his daughter who would never know her father, and his wife, left helpless.

It was eight a.m. Two trucks, one coming from Port-au-Prince, the other going to the city, sped by them without noticing anything. He was given the order to lower his head and not raise it again unless one of them asked him to. Orélus lowered his head. From the questions they asked Dudley in a threatening, cold, sarcastic tone, like killers in a movie, Orélus became acutely aware that not only was he caught in the middle of some dirty business—some very dirty business—but he knew nothing about it.

"What did you do with the packages that were unloaded at Fort-Liberté? Where's the money from the sale of the merchandise? This is the last time you're gonna enjoy yourself with other people's money. The party's over—got it, Dudley? Over. Because, you know, the boss, he's not happy. Like, really not happy. You thought you could be a wise guy, well, forget it. Take a deep breath, because you don't have long to live."

Then Orélus remembered a piece of news that had made the headlines two months back: a plane crashed in the middle of the countryside in the Fort-Liberté area and two SUVs arrived on the scene a few hours later to take away the cargo. So he was caught in an affair involving the drug cartels.

When they asked Dudley who his companion was, he answered without a tremor in his voice: Orélus had nothing to do with the whole thing, a friend had simply asked him to drive the guy to Port-au-Prince, and that was it. He hardly knew him. Orélus thought he was home free until one of the three men observed that as he had seen everything, he was becoming a potential witness. Orélus didn't hear any response from the two others. Since he couldn't see them, he imagined they must have made simple hand gestures to decide his fate. Orélus had a strong urge to pee in his pants. But he held it in and decided he had to keep up his strength so he could explain himself when the time came.

After another ten minutes, the car turned off to the left.

There was no more asphalt, just a bumpy road heading far into the countryside. Orélus prayed to God and invoked the eighty-third psalm. After the tenth invocation, the car stopped suddenly. The driver honked three times and a gate opened. Orélus had no strength left to pray. Entering a gated property meant it was all over for him. The driver of the car that had followed Dudley from Saint-Marc stood before the open gates and told the three thugs in Dudley's car to get out. The men dragged Dudley with them. But in a burst of frantic energy, he decided to resist. They shoved him brutally to the ground and ordered Orélus to keep his head down. Orélus heard words being exchanged between these men, violent blows raining down on Dudley, the dull sound of a bullet from a silencer, and a noise like someone clearing his throat. Dudley made the noise twice. Then nothing.

When Orélus heard the steps of someone coming over to the car, he said a last prayer to God and commended his daughter to Him. As the man reached the car door, he ordered Orélus to lift up his head. Orélus obeyed and told himself he would not be weak: he would die with dignity. He raised his head and saw the man who had been driving the other car, and seemed to be the boss of the squad, make a little gesture of surprise. Then he said, "You don't recognize me?"

Orélus shook his head; no sound could come out of his mouth at that moment.

The man went on: "Do you have a baby who was born fourteen months ago?"

Orélus nodded.

"Do you remember someone coming into the waiting room in the hospital that night and asking for money to buy medicine for his wife, who was at death's door?" The event returned to Orélus's memory. "You're the only one who took out his wallet and gave me money. You forgot my face but I will never forget yours. Get out of here right away or you're a dead man. Don't ask me any questions. I'll say you ran away."

Orélus grabbed the few sheets of his report within his reach.

"Hurry up. If the others come back, you're dead."

A part of the health survey would have to be redone.

The stranger opened the gate and Orélus ran out and never looked back. He kept moving until he met a passerby and asked where he was. The answer: "You're at Santo 19." He asked where he could catch a tap tap and followed the man's directions. He crossed through town in a mental fog as if he'd come back from the grave, from the other side of life.

When he got to the office, he collapsed and told his fellow workers every detail of his misadventure. They gave him unsweetened coffee and herb tea to calm him down.

In the truck bringing him back to Saint-Marc that afternoon, he resolved to say nothing to his wife. Women talk too much. Even the least talkative end up talking. The experience he had just lived through must not be known in Saint-Marc.

Orélus met Pierre four days later, and when his friend asked him how things were going, Orélus thanked him warmly for helping him get to his appointment in Port-au-Prince on time. Pierre left without asking any more questions, without any particular emotion showing on his face. Orélus listened attentively to the news on the radio, hoping someone would talk about the incident he'd just lived through. But no, nothing. Absolutely nothing.

That night, Orélus stayed up until almost two a.m. A light breeze was coming in from the sea. He eventually went to bed without having solved what would be the enigma of his life from now on. Who was the man he happened to get a ride with in that SUV going to Port-au-Prince?

MERCY AT THE GATE

BY MARIE KETSIA THEODORE-PHAREL

Croix-des-Bouquets

T he contrast of jet-black, knotted pubic hairs against the squirmy white objects confirmed for Moade, called Moah, that what she was seeing was not rice or lice, but maggots.

"Aunt Haba, do you think the man is dead?" Moah asked in a voice no more audible than the flapping of butterfly wings.

The hustle and bustle of the early-September morning in Croix-des-Bouquets was well underway. The man in question was lying still; his naked legs, naked ass, ashen penis, exposed for all of Croix-des-Bouquets to see. Moah lifted her gaze from the sprawling man's scantily clad body and the tattered doctor's lab coat. Leaves covered his forehead and hair. There was the matted fur of an unrecognizable animal next to the man. Flies swarmed the animal's carcass.

Moah looked at her aunt who was wrapping her old, frayed scarf, the color of budding okra flowers, around her nose. Moah watched and admired her aunt's long, slender fingers as Haba broke a stick from a nearby bush to poke the body. The man winced faintly. Haba flung the stick to the side and took a step back.

Slowly, a mud-clad hand arose from beneath the pile of leaves. It had a scar the size of a nickel between the thumb and the index finger. Another scar, like a miniature Earth, was centered in the middle of the man's palm. The hand lifted up from the top of the body. Moah flinched as it flung the debris from the man's face. Moah realized that her aunt had been squeezing her hand. She couldn't feel her fingers. She looked at her aunt, perhaps for confirmation, permission, or condemnation; however, unlike Moah, Haba hadn't focused on the dark patches of matted pubic hair. Instead, Haba noted the brown eyes sunk deep into the man's head. Those eyes looked as if at anytime they might become submerged into some deeper place in his head.

The man stared back at Haba. His gaze narrowed slowly like the lens of an old camera. He smiled a decayed smile. In shock, Haba's face closed as though choking. Her left eye and cheek twitched involuntarily. Haba's eyes grew wide not with fear, but with seething anger. A boiling swell of rage climbed out from deep inside of her and poured out of her eyes.

Moah looked at the half-dead man and wondered about his identity. If she asked her aunt, Haba would ignore her or change the subject, like she always did when Moah asked about her father and mother. When really pressed for an answer, Aunt Haba would only say, "Isn't it enough to have an aunt who loves you? Isn't it marvelous to have a name like Moah, 'the word'? The word today is obedience."

The look Haba was giving the man at that moment was further proof that this was a subject not to be broached. It was as if Haba had seen a ghost. No, the devil. At least that was the look Moah would give the devil, she thought, if she ever saw him. It was an I-don't-have-any-fucking-business-with-you look. While she stood there unable to move as everything seemed to go in slow-motion, the wind howled as if to echo the complaints of an oppressed world. The butterflies humped the wind because there were so few flowers in Croix-des-Bouquets.

Moah thought back to the crowd she had seen in that exact spot only a few hours before as she and her aunt had made their way to morning mass. Her aunt had avoided the throngs of people by crossing the street and cutting to rue Stenio Vincent. They had rushed past the Charlotin boys' school, the massive khaki-colored walls of the military headquarters, then into the yard of Our Lady of the Rosary. Now Moah knew that the crowd must have been looking at the man too.

Moah assessed the situation, trying to ascertain its advantages. After all, in addition to her beauty, a quick mind had made her the object of desire for three old men. Even though this was something she was proud of, she knew at that moment that there would be no more fooling around with old men. There would be no more Mondays with Jacques who visited while Haba was at mass. Jacques who always brought five green bananas or plantains. And for that, Moah allowed him to cup her breast for five minutes. No more than that. She counted every second. He held her generous breasts in his wide, rough palms, as if they were some mythic goose eggs or gifts from God. Afterward, he would brush her cheek with his index finger, put on his hat, and walk his long, lean body down the winding path back to Beudet where he lived in a small shack on a small farm.

Equally, there would be no time for old Pierre-Paul who paid her two gourdes for a medicinal foot bath and her listening ear. He talked of his exploits as a bodyguard during the olden days of the Paul Magloire presidency.

"Magloire was the best president because he loved to party with the people. This made my job very hard. I was shot at least five times when I was protecting him." He repeated the same facts every ten minutes, as if he were meeting her for the first time. The story she most liked to hear him tell was how her town got the name Croix-des-Bouquets. "There's a curse of violence that constantly looms over this place. It's from long before Croix-des-Bouquets was the famous place that allowed the slaves to seize Port-au-Prince during the Revolution because of how they massacred the French. There was a famous battle fought right here. However, long before that, it was the cradle of secret societies. Open your eyes and see. Wives go missing. Husbands die young. The curse I'm talking about is from a love affair that ended with a cross and a bouquet by the side of the old road at the onset of colonialism. This is how people came to know and name the town. There was a cross by the side of a road from Port-au-Prince. This cross was surrounded by a bouquet of flowers that never died. It marks the body of a beloved, unjustly killed lover."

She never challenged Pierre-Paul's assertion that the town grew from a foot-carved path from Port-au-Prince to a vibrant small town where centuries later the Duvaliers had built a lavish ranch. Pierre-Paul would gloat and say, "This ranch also fell under the curse."

Pierre-Paul also loved to have her clean his guns and taught her how to hold them. He was surprised at how naturally it came to her. She could now shoot a bird from a hundred feet.

However, right now what concerned Moah was that she couldn't stop playing visions of that half-dead man's pubic hair in her head. She was sure that those visions would keep her away from her retired priest, Father John, who never returned to Grand Marais, Minnesota, where he was from and of which he talked extensively. He no longer attended mass at Our Lady of the Rosary either. He spent his days gossiping and playing bezig. When she picked up his laundry for washing, she would have to ignore the dollar that he always forgot in his pants pocket, and which she always replaced with a pair of her unwashed underwear.

Moah was completely turned off from sex after looking at that half-dead man. The sight of the man's limp, grayish, flaky, peeling penis fixed itself in her brain. Over and over she saw the maggots crawling around his pubic area. At that moment, she could have just joined a convent.

Later and for the remainder of the day, Haba stayed in bed with a headache and a mild fever. Soon after she had sent Moah to the garden to collect leaves, Haba's best friend, her cousin Clotide—whom she called Titide—flung the door of the one-room house open. Clotide's voice was the perfect match for her flamboyant personality. Her dark brown flesh jiggled under her orange muumuu with bold yellow sunflowers. Moah crouched under the window, waiting to hear what the two women would say as they lay next to each other, chatting in Haba's bed.

"Come on, Haba. You have to talk about it. They found him hugging a dead dog, his only friend since they let him out of jail three years ago."

"Three years ago? He's been out for three years? Where's he been?" Haba turned onto her back to look at Clotide's face.

"They say mostly roaming around like a lost soul. You wouldn't know that now. Within two hours, Lamercie had found out and sent her people to collect him from the side of the road where he and his dog had been dumped. She's totally cleaned him up. Two of the girls who serve under her told me they saw him and he looks great. I guess Lamercie finally got to him. I guess, judging by his state, her magic worked. It's like a second Lazarus."

"That stuff's all bullshit. She's got no more power than the fart I'm about to lay if you don't leave me alone."

Clotide reached over Haba's head to the makeshift table where there was a pail of water. She grabbed the cloth, squeezed it, and wiped her cousin's face with it.

"It's been sixteen years since the incident and thirteen of those he spent in jail and you still can't forgive him?"

"Forgiveness is not for the giving; the offender has to earn it."

Haba tried to do what she usually did when she was in church. She tried to block out her surroundings and visualize God. Everyone saw her as a devout person. Last week Sister Imadresse stopped her after church to tell her how serene she looked during mass and asked her if she ever saw God during her peaceful moments.

Haba attended three services a day if they had them. But people had no idea that church was where she went to curse God. She knew for sure that God would be in church and he couldn't avoid her there; so she went religiously. In her mind she'd called him all the bad words she knew at least a thousand times. She spent days making up words and thinking of bad thoughts to throw at God.

"I heard he named the dog after you, Habakkuk."

"He should thank the missionary who convinced my illiterate mother to accept that ugly name in exchange for a bowl of food."

"Haba, don't be so mean. I heard he really loved that dog. He used to save the scraps of cornmeal they gave him and feed the dog through the hole in the wall of his cell. And the dog never left his side. That's loyalty."

"Something he knows nothing about."

"You can't blame the man. They arrested him and didn't even give him a trial."

"Titide, if you came to torture me, it's working."

"Okay, answer me this one question and I'll go away."

Haba lifted the compress from her head to look at Titide's round, brown face.

"Tell me: when you saw him, didn't your heart beat faster? Didn't your knees go weak even though he was completely filthy?"

It was a question she wasn't ready to answer. Titide hovered over her waiting. Moah stooped closer to the window to hear, but Haba didn't answer it for fear it would unleash all the feelings she had locked away for sixteen years. She couldn't stop her mind from going to those days that she had folded away. She'd folded them the way a widow folds a shirt or a pair of pants previously owned by her dearly departed.

She tried everything to keep her mind still, but it was like a raging bull, charging and pushing to let the memories flood over her body. Her mind went back to the first summer of nursing school. She had been unable to pay the tuition and had returned home to Croix-des-Bouquets from Port-au-Prince. At that time, she had been hoping the Church would help her go back. At that time, Father John from Grand Marais, Minnesota, was young and committed to educating the people, so he told her to come work at the dispensaire, the community health center that the white missionaries had built. At that time, it was the only hospital-like establishment in Croix-des-Bouquets. That's where she'd met Colin Didier. She hadn't known anything about him except that he had been sent to medical school in Cuba and he had actually returned. He spoke Spanish and French with as much ease as Creole, but when he spoke Creole, there was a song in his voice. His words dragged—an indication that he was not from

La Plaine. He was from the North where people didn't speak Creole; they sang Creole.

Now she was remembering the perspiration that rolled behind her ears as she assisted him in cleaning the gunshot wound of a "troublemaker" brought to the clinic. In those days, the less you knew about someone's injury, the better. The three hundred and ninety-two days that followed proved to be sweeter than icing on cake. There were stolen kisses and fondling in the storage depot. She danced for him in the river as water rolled over her body. Afterward, he wrote her a poem and the first line said, *Dieu sourit quand l'africaine danse.* God smiles when a black girl dances. She remembered the kisses on her toes. He borrowed words from that golden-tongued bard Francis Cabrel to serenade her with his guitar. Indeed, he drew from the wells of her eyes to write love letters. Then there was the way he made love to her breasts. He wanted to wait until they were married to penetrate her. But each day they came closer and closer, until they couldn't wait anymore, and like a deluge they drowned in the rhythm of each other's body.

Then one evening, on day three hundred eighty-nine, she sat on her veranda shelling Congo peas with her then pregnant sister-in-law Mimose, and God let the world step on her throat. Her brother had been on a two-month contract to cut sugarcane in the Dominican Republic. That night, a woman dressed all in purple, with enough jewelry to sink a ship, accompanied by two men stood at the gate about ten feet from the veranda.

"Is this where a certain Habakkuk lives?"

Haba's heart skipped. Very few people knew her real name. Outside of family—her brother, sister-in-law, her cousin Clotide, two aunts in Port-au-Prince and their five children—

only Colin knew. She wondered if something had happened to him. She put the pan down and went to open the gate. The woman and her entourage entered.

"Would you like some coffee or water, miss?"

"Madame Lamercie Didier," the woman said, with emphasis on the last name. "And no, thank you for offering. I don't intend to stay long. I just wanted to see what the slut who refuses to leave my husband alone looks like."

Haba felt faint and grabbed on to the post closest to her. Mimose dropped the pan and came to stand next to her.

The woman continued: "Be careful. I made him. I sent him to medical school for my purposes. No small-town tramp is going to take him from me. Back off. I hear he proposed to you. Be careful or the dress you marry him will be the dress you're buried in."

Haba stayed home and refused to return to nursing school even after Father John had found two months' tuition for her. By that time, she knew she was pregnant. The torture didn't end with Mrs. Lamercie's threats. There were dead animals found in her yard. A snake in her bed.

Colin didn't let up either. Every night he played a new song at her gate. She would go outside and throw rocks at him. Once she hit him on the head. He simply kneeled and asked her to do it again. He even brought more rocks for her to hit him with, but she couldn't do it. She fell into his arms and they were both wracked with sobs not knowing what to do.

Then, on day three hundred ninety two, while Haba, still in her first trimester, was napping and her sister-in-law was in her last days, a little girl brought a plate of food from Mimose's aunt who sold at the market. Mimose couldn't resist. After eating this food intended for Haba, Mimose spent two days throwing up blood and she became so dehydrated that the baby couldn't be saved. The young girl who had brought the food was never located.

One evening soon thereafter, Lamercie walked past the front of the house and sang a song that made Haba's brother Jules run after her with his machete. It took about eight people to peel him off of her.

"You've signed your death certificate," Lamercie had said. The next night, in front of Our Lady of the Rosary, in front of the usual joke-seeking crowd, Colin announced that Lamercie was not his wife and asked Jules for Haba's hand in marriage. Jules, his head and heart numb, accepted. The next day, Father John conducted the ceremony. Haba moved into the one-room apartment he had rented above the clinic. They were going to stay there until the baby was born and then move to Léogâne where he had received a position at a new hospital.

Then, one night, there was an emergency he had to attend to, and he didn't return. The next day, the police paraded him up rue Stenio Vincent en route to the jail for booking. Even before he had reached the destination, people were whispering that the police had found him next to the dead body of a thirteen-year-old girl. The police said that the child had been raped. Haba didn't dare show up at the jail and they sent him straight to Port-au-Prince, which had a jail fit only for the devil. This had all taken place sixteen years ago, but it felt to Haba like it happened yesterday.

In the days following her encounter with the half-dead, filth-ridden Colin, he came to Haba the way thread comes through the eye of a needle. Every shadow and scurrying animal was Colin. She wondered if he would come seeking her. As Clotide liked to remind her, "You are still his bona fide wife."

After two months of jumping at every noise outside of her house and running from shadows, Haba finally started to relax. She returned to her gardening and even resumed tutoring the neighborhood children in her home, as she had been doing for several years.

One day after a particularly hard-headed third-grader left, Haba was reviewing her notes for the next student when a pair of shiny brown shoes appeared in front of her. Slowly, her eyes climbed up the beige pants to the matching linen shirt tucked in by a belt of that same reddish-brown tone as the shoes. Her gaze froze there because she knew what the head looked like.

Colin lifted her chin so softly that she couldn't pull away. Slowly, he dropped down and kneeled in front of her. Their foreheads touched the way they used to. They remained in this position for a great while—just drinking in one another.

Once inside, their bodies spoke an inexplicable language that only they could explain. It apologized. It told of the aches, the yearnings, the angers that had built up over the years. It screamed of joy and forgiveness. It was a rhythmic dance that Haba imagined would make God smile.

That same afternoon, after school, as Moah rounded the corner of rue Stenio Vincent, cut through the closed toy factory, now a soccer field, and pranced the hundred yards to her fence, she bumped into Tiboguy. He was somebody's child. Somebody with a lot of children but no one could really remember who. He ate at any "aunty's" house, anyone who would feed him for whatever chore they needed done. His stomach protruded over his dingy Superman underwear which he was too old to wear.

"Seems like your auntie's husband has come home to see her."

"Mind your own business, Tiboguy. How do you know all this?"

"I saw him there on his knees making love faces."

"Get out of here or I'll beat you to a pulp."

Tiboguy ran. At a safe distance, he spread his butt cheeks at her. Moah pretended to chase after him, but when he had gained a good distance, she took the footpath behind the marketplace and headed for Pierre-Paul's house.

She found him on his veranda, in his green rocking chair.

"Moah, Mo pa mwen, why are you so beautiful? You just want to break an old man's heart, make me wish I could be thirty years younger."

"You were never young. Why would you want to be young, old man? Where's the pail? I want to give you a foot bath."

"You know where—under the bed. The leaf vendor brought some nice, fresh medicinal leaves. They are on top of the table. Use those cause I've got a lot of swelling today."

Moah went straight for his drawer. She knew he kept money there. Lots of money. There were medals, gold, jewelry, and two old guns. She knew he would not miss anything. She took what she needed and quickly grabbed the bucket.

"Today, I've got a story for you. This is going to make you believe the curse of Croix-des-Bouquets."

"Does it involve you?" she asked.

"No, put this picture in your mind. It's the heyday of the Duvalier regime, when we were flirting with Cuba and the United States acted like a married man whose mistress was cheating on him. The political air was intense. Many young men had gone to study medicine in Cuba. There was a brilliant young guy who grew up a few blocks from here. His mother was of questionable vocation and thus no one knew his father. He was handsome and smart, so, like we do here in Haiti, he became everybody's child. When he was about fifteen or sixteen, his mother died. He was taken in by the manbo next door."

"Wait a minute, does this boy have a name?'

"Yes, he does, but it doesn't matter because this is your story, my story, our story. He was about twenty when I heard that the manbo married him to Èzili. He became the groom of Èzili. Whether he knew or understood the implication, I'm not sure, because he fell head over heels in love with a local girl. She was nice. She had been sent to Port-au-Prince to study nursing, but once she fell in love with the boy, she never gave nursing another thought. The boy made a fatal mistake and married her. The manbo became raving mad. She killed the girl's brother, sister-in-law, and their unborn baby. Then one day soon after, in the manbo's compound, a young girl was raped and killed. Even though the young doctor was nowhere near the girl or the site, the police arrested him. He spent sixteen years away from the woman he loved and his baby daughter. Finally one day, he finds his way back to her. The manbo found out and killed them both."

"This happened in Croix-des-Bouquets?"

"No, this is *happening* in Croix-des-Bouquets."

"This is the best story you've ever told me." Moah worked methodically as she nursed Pierre-Paul's swollen limbs.

Everyone knew that Lamercie was going to kill Colin and Haba. She left her compound, machete in hand, her large blue dress flapping in the wind. At first it was the neighborhood kids who followed her. Then the neighborhood gossips. Pretty soon, all of those who lived in the bouk with nothing to do followed her past the cemetery. They followed her past Our Lady of the Rosary, Charlotin, and onto the busy rue

Stenio Vincent. She cut through the yard of the old abandoned factory. By the time she got to the front gate of her destination, she was a woman possessed. She pounded on the half wall that held the makeshift gate. She trampled the patch of wild flowers struggling to hold on to the undernourished soil. Somehow, through it all, she heard the clicking of a gun. The crowd looked up.

Some will say that she wore her hat crookedly like some cowboy out of an old western movie. Some will say that Lamercie raised the machete intending to fling it at her. But everyone saw Moah raise the old gun and shoot straight for Lamercie's heart. Everyone gawked as Lamercie thrashed like a chicken at a Vodou ceremony. Six of Pierre-Paul's old bullets had penetrated her blue-clad body.

A week later, two gentlemen with serious looks on their faces claimed they had heard about some gunshots and had come to investigate.

"I was shooting birds," Moah said. They paused; looked at her pretty face and her perky breast peeking from her sundress. Then they commented on how beautiful and tall the flowers next to the gate were. The flowers and a small cross had been planted over a tall mound at the gate. Although the men had long legs, they almost trampled the mound and its flowers when they tried to enter the yard. As they left, one of them kept repeating, "My, how do you grow such lovely flowers?" Moah simply smiled.

The police canvassed the neighborhood looking for witnesses who might know something about why Lamercie had vanished. No one had seen anything or knew anything. But everyone agreed with the officers that the flowers at the Didier family's gate were the prettiest they'd ever seen in Croix-des-Bouquets.

THE LEOPARD OF TI MORNE

BY MARK KURLANSKY

Gonaïves

I zzy Goldstein felt in his heart that he was really Haitian, although no one who knew him understood why he felt that way.

"Izzy, you're Jewish," his mother would say with sorrow showing on her brow as she examined the Vodou artifacts displayed in his Miami Beach apartment. He had a particular affection for Damballah, the snake spirit, and there were steel sculptures, beaded flags, and bright acrylic-on-masonite paintings of snakes. He had thought of getting a terrarium and keeping actual snakes, but then there would be the responsibility of feeding them.

His original connection with Damballah began when he became convinced the spirit was Jewish. True, he was a lwa of Haitian Vodou and of African origin, but when not a snake he was often portrayed as Moses, and there were several richly colored chromolithographs of Moses holding the Ten Commandments on Izzy's wall that he had bought in Little Haiti. This was little comfort to his mother since Moses was shown with horns. But even worse, from his mother's point of view, was the other Damballah poster in which he was depicted as St. Patrick dressed like a Catholic cardinal with a Celtic cross and snakes at his feet.

Izzy argued that the name Damballah ended with an "h" and that Creole words never have a final "h." Hebrew words, on the other hand, frequently do. His mother did not find this argument convincing. He also had an ason, a gourd covered with a net of snake vertebrae, that he had bought in Little Haiti too, and had the habit of shaking it when making a particular point, to the general annoyance of friends and family. Also in his apartment was a picture of an admiral. This was in fact Agwe, who Goldstein tried to consult regularly because he was in charge of the sea. The sea was important in Izzy's life. He had learned to sail in small boats handling a mainsail and a jib across Biscayne Bay, running to a causeway just so he could go beating in the wind to the other end of the bay. He tried to get away from the sea by going to college in Wisconsin, but after three semesters he dropped out and joined the merchant marines and spent five years on freighters across the Atlantic.

Five years of that was enough, and he was back in Miami trying to find a direction for his life.

Damballah offered fertility, rain, and wisdom. Yet it was only the last of these that interested Izzy Goldstein. Back in Miami he kept reading about Haiti. Then he started to go to Little Haiti, eat griyo, fried pork, and bannann peze in the restaurants and learn about Vodou. He even started going to ceremonies late at night. He wanted to be possessed by a lwa. He wanted Damballah but would have accepted whichever one took him. Only it reminded him of that period before his bar mitzvah when he would wrap himself in his tallis, close his eyes, and bob his body up in down in rhythmic rapture as he recited ancient Hebrew and Aramaic, languages—to be honest—he understood even less than he did Haitian Creole. But no matter how hard he had tried, the Hebrew God did not stir within him, and now, neither did the lwas.

At the lunches in the little restaurants, at the late-night

ceremonies, at the clubs where groups played konpa and merengue and the people danced so perfectly while hardly moving at all, he asked, *What can I do for Haiti?*

No idea came to him. There was no wisdom from Damballah. The lwas were as silent as Yahweh. Until one day . . .

A 110-foot rusted Honduran freighter was for sale for so cheap that he could buy it with the money he had saved from the merchant marines, with enough left over for the repairs. The engine only needed a little work, which he could do himself, the shaft was straight, the screw was almost new, and he only had to spend a small amount on scraping and repairing the hull. A forward pump needed a little work. And then Izzy Goldstein was captain of a freighter.

He was going to name it *Damballah*, but then a better idea came to him in Little Haiti on a block of two-story yellow buildings shining hot in the Florida sun. He could form an organization that brought relief to Haiti on his freighter. What kind of relief? Doctors? Medicine? Food? Tools? What should he bring them? He went to the Jeremie, a little bar where he could find his friend DeeDee.

DeeDee, whose real name was Dieudonné, was a light-skinned Haitian with graying hair. He kept moving back to Haiti and then back to Miami, back and forth as regimes changed and he was in or out of favor. DeeDee took him to a lawyer in a gleaming white office on Brickell Avenue. The lawyer's name was Smith. He was tall and lean and had his hair slicked back in that way that had become fashionable for men with that kind of straight hair. He was from the rare group known in Miami as Anglos. This was a negative grouping. If you did not speak Spanish and you weren't black and you weren't Haitian and you weren't Jewish, you were an Anglo. Smith wore powder blue–striped seersucker and this worried Izzy. He never trusted men who wore seersucker suits. Izzy was surprised that a lawyer who specialized in Haitian clients would have such a luxurious office, but whatever reservations he had about the lawyer were laid to rest when he told Izzy that he was not going to charge him. "I'll just do it for Haiti."

Wasn't that wonderful? The lawyer showed him how to establish a nonprofit organization with tax-exempt status and a fund-raising program. Izzy called his organization National Assistance for a New Haiti and had the letters *NANH* painted on the hull of his freighter. Haitians pronounced it like the Creole word *nen*, which means *dwarf* and made them laugh, but Izzy Goldstein didn't know anything about that.

What he did know was that thousands of dollars from concerned Americans were contributed to NANH, and with that money DeeDee loaded the freighter at night. He said it was too hot during the day. When they were set to leave, Izzy was surprised to see his deck stacked high with used cars, bicycles, and even a few Coca-Cola vending machines.

"I don't know, DeeDee. Is this the kind of stuff they need in Haiti?"

"They need everything in Haiti," the man replied with a big sweep of his arms. "Even bicycles."

"But shouldn't we bring medicine?"

"We are gonna do that too. But you have to be careful with medicine."

"How do you mean?"

"Not everybody is happy to see white people come with medicine." Izzy looked worried; he didn't like being reminded of his color. "We will go to Ti Morne Joli and Madame Dumas will explain everything, man," added DeeDee with a reassuring smile. The lawyer had talked about Madame Dumas too. She was going to be important for NANH.

They pulled up the anchor and made their way around the curve of the Miami River into the bay Izzy had always loved, and set a course for Gonaïves, Haiti. In the pilothouse, Izzy Goldstein was too excited to sleep. Help for Haiti was on the way.

When Haitians die, it is Agwe's work to carry them across the ocean back to Africa. But Agwe didn't always have to do this work. In ancient times, when Haiti was still connected to Africa, life was much easier for Agwe and, in fact, for all the old lwas. In those days, all the lwas and all the animals of Africa could easily walk to and from Haiti. Haiti had lions and elephants and tigers and giraffes and leopards. The forests were thick with vegetation and the tree branches were heavy with every kind of fruit. But that was in the old days.

Gonaïves looked white under the hot sun with a black sky behind it filled with rain that would not fall. It was even hot at sea, and it got hotter as they approached the stone and cinder-block ramparts.

The quay below was chaos. There were trucks and cars, but mostly large handcarts and children chasing them, hoping for something that dropped. The port official boarded and Izzy Goldstein told him it was "the *NANH* from Miami," and the official, hearing "the nen from Miami," smiled. Izzy supposed that the man was laughing at his French. The official said something in Creole and Izzy looked confused, and then the man said in very good English, "How much are you gonna pay to dock here?"

DeeDee took over and Izzy was led by a deckhand down to the crowd, and in the middle of it he was introduced to the most beautiful man he had ever seen. Jobo was tall, broad-shouldered, lean, and muscular, and his skin had the satiny luster of burnished wood, perhaps a very dark walnut. He escorted Izzy to a polished white Mercedes that clearly did not belong there in the ramshackle port.

Jobo seemed a pleasant young man, there was a sweetness to him, but when he sat in the driver's seat and turned the key, he was transformed. With his fist he pounded ferocious blasts of the car horn and left no doubt that anyone in his way would soon be under his tires. The crowd parted and they were on their way, climbing only slightly as they left the steamy dilapidated city and entered the last green village on the edge of a bone-colored Saharan landscape that rolled on and on like a sea.

Again Jobo honked the horn insistently in front of an iron gate, which, to the great excitement of Izzy, was fashioned into a swarm of black metal snakes. A boy appeared, and with every ounce of his small body managed to push the gate open. They entered a lush tropical world of ponds and fountains and green and orange broad-leafed plants and drooping magenta bougainvillea and coral-colored hibiscus sticking out their tongues suggestively. Rising above this forest were high-pitched roofs and wide balconies.

They got out of the vehicle and stepped up to a wide, high-ceilinged porch with a tiled floor and large potted plants. Between two lazy banana bushes was a tall cage about two yards square. Inside was a leopard, lean with angry yellow eyes and ears cocked back and fur like silken fabric in black and rust and ocher. The cat was pacing back and forth, as though exercising to keep in shape. But Izzy couldn't help thinking about himself. He was hoping someone was about to offer him a tall, cold drink.

* * *

*When Haiti was sent away, many of the lwas—including Damball-
lah, Èzili, Legba, and Agwe—went as well, but most of the animals stayed in Africa. However, the goddess of love, Èzili Freda,
kept one leopard because she could not resist beautiful things. She
wanted to keep the leopard the same way that she kept closets full
of beautiful dresses and fine jewelry. The leopard tried to run away,
so she kept it in a pink-jeweled cage.*

Jobo ushered Izzy inside, holding open a large glass door that
did not fit with the rest of the house. Izzy's body instantly
hardened to a tense knot. It was as though he had walked into
a refrigerator, possibly a freezer. He was not sure but thought
he saw traces of vapor from his breath. A furry red creature
glided toward him speaking the same formal and emotionless
French of his ninth grade teacher who had always called him
Pierre because she said there was no way to say Izzy in French.

"Bonjour, bienvenue. Comment allez-vous?" she said with
a smile made of wood. She was wrapped in a thick red fox
coat. Her body stuck out at angles, a hard thin body. Her
straightened black hair was swept up on her head. She wore
shiny dark-purple lip gloss with an even darker liner. Her
green eyes were also traced in black, which matched the carefully painted polish on her long nails filed to severe points. All
this dark ornamentation on her gaunt face made her skin look
pale with a flat finish, like gray cardboard.

On one finger was a very large emerald that was close to
matching her eyes, and when she held her long hand to her
face, the stone appeared to be a third eye. She would have
been attractive except that everything about her seemed hard.
Even her face was boney. Maybe, Izzy thought, she understood
this and wore the fur to try to appear softer.

She turned to Jobo and ordered him in French to fetch a

cold bottle, which was exactly what Izzy wanted to hear. To Izzy it seemed odd—here he was, trying to learn Creole—that a Haitian would speak to another in French, even though Jobo answered only in Creole. Izzy soon realized that she also spoke nearly perfect American English. So who was the French for? Even when she spoke English, she punctuated everything with "N'est-ce pas?"

Jobo returned with two very long crystal champagne flutes and a bottle of champagne, which he opened with the craftsmanship of a well-trained wine steward. It was cold and bubbly with a flush of rose like the blush on her protruding cheekbones, though probably more natural.

"Pink champagne, n'est-ce pas?" she said. "Don't you love pink champagne?"

"Èzili's drink," said Izzy, who knew that the goddess loves luxury and her favorite color is pink. The smile flew off her face like a popped button, leaving Izzy to wonder what he had said that was wrong.

She offered him a building near the port that he could use as the NANH warehouse, although when he said "NANH warehouse," she smiled. She could also provide a staff for distribution of the goods he brought in so that he simply had to bring them in and the rest would be taken care of. She asked nothing for this service, simply explaining, "I am Haitian and I love my people." He was moved but he thought he detected a certain angry glow in Jobo's eyes while she was speaking.

"All I ask, mon cher . . ." She paused and he thought maybe she was going to ask about aid to a favorite cause. Which in fact may have been the case. "Gasoline, N'est-ce pas?"

"Gasoline?"

"Mais, oui. Beaucoup, beaucoup. I will tell you how many barrels."

"But, ah, Madame Dumas?" He was now so cold his teeth were chattering.

"Oui," she said softly like a kiss.

"How do I justify spending relief money like that?"

"Ah-bas, c'est tout correct, n'est-ce pas. It is an operating expense, n'est-ce pas? It's for my generators," and she moved her green eyes across the ceiling. "This takes a lot of gasoline, n'est-ce pas? And then there are the freezers for the meat, n'est-ce pas?"

He supposed that she was keeping meat for the village and that would be a worthwhile thing to subsidize. Far safer than leaving meat out in this tropical heat. Although you could keep food fresh forever in this living room.

"As a matter of fact, I am going to buy a freezer compartment for your ship. You can bring down meat."

"That is a wonderful idea. Put some protein in people's diets."

"Eh, oui," she replied in a distant philosophical tone. "Jobo, this reminds me. Feeding time." And then she said something in Creole that Izzy didn't grasp, though it sounded like a comment about Jobo's shirt, which he then removed as he went out into the heat. She smiled at Izzy and added, "He is too beautiful for clothes, n'est-ce pas?"

Izzy nodded, unsure of how to answer.

"So it's all arranged. My man is paying them off so you can unload right now"

"Paying the . . . ?"

"All taken care of," she said merrily, with a gesture like washing her hands. He was informed that he would be staying in Madame's house, which he did not feel entirely comfortable about, but he had no other ideas of where to stay.

He was put in a room just as cold, with carved wooden panels and a ceiling fan for which there was no real use. Evidently the air-conditioning could not be turned down or off, and the windows did not open. But the bed was equipped with fluffy goose-down quilts imported from Austria.

Izzy went outside to warm up. Jobo, with a large ring holding many keys, was coming from a wooden shed with a package. He stepped up to the porch and over to the leopard cage. He unwrapped the package and took out what looked like two sirloin steaks. Izzy assumed he was mistaken about the cut, but the steaks were nicely marbled. All the while the leopard paced, stopping only for a second to snarl. The animal was dangerous and Izzy could see claw marks—parallel lines on both sides of Jobo's shirtless back.

"Jobo, is there some kind of a ceremony I can see?"

Jobo showed a sweet smile. "You want to see some real Vodou?"

"Yes, exactly."

"I can arrange it, but it koute chè."

"How expensive?"

"Anpil. Anpil. I will take you to Kola."

"Kola is the ougan?

"He's a bòkò. He can fix it. I'll go talk to him now." And with that, shirtless and with claw marks showing, he walked down the driveway and out the gate of iron snakes.

Izzy sat on the porch watching the incessant pacing of the leopard. The cat had one of the steaks in his mouth but he didn't stop moving, not even to eat. Izzy thought about the Vodou priest named Kola. Did "kola" mean a line? A queue? It must mean something.

The leopard pleaded with Agwe that he did not want to be locked in a cage and asked to be taken back to Africa. But Agwe said, "I can only take spirits back after they die."

"Then kill me. I want to go back," said the leopard.

Haitians like nicknames. Dieudonné was DeeDee. Ti Morne Joli was always called Joli. Madame Dumas was Lechat, the bòkò was Kola, Jobo was Beau. And Izzy? Everyone in Joli called him Blan.

"What is this blan up to ?" asked Kola, a short stocky man with a powerful body, shirtless like Jobo, sitting under a leafy tree, on the stripped-bare engine block of a long-dead car. All the other parts had been sold and someday the block would be too. He dug in the earth with a trawl and pulled out two small green Coca-Cola bottles, felt them to see if the ground had kept them cool, dusted them off with his thick but skilled fingers, and handed one to Jobo.

Jobo smiled. "What do blans want? He wants a Vodou ceremony."

"A Vodou ceremony?" Kola had a wide toothy smile. He rubbed his stomach. He was proud of his belly because he was the only one in Joli who had one. "San dola. Tell him there is a nice ceremony for a hundred dollars. For one-fifty I can show him something special."

Jobo nodded.

"But what does this blan want? Is he bringing blan doctors and their medicines?"

"No, I don't think so. But I wanted to talk to you about your medicines."

"You need a powder?" asked Kola.

Jobo looked at the ground and shook his head.

"Do you have money for my powders? What do you need? A rash, a headache, a fever, the stomach? What would you like to do?"

"You know my aunt's baby died today?"

"I know."

"Do you know how much meat Madame Lechat has? Do you know? Anpil, anpil. Three big freezers. It all goes to that cat. If she died, everyone in Joli could eat meat for three weeks."

"Yes, but for a great lady like that, that koute chè. Do you have that money?"

"No. But if I did, you could help me?"

"It would cost less to kill the leopard. Then she wouldn't need the meat. Maybe you could take it."

"I don't just want the meat."

"What do you want?"

"M vle jistis."

"Ah, justice. Justice costs. Justice is very expensive."

Izzy was pacing the porch, almost the same strides as the leopard, though he didn't realize it. Something about that animal made him restless. That and an occasional harsh cry from upstairs. "Jobo! Jobo!" Finally, she came downstairs and out onto the porch. The light from inside was shining on her. She was wearing a long silk shift and he could see that there was no shape to her body—just long and thin. He also saw through what was left of the makeup that she was a bit older than he had first thought.

"Have you seen Jobo?"

"He went to the ougan to arrange a ceremony for me."

"The oun . . . ?"

"Kola?"

"Ah, the bòkò, Kola." Then her green eyes darted past him. It was Jobo coming back. Izzy sensed that he should retreat to the other end of the long tiled porch.

"Jobo," she called out. "Jobo, viens ici. Viens." She spoke

in that melodious high pitch used by Frenchwomen when calling their pets.

And he did come, and she put her arms around him, her cardboard gray hands looking bright against his dark back as she dug her black-polished nails into his skin.

"DeeDee, can you help me?" asked Jobo.

"What do you need?"

"Money."

DeeDee laughed.

"I need to pay for something very expensive. Just one time I need some money. I can work."

"Why don't you ask the blan?"

"This is not the blan's business."

DeeDee understood and told him that he was loading a shipment of mangoes on the NANH late that night.

"I'm not sure I can get away at night."

"Late-late. I am paying very well for this particular shipment—of mangoes. Give her a lot of champagne."

"Mais oui."

DeeDee paid off all the port officials with money from Madame Dumas and the NANH untied and set her bow northwest to round the peninsula and head to Miami. The mangoes helped the ballast but the freighter was still sitting a little too high in the water. They had to hope there were no storms. Izzy was surprised when he inspected that the mangoes were just piled in the hold without any crates. "It will take forever to off-load," he complained. DeeDee shrugged.

Then Izzy noticed they were off course, but DeeDee explained that they had to make a quick stop.

"To take on more ballast?" asked Izzy.

There was no answer, but DeeDee was busy navigating. They dropped anchor by a reef—a strip of white sand and a grove of palm trees in the middle of the turquoise sea. Izzy saw nothing heavy to load on the boat.

Then the crew lifted the cover off the hold and Izzy was astounded by what he saw next. Haitian men and women, one child of about eight, under the yellow mangoes. They staggered up, their limbs stiff and their eyes blinded by the hot light. Some were almost naked. They were hurriedly helped to the beach on their shaky legs. There were eleven of them, including three who were dragged and appeared to be dead.

Shouting erupted in Creole. Arms flayed the hot air angrily. They were saying, "This is not Miami! You took our money!" Some pleaded, "Please, don't leave us." But DeeDee insisted that this boat was too big to bring them in and that small boats would come tonight to drop them on the Florida coast.

Izzy was angry and fought with DeeDee all the way to Florida. DeeDee's answers made no sense to him.

"Why are we doing this?"

"Because we can't bring them into Miami."

"Why were we carrying them at all?"

"They needed the help, Izzy."

"I have to tell the Coast Guard. They'll starve in that place."

"No. It's all arranged. Boats will come for them tonight."

"They said they paid. Who got the money?"

"The mango growers."

They tied up on the Miami River. But they were not going to be able to return to Haiti: there was a coup d'etat. Little Haiti was intoxicated with the news. A new government was being formed. There were curfews. There was rioting in Port-au-Prince. In Gonaïves, a mob attacked the NANH warehouse, took everything, then tore down the building a chunk at a time with rocks and machetes. After a day, all that remained of the two-story building was a few steel reinforcing rods sticking out of the ground. DeeDee soon vanished and it was said in Little Haiti that he was now an official in the new government. Izzy hadn't realized he was involved in politics. He had never seemed interested in anything but commerce. Then a man approached Izzy one afternoon alongside his boat on the river. Izzy recognized him. He was usually in Bermuda shorts with an *I Love Miami* T-shirt, a Marlins hat, and a camera. But this day he was wearing a suit and showed Izzy something that said he was an FBI agent.

Kola had a new Coca-Cola cabinet. It was red-and-white metal with a glass door. A stray rock from the riot had dented one side but the door was intact.

Of course, it didn't keep anything cold because Kola had no electricity. But it was a good cabinet and he kept it behind the temple to store his bones, herbs, potions, and powders. His Coca-Cola was still in the ground where it was cool.

Soon Madame Dumas began experiencing something completely new to her. She started to sweat. Even in her air-conditioning she was sweating. It poured out of her forehead and ran down her fine cheekbones, and from under her arms a rivulet flowed to the small of her back; under her breasts, sweat soaked her stomach. Her pink silk shift had turned cranberry with wetness. And as the sweat poured out, she became weaker and weaker—while Jobo watched.

Madame Dumas collapsed on the living room floor and

crawled to the couch. She looked up at Jobo with her arm reaching out at him. "Jobo, aide-moi." Help me.

He only stared at her.

"I need a doctor."

"I can't get a doctor. The roads are closed. The coup."

"Oh, yes, the coup," she muttered, as though there was a secret irony to this that only she could appreciate. "Then the bòkò. Can't he make a powder to fix me?"

"Mais oui," Jobo answered, appreciating his own secret irony.

"Vas-y. Get something!"

Jobo left and did not come back for hours. When he did, Madame Dumas was not sweating anymore. She was stretched across the cool floor tiles—dead.

Jobo unceremoniously removed all her clothes and carried her out to the leopard cage. He opened the door and dumped her on the floor. The leopard, who he had not fed in three days, was so startled that he stopped pacing. He walked over to the body and sniffed it as Jobo started to close the cage. Suddenly, the cat leapt over Jobo, knocking him down, and off the porch into the bush, over the wall in graceful flight, and was never seen again. He might have run to the arid desert in the northwest and managed to find a way to survive there. Or maybe he ran along the Artibonite River to hide out in the mountains above the valley where many others have hidden.

The leopard had left Jobo with the question of what to do with the unwanted remains of Madame Dumas. He consulted Kola but neither could come up with a good solution. Several days later, while Jobo was still contemplating this dilemma, someone started clanging the locked gate. Jobo ran down and saw Kola framed in black iron snakes. He explained that Madame had a family that wanted both the house and the body.

They wanted to bury it in France, but Air France had suspended flights because of the coup.

"Eh oui," said Jobo, who had never seen an airplane close up, with feigned comprehension.

"Poutan!" shouted Kola, raising his stubby index finger to make a point. "I told them if they want to come get the body in a week or even two, I can use magic to keep it in perfect condition."

"Magic?"

"Mais oui. And you have that magic in your house. It is the magic of meat."

Now Jobo understood. "And they will pay?"

"Gwo nèg koute chè," Kola said. You have to pay a lot for an important person.

Jobo smiled. "Anpil, anpil dola?"

"Anpil. Very expensive."

After Kola left, Jobo went back to the cage and picked up Madame. She still had not stiffened much. He emptied one of the big top-loading freezers and dumped her in. She landed in a most undignified pose and was soon petrified in ice, to be thawed and served up properly by magic in due time.

Jobo was right. Once the freezers had been emptied, the people of Ti Morne Joli ate meat for three weeks. Many became sick because they were unaccustomed to such a rich diet. But it was not likely to happen again.

It was Damballah who finally confronted Èzili, bribed her with dresses and bracelets and pink elixirs until she set the leopard free. The animal ran and ran and ran, as though he could run all the way back to Africa. But the ocean was there now. He ran so hard that he turned into a man. That was the first Haitian, and that is why Haitian people always struggle so hard to be free.

* * *

"I want to talk to my lawyer," said Izzy.

"I think you need a new lawyer. He's been arrested. Seems you were just a small part of the operation."

Izzy thought, *They arrested the Anglo. Isn't that something? They got the Anglo.* Then he spoke: "Why do you say that the goods were stolen? Everything was paid for."

"We were watching you. What tipped us off was that you had Coca-Cola machines. You can't buy them. Only the Coca-Cola Company owns them. You're not the Coca-Cola Company, are you?"

THE BLUE HILL

BY Rodney Saint-Éloi

Ozanana

Translated by Nicole Ball

The stench of sulfur mixes with the reeking blue toxic trash that was dumped on the hill that January day. It has been named "the blue hill" ever since. Everyone is afraid to say who is responsible for this open gash in the earth that poisons everything and will, eventually, eat up the legs of children and rot the roots of plants, cause the dogs, the flies, and the fish to disappear. Even the mosquitoes won't survive.

Rumor has it that the garbage comes from a friendly country that has an overload of chemical refuse and needs to find generous neighbors who can house it for them. So far from God indeed. Proximity is sometimes a curse. That's how a dump like this came into our backyard. Except that at City Hall, under the pretext of us being the twin city of God-knows-where, they pocketed the cash that was exchanged for this so-called favor. On top of that, the military, the ministers, and the honorable members of the government have all made tons of money.

One fine Monday, at exactly noon, the ship, sailing under the friendly neighbor's flag, reached the harbor. The kids swam close to it, performed amazing pirouettes and somersaults, acrobatics meant to impress cruise ship tourists in the hope that the visitors would enthusiastically throw their pennies into the water. In no time at all, instead of being filled with generous tourists, the wharf was under military watch. The ship was full of guards with the faces of unleashed and trained dogs eager to stuff themselves with nigger meat. You could see battle dress, golden flashers, and a thousand boots of the Special Forces. On their heads were green berets and on their clean-shaven faces were plastered a kind of cynical seriousness, a conquering look of *What do I care about petty local squabbles?* They spoke sternly into their walkie-talkies, surely of matters of state. The seaside was promptly evacuated, with a huge deployment of troop vehicles whose sirens and tinted windows scared the locals. Trucks transported hundreds of suitcases up the hill. Shops and businesses were forced to close their doors. The chemical trash–dumping troops went around every street, every neighborhood, showing off their machine guns at every window. They imposed a curfew without warning. It was just a matter of military strategy, letting people know that they had taken over the city. So every mouth stayed quiet. Local men were rounded up and forced to work day and night for a whole week to burrow everything into the blue hill.

That blue dirt didn't look like the sky, the locals joked.

Soon, many residents became covered with blue pustules, large blue stinking marks. Lacerations invaded bodies. Slashes marked their faces. Gashes on their bellies.

Yes, it's the blue disease, brought to us by the fatra pwazon, they said. Forced to remain silent, the few doctors in the area couldn't give a name to that blue body-and-mind disease which was spreading as quickly as mad grass. They say it's a matter of national security, and that's why it's not being mentioned in the papers or on the radio.

Detective Simidor, whose local police duties had been immediately neutered by the invasion, refused to accept the curfew. Even though his massive, muscular physique hadn't been affected, he immediately began to feel his mind slipping. For one thing, he could not remember any specific moments from his past. Had he always been a bachelor locked up in a one-room house by the blue hill? Did he have a wife, children, who somehow never made it home? Was he a brother? An uncle? A nephew? Did he have a living mother? A father?

He hadn't slept since the blue invasion began. All he could think about was what he knew had once been a city—his city?—and the blue hill. How can the city defend itself, he wondered, when the people have barricaded themselves inside their homes, becoming accomplices of their own confinement, while peeking from behind their windows at the invading blue trash army? Watching the trucks full of blue chemicals being dumped on the hill by his countrymen, he felt like shouting out that the plot must not succeed. But it was already too late. He wanted to loudly preach to everyone, hammering the truth into them. Our cowardice is our suicide, he wanted to say. Our silence is our coffin. It seemed, however, that he would have to pursue this job of enlightening people singlehandedly. The next day he would go into the streets and declare to whoever was willing to listen that the ground was soiled and that everything had been contaminated, that they would have to yell to be heard, that they would have to move heaven and earth to shed light onto the graveyard the country has become.

Life on your knees is no life at all, he would say. Pito nou lèd nou la. What was the point of this horrible, stupid charade, clinging to the remnants of day-to-day existence, an absurd life, as absurd as the bright spots that once in a while made you think that light was awaiting us at the end of the tunnel?

Dragons now routinely walk on the sea, he would tell them. They unwrap their wings, their mouths of fire. In the mythical world from which these invaders and their blue trash have come, giant creatures swallow entire schools of flying fish and set ablaze incandescent beams that wipe shores clean. Millions of gallons of oil spew out of the core of the earth, from deep beneath the sea. A sign of the times: the end of the world is striding in. At the first ring of the church bells, the residents must not scurry off and seep into burrows under the sand like spider crabs, hiding their faces under seaweed flowers of transparent green.

Some of them, paralyzed with fear, are still hiding under their beds, reciting their rosaries, purring strange words in strange languages: God of Mercy, may our prayers be answered! And there are those who are stronger and pick things up: this one a chair, that one a mattress, that other one a bucket, and in the daytime, before the next curfew, they follow the path to the hills to take shelter on the mountainside. But what is the point? Despair is the only certainty here. If it doesn't kill you, they say, it will strengthen your veins, your muscles. Despair sticks to your skin; it's your sweat, and the air you breathe. Despair is second nature from which everyone draws the joy of laughter and resilience together, so we can go peacefully to cockfights, bet on the winning numbers at the lotto, and pretend that the crystal ball of luck is turning smoothly—but doom, like a valiant soldier, always comes hounding.

Apocalypse, Apocalypse, he would tell them. In the last days, dogs will not recognize bones. Sons will not recognize their mothers. Cats will think they are lions; birds will have beaks of fire; oceans will be large mouths of flame. The sky will sweep down on us like a vulture. The blue priests and their blue cassocks will come from everywhere, but they will be of no use.

Now sweating in his room behind the police station where he believes he has barricaded himself, Simidor fights the blue fever madness that has turned the entire town into blue-hill-digging zombies and thinks that perhaps it would help them come out of their blue fog if he told them the story of the little black saint named Santik Du.

Around the year 1350, a plague was terrorizing the country. Santik Du was living a life of hardship and charity. He went around barefoot in the hope of relieving the wounds of the sufferers. He promised them eternal life and solace. That is how Santik Du contracted the plague and died. Simidor would not make the same mistake—though he, like Santik Du, was on the side of humble people. He could not remember ever being a praying man. But this was finally something he could remember. He had learned the story of Santik Du at the school-required catechism, just like the rest of them. That is, those whose parents could afford to send them to school. Even those who hadn't learned this version of the story still knew to pray to Santik Du when they had small ailments: headaches, colds. They even prayed for compensation from petty thefts. Sometimes he would joke to them that Santik Du was making his job insignificant. Yes, he could still remember that. When someone loses something, all he has to do is say the Santik Du prayer: help me, Santik, to find my wallet and I will give you five pyas. And that's why you can find near the Virgin Mary, along with many written prayers, small bills wrapped in handkerchiefs, and a prayer specifically addressed to the black saint, gourds filled with offerings. Often, for lack of money, they will leave a mere piece of bread and a few peanuts. It's reassuring for the people to find a saint who resembles them for a change; Detective Simidor could maybe talk to the city's patron saint who fastened the rope of bad luck around the whole nation. Santik Du, help my people come out of the blue fog. Save me, too, who wants to save them. Don't let me die before I tell them all this. Don't let the fatra pwazon take over our brains before it kills us.

Simidor imagines himself as Santik Du on a crusade, making signs with his big cross: get rid of your superstitions, destroy your dolls of wax, get rid of your lwas, throw away your rituals and your damned souls in the morning ashes; throw away, brothers and sisters, the rogations of your gods and those holy pictures you worship. Throw away your stinking blue marks and pustules, the lacerations on your faces, the gashes on your bellies. The scent of the ylang-ylang tree, mixed with the smell of sulfur, will cure you, along with invocations of three-leaves, three-roots, three-drops of your tinctures. The dragons move forward a lot faster on the water, opening their mouths of fire once more, smashing up pirogues. They tread forward on the rough sea, flames tearing into the horizon. Time and again the stars turn off at the same moment as the kerosene lamps. The mountains swallow up the stars and the angry wind rises. The tree branches play lago, hide-and-seek, in a macabre clatter, the endless moaning of the dead. Windows turn into kites. Tin roofs fly from house to house. The waves come knocking madly on every door. The candelabra, lilac, and hibiscus fences are on their knees; the coconut trees creak and come crashing down with sharp noises.

Simidor imagines himself crossing the waters. He stretches out his hand as a sign of respect for Agwe, the god of the sea. He invokes Ogoun, the god of war.

Ogoun down wind

Down raging waves
Down down fire

Ogoun, he sings, we inhabit an isolated, pristine, gentle island with vegetation that escapes human comprehension. Rare species with names of flowers and trees that nobody knew existed. Before the blue hill, you could rest here in peace. There was nobody and nothing to bug you, no longing. We had named this place Ozanana, the new Promised Land. We sang the songs of the hills. Happiness was avoiding the anger of the gods. But what unites us now is the catastrophe of the blue hill, sings Simidor. Ozanana, the word must be repeated over and over again. For isn't it true that only words exist, and only words give shape and flesh to the universe?

Lying there dying from the blue fog that is killing everyone, Simidor wishes he could tell his compatriots to pay attention, for the last days seem to be coming nearer. Write down the spectacle of the last hour, he would say, record all the details. Chain all the demons that are inside of you and outside of you! Describe everything you feel. We will at least have the elegance to bear witness. Our words will have served as breviaries for the castaways if any of them survive. If you see a black lamb astray, do not kill it; show it the way to the caves that the gods tell us were our first homes. Show it the way to the trees that the gods tell us were our first places of worship. If you see a horse of fire being whipped, a big black horse, gallop with it and hold its bridle. If you spot a glorious knight, beg him to give up his armor, his wine, his wheat, and his crown. If, God forbid, you happen to touch the dying lamb with seven horns, the horse with golden eyes, or the knight with the shark head, the sun and the moon will come down over your head and their fire will burn you. Then you will know thunder, typhoons, volcanoes, earthquakes like you have never imagined.

In his mind, Simidor starts to play a barbaric opera, a funereal song that pierces the air with all the wrenching cries of those dying around him. The agony of the earth is beginning today. The roosters are singing their last cock-a-doodle-do before passing away under the demented clouds. The trumpets are sounding for the most beautiful women, the bravest men, the gentlest children. The trumpets bore through your ears, drill into your insides, and make your hair rise straight up on your head. That's when the beast with the thousand horns appears. It sets up its gigantic legs on the clouds, trampling down whatever is still on earth: limbs, faces, and human traces. The music swells in Simidor's head. The trumpets shiver, play a staccato that makes the stars fall. The sun, which feeds the belly of the garden, is fading. On that very day, what is said is done. The sun rolls over the river and dies abruptly of a stroke. Latibonit o! Even the sun cannot protect itself against death now. The sun is dying. Tell me, my friends, tell me, my comrades, how should I bury the sun?

Down, down, tongues of the men of this country! Simidor's delirium shouts. The beast with a thousand horns has overtaken me. Is that really his goddamned mouth of fire? Is it the Apocalypse? The coffin is swaying over the crowd like a tongue. The army has risen from the waters. The stench of blood and mud on the faces of the dying. The images loop by, immense, worse than in the nightmares of the darkest days. What can we do with these dragons? Why this fire, taking the shape of a huge rainbow? Why are these myths merging in my head?

Simidor rubs his eyes, turns to the other side of the bed and switches on the light for the last time. Is it day or night? The alarm clock says 4:53 p.m.

ABOUT THE CONTRIBUTORS

Jerome de Perlinghi

MADISON SMARTT BELL is the author of twelve novels and two story collections. In 2002, his novel *Doctor Sleep* was adapted as a film, *Close Your Eyes*. Bell's eighth novel, *All Souls' Rising*, the first volume in his Haitian Revolution trilogy, was a finalist for the 1995 National Book Award. *Toussaint Louverture: A Biography* appeared in 2007. Since 1984 he has taught at Goucher College, along with his wife, the poet Elizabeth Spires. He lives in Baltimore.

Jared McCallister

MARIE LILY CERAT is an educator and writer, and co-founder of the group Haitian Women for Haitian Refugees. Cerat has published a West African folktale in 1997; a commentary for NPR as part of the 2001 Conference on Racism in South Africa; and two essays in the Ten Speed Press book *Vodou: Visions and Voices of Haiti*. She is a contributor to *Haiti Liberté* and at work on a novel, *In the Light of Shooting Stars*.

Patrick Box

LOUIS-PHILIPPE DALEMBERT is a novelist, short story writer, poet, and essayist born in Port-au-Prince. His books have been awarded the Villa Médicis and Casa de las Américas prizes, and he has been honored with grants from DAAD in Germany and UNESCO-Aschberg in Israel. Since his departure from Haiti in 1986, Dalembert has lived in many cities, including Paris, Rome, Port-au-Prince again, Jerusalem, and Florence. He now lives in Berlin.

Jill Krementz

EDWIDGE DANTICAT was was born in Haiti and moved to the United States when she was twelve. She is the author of two novels, two collections of stories, three books for children and young adults, and three nonfiction titles. In 2009, she received a MacArthur Fellowship. Her most recent books are *Eight Days* and *Create Dangerously*.

Lorrie Jean-Louis

RODNEY SAINT-ÉLOI was born in Cavaillon, Haiti. He is a poet and memoirist, as well as the founder of Memoire d'encrier, a Montreal-based publishing house. His poetry collections include *Graffiti pour l'aurore (Graffiti for the Dawn)*, *Pierre anonymes (Anonymous Stones)*, and *J'ai un arbre dans ma pirogue (I Have a Tree in My Canoe)*. His memoir on the January 12, 2010 earthquake in Haiti, *Goudougoudou*, was published in France in the fall of 2010.

Nathalie Fievre Belizaire

M.J. FIEVRE'S short stories and poems have appeared in *P'an Ku*, *The Mom Egg*, *Healthy Stories*, *Writer's Digest*, *Caribbean Writer*, *Pocket Smut*, and *365 Days of Flash Fiction*. She is a regular contributor to the online publication the Nervous Breakdown and a contributing editor for *Vis.A.Vis* magazine. She is the founding editor of *Sliver of Stone* magazine.

Sylvia Plachy

MARK KURLANSKY has written twenty books of fiction, nonfiction, and children's books, and has translated a novel by Emile Zola. *Cod: A Biography of the Fish That Changed the World*, *Salt: A World History*, and *Nonviolence: The History of a Dangerous Idea* are among his best-known books. As a newspaper reporter, he covered Haiti and the Caribbean for eight years, and he continues to write on Caribbean themes.

Jacques Lenbart

YANICK LAHENS is the author of three short story collections, including *Tante Réisa et les dieux*, *La petite corruption*, and *La folie était venue avec la pluie*; and two award-winning novels, *Dans la maison du père* and *La couleur de l'aube*, which has been translated into Italian and German. Her next book, *Failles*, about the earthquake in Haiti, will be published in France in 2011. She lives and works in Haiti.

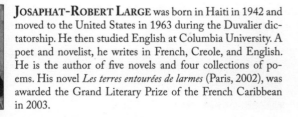

Herve Large

JOSAPHAT-ROBERT LARGE was born in Haiti in 1942 and moved to the United States in 1963 during the Duvalier dictatorship. He then studied English at Columbia University. A poet and novelist, he writes in French, Creole, and English. He is the author of five novels and four collections of poems. His novel *Les terres entourées de larmes* (Paris, 2002), was awarded the Grand Literary Prize of the French Caribbean in 2003.

Pascal Huee

KETTLY MARS was born in Port-au-Prince in 1958, and she started writing at the beginning of the 1990s. Since then, she has won two literary prizes and her work has been translated into English, Italian, Dutch, German, and Japanese. She is a member of the Prix Littéraire Henri Deschamps.

NADINE PINEDE is a graduate of Harvard University and was a Rhodes Scholar at Oxford University. She earned her PhD at Indiana University and is an Elizabeth George Foundation Scholar at the Whidbey Writers Workshop MFA program. Her writing has appeared in numerous publications, including the *New York Times, San Francisco Chronicle, Sampsonia Way, Radcliffe Quarterly, Literary Newsmakers, The Other Journal, A Lime Jewel,* and *Soundings Review.* She is working on a novel.

Jalene Tamerat-Sylvain

PATRICK SYLVAIN is a poet, writer, photographer, and social critic. He works as a Haitian-language and -culture instructor at Brown University. He has been published in numerous anthologies and journals, and his work was recently featured on *PBS Newshour* as well as on NPR's *Here and Now.* His bilingual poetry collection, *Love, Lust & Loss,* was published in 2005 by Mémoire D'Encrier.

Marie Ketsia Theodore-Pharel

MARIE KETSIA THEODORE-PHAREL was born in Port-au-Prince and now lives in Homestead, Florida, with her family. Her writing has appeared in *Compost Magazine, Onyx, African Homefront,* and *Butterfly Ways: Voices from the Haitian Dyaspora in the United States,* edited by Edwidge Danticat.

Philippe Elie

EVELYNE TROUILLOT was born, lives, and works in Port-au-Prince. Her first novel, *Rosalie l'infâme,* was awarded the Prix Soroptimist de la romancière francophone in 2004. She has published three more novels, three collections of short novels, and two books of poetry—one in Creole and one in French. Her latest novel is *La mémoire aux abois.* Her work has been translated into German, Italian, and English. She has also written for theater.

JMJ

KATIA D. ULYSSE was born in Haiti. She holds a master's degree in education from the College of Notre Dame, Maryland. Her stories and essays have appeared in *Phoebe,* the *Caribbean Writer, Poui, Macomère, Wadabagei, Calabash, Haiti Progres, The Butterfly's Way* (edited by Edwidge Danticat), *Mozayik* (an all-Creole anthology), and other journals and anthologies. She is currently finalizing *Mouths Don't Speak,* a collection of pre- and postquake stories. She lives in Baltimore.

GARY VICTOR was born in Port-au-Prince in 1958. He is a longtime contributor to *Le Nouvelliste*, Haiti's best-known daily newspaper. He began his career by writing fiction for young adults in the youth edition of the newspaper. He has published nine collections of short stories and twelve novels, including *Saison de porcs (Pork Season)* and *Le cercle des époux infidels, (The Adulterer's Circle)*. He has also written for theater, television, and cinema.

MARVIN VICTOR was born in Port-au-Prince in December 1981. He is a painter and filmmaker. In 2007, he won the Young Francophone Writer Prize in France.

IBI AANU ZOBOI was born in Port-au-Prince as Pascale Philantrope. Her writing can be found on the web, in literary journals, and anthologies including the award-winning *Dark Matter: Reading the Bones*. She is a recipient of a grant in literature and writing from the Brooklyn Arts Council for the Daughters of Anacaona Writing Project, a program for Haitian teen girls, and she has completed a young adult fantasy/science-fiction novel based on Haitian mythology. She lives in Brooklyn.

Also available from the Akashic Noir Series

TRINIDAD NOIR
edited by Lisa Allen-Agostini & Jeanne Mason
340 pages, trade paperback original, $15.95

Brand-new stories by: Robert Antoni, Elizabeth Nunez, Lawrence Scott, Oonya Kempadoo, Ramabai Espinet, Shani Mootoo, Kevin Baldeosingh, elisha efua bartels, Tiphanie Yanique, Willi Chen, and others.

"For sheer volume, few—anywhere—can beat [V.S.] Naipaul's prodigious output. But on style, the writers in the Trinidadian canon can meet him eye to eye . . . Trinidad is no one-trick pony, literarily speaking."
—Coeditor Lisa Allen-Agostini in the *New York Times*

HAVANA NOIR
edited by Achy Obejas
360 pages, trade paperback original, $15.95

Brand-new stories by: Leonardo Padura, Pablo Medina, Carolina García-Aguilera, Ena Lucía Portela, Miguel Mejides, Arnaldo Correa, Alex Abella, Moisés Asís, Lea Aschkenas, and others.

"A remarkable collection . . . Throughout these eighteen stories, current and former residents of Havana—some well-known, some previously undiscovered—deliver gritty tales of depravation, depravity, heroic perseverance, revolution, and longing in a city mythical and widely misunderstood."
—*Miami Herald*

BOSTON NOIR
edited by Dennis Lehane
240 pages, trade paperback original, $15.95

Brand-new stories by: Dennis Lehane, Stewart O'Nan, Patricia Powell, John Dufresne, Lynne Heitman, Don Lee, Russ Aborn, J. Itabari Njeri, Jim Fusilli, Brendan DuBois, and Dana Cameron.

"In the best of the eleven stories in this outstanding entry in Akashic's noir series, characters, plot, and setting feed off each other like flames and an arsonist's accelerant . . . [T]his anthology shows that noir can thrive where Raymond Chandler has never set foot."
—*Publishers Weekly* (starred review)

BROOKLYN NOIR
edited by Tim McLoughlin
350 pages, trade paperback original, $15.95
*Winner of Shamus Award, Anthony Award, Robert L. Fish Memorial Award; finalist for Edgar Award, Pushcart Prize.

Brand-new stories by: Pete Hamill, Arthur Nersesian, Ellen Miller, Nelson George, Nicole Blackman, Sidney Offit, Ken Bruen, and others.

"*Brooklyn Noir* is such a stunningly perfect combination that you can't believe you haven't read an anthology like this before. But trust me—you haven't ... The writing is flat-out superb, filled with lines that will sing in your head for a long time to come."
—Laura Lippman, winner of the Edgar, Agatha, and Shamus awards

MIAMI NOIR
edited by Les Standiford
356 pages, a trade paperback original, $15.95

Brand-new stories by: James W. Hall, Barbara Parker, John Dufresne, Paul Levine, Carolina Garcia-Aguilera, Tom Corcoran, Vicki Hendricks, Preston Allen, Lynne Barrett, Jeffrey Wehr, and others.

"This well-chosen short story collection isn't just a thoughtful compilation of work by South Florida's best and upcoming writers ... [it] is also a window on a different part of Miami-Dade and its melting pot of cultures." —*South Florida Sun-Sentinel*

DELHI NOIR
edited by Hirsh Sawhney
300 pages, trade paperback original, $15.95

Brand-new stories by: Meera Nair, Irwin Allan Sealy, Uday Prakash, Radhika Jha, Tabish Khair, Ruchir Joshi, Omair Ahmad, and others.

"All fourteen stories are briskly paced, beautifully written, and populated by vivid, original characters ..."
—*Publishers Weekly* (starred review)